Cozen

BETHANY-KRIS

Published by Bethany-Kris

BK

www.bethanykris.com

eISBN 13: 978-1-988197-60-9

Print ISBN 13: 978-1-988197-61-6

Cover Art © London Miller

Editor: Elizabeth Peters

For D—the man who stole my heart like a thief.

Contents

PROLOGUE 7

ONE 11

TWO 26

THREE 35

FOUR 46

FIVE 55

SIX 66

SEVEN 76

EIGHT 86

NINE 95

TEN 105

ELEVEN 115

TWELVE 124

THIRTEEN 133

FOURTEEN 142

FIFTEEN 150

SIXTEEN 165

SEVENTEEN 174

EIGHTEEN 184

NINETEEN 194

TWENTY 203

TWENTY-ONE 210

TWENTY-TWO 221

TWENTY-THREE 228

Prologue

December 24th, 2012

A family with a history as old as time, and one they refused to muddy or be ashamed of, the Astors were a force to be reckoned with. And not one very many people felt comfortable going up against in any kind of way.

They controlled the gun trafficking business—carving out a mark as the biggest, and likely only, gun trafficking organization in North America. They dominated politics by either being directly in the Senate, or having a foot-long list of politicians they could call on at any time to do their bidding. They owned one of America's biggest banks, newspapers, and a branch of television media.

It meant they could control what was put out in the world, and in a way, influence the goings on in their own country. They had the means, the tools, and the wherewithal to use it to their advantage, too.

They couldn't stand competition.

They were excessive to a filthy point.

They never backed down.

Proud.

Arrogant.

Dangerous.

They earned it.

And they knew it.

When an Astor summoned someone—today, it was Ace, a black market broker able to find anything or anyone that might be needed to get a job done, or a deal made—that someone picked up their shit, and they went. No one needed the trouble of ignoring an Astor's call or request.

"The mansion is quiet today," Ace noted.

Pearl Astor glanced over at the broker she had called in, and smiled. "I had to get the rest of them out of my hair for this."

Ace lifted his brow at that. "Oh?"

"Fourth thinks the best way to go about doing this is the flash and dash. Make a big scene, and deal with the clean up later."

"That might be a *faster* way, sure."

Pearl shook her head. "The Astors cannot afford any kind of problems in the criminal world at the moment. We're gearing up for some … well, that's none of your business, but I meant what I said. We're going to have enough to deal with soon, and we don't need to be adding anything else to our list of problems."

"Fourth does have his ways," Ace said.

"Usually, I'm tempted to go with his ways," the old woman said, smiling in that unsettling way of hers, "but not this time. Are you going to show me what you have, or diddle around longer, Ace?"

Straight to the point.

As always.

"Pearl, you have a call—"

"I am not taking calls, Mathieu," Pearl said, never looking away from Ace.

The butler—a man in his fifties, at least—continued to stand in the doorway. "It is your son, ma'am."

"And Senior can wait, I am busy."

"If you're—"

Pearl's sharp gaze drifted to the side, and narrowed when she had Mathieu in her line of vision. "Child, if you ask me if I am sure about the words that just came out of my mouth …"

Child.

The butler was not a young man, but maybe to a woman of Pearl's age, he seemed like it. Ace couldn't be sure, but his amusement came out in the form of a grin that he hid by looking down at the tablet in his lap.

Nonetheless, the warning in Pearl's old voice could have cut glass. Her age, Ace decided, was nothing more than a number. She was just as dangerous as anyone else who laid claim to the Astor name.

"Don't interrupt my meeting again," Pearl said.

"My apologies," the butler muttered.

He was quick to scatter. His footsteps couldn't even be heard as he left.

Sighing, Pearl turned back to Ace. "Now, are you going to show me what you have? Prove the thief you chose is the right one for the job?"

"She is the right one," Ace returned, "and actually, she may be the only one."

Pearl lifted a brow, and a jeweled finger to wave. "So *you* say."

"Cozen is exactly what you need. She integrates into a mark's life, gains their trust, and gets the job done. It may take two weeks, or it may take six months. It doesn't matter because when she is done, she leaves

8

quietly and without the fanfare another thief might cause with a quick heist."

"Problematic."

"Pardon?"

"That would be problematic for us," Pearl said, "and so, you think this woman and her partner will be—"

"I never said Cozen has a partner. She works alone."

For a long while, Pearl stared hard at Ace. It almost felt as though she were weighing his words, and how she felt about them.

"No partner?" she finally asked.

Ace shook his head. "She doesn't need one."

"And what if she fails—what is her backup?"

"She has never failed."

Pearl rested back in the couch, and the lines of her aging face deepened with her contemplating frown. "Never?"

"Her way of working takes time, and sometimes it feels like very little is getting done, but it is always successful. If you give her a little bit of faith, I promise you will receive everything you want in return."

"Fine, show me."

Ace turned the tablet on, and typed in in his four-digit passcode. A few swipes across the screen, and he had the video brought up. Turning it around for Pearl to get a good view of what was happening on the screen, he waited.

Pearl watched in silence as a party was caught on camera in what had been an art gallery—the famous theft of the Van Gogh painting had basically bankrupt the place when the rich who had been using it to show off their art under the guise of possibly selling it no longer had a client list to keep them relevant.

The camera was directly on the wall that showcased the Van Gogh—a small painting no larger than twelve by eight inches, or so—and a few other pieces that any respectable art dealer would die to put on the market.

The crowd swelled once in the video.

They dispersed.

"I'm sorry, what is happening?" Pearl asked.

"Wait for it," Ace murmured.

The crowd swelled again, but this time when they dispersed, the painting was gone. The Van Gogh was taken.

Pearl sat back quickly. "I missed it, didn't I?"

"No," Ace assured, "but you'll never *see* her actually doing it. This took her three months, according to the broker I talked to who approached her for this job. She integrated into the mark's life, as she does, and then planned her heist according to his ways and rituals. I don't have all the details of this particular heist, but as you can see, she clearly took her time to know the room, the cameras, and which way would be safe and clean for her to get it done. This is her style, and her signature. Exactly what you want."

Ace let the video play through the end at a slightly faster speed before stopping at just the right point, saying, "There she is."

The woman with the russet eyes glancing up at the camera as the guests finally noticed the painting was gone wore a ghost of a smile.

"They have this video, clearly," Pearl said, hedging at something.

"They never even looked at her for this. The man who I talked to stated she stayed about two weeks after this, and then left quietly."

Pearl tipped her head to the side. "Cozen, you said?"

"Yes."

"Appropriate name."

Ace smirked. "You could say that."

"Does she always use that name?"

"Depends on the situation, or the mark."

"And you are *sure* ..."

Ace set the tablet aside. "Pearl, I will do a lot to get a deal done, but I promise you that Cozen is the thief you need for this. Let me approach her with the job."

"Fourth isn't going to like this," Pearl muttered. "He thinks he can do this quicker."

"I'm sure he could, but Cozen will be clean. Therein lies the difference."

The Astor queen nodded once. "Fine, approach her."

January 8th, 2013

"What is it, do you think, that keeps you coming back for more?"

Cozen Taylor shifted on her perch at the end of the reclining lounger, and passed her companion a look. "What, are you shrinking my head now, Ace?"

Zander "Ace" Everston laughed hard and loud. "No, but I'm always curious about thieves like you, Zen. Frankly, I'm curious about anyone in our world, and what keeps them going from one job to the next."

"I get that."

"So do tell, then. What keeps you coming back for more? The last one was the *last one*, right? That's what you told me when I came to offer you the deal on this job. Yet, here you are taking it."

Fair is fair.

"The last one *was* the last one."

"And as I said, here you sit in South Beach waiting for the next call."

Cozen smiled out at the tide starting to rush up the edges of the beach. The smell of the ocean clung in the air, and despite it being January, Miami was still warm enough that all she needed to wear was a thin shawl over her black, bodycon dress.

Sand touched her toes when she dug her ruby red stilettos further into the beach. Even the sand still had a warm quality to it, and the beige color matched some of the streaks lighting up the sky. Miami was a beautiful place to visit, or relax. She tended to stick to the other side of Florida, though. More tourists, she supposed. It was easier to blend in with the crowd.

"Does that mean you're not going to answer me?" Ace asked.

"Are you ever going to tell me how you earned your nickname?"

Ace flashed her a grin.

For a second, she was caught by how handsome Ace could be when he was *trying* to be charming. Usually, he tried most of the time. Had it been years ago and he graced her with that kind of smile, Cozen might have felt a twist in her stomach—unsure of how to react to a handsome man grinning at her.

But she was no longer a young, simple girl—twenty-five years on earth had brought with it a sense of understanding, and difficult life lessons for Cozen. Smiles from this man did little for her. Smiles from anyone did little for her.

"Well?" Cozen asked. "Your nickname?"

"Nope," Ace said.

That was that.

"It was supposed to be the last time, though," Cozen said quietly as she peered back over the water. Outside the café overlooking part of South Beach, she should have been enjoying the cold margarita in her hand, and letting the stress fall from her shoulders. Instead, she was going over all the reasons she had decided to come here when Ace sought her out for another job. "At least," she added, shooting Ace a look, "it should have been the last time on this continent for a while."

Ace grinned like he understood, but quickly sobered as he looked into his glass of whiskey. "This job was by special request."

"It's always special when the Astors call someone in to do a job."

At the mention of the family who had asked for Ace—a broker, of sorts, in their underground world of criminal kings, thieves, and far more—to bring in a thief worth their weight when it came to a heist, the two quieted.

"My last heist was in Boston," Cozen said. "Two years ago."

"Mmm. A Van Gogh, right?"

How did—

"You didn't broker me that job," she said.

Ace cocked a brow, saying, "No, but I know the person who did. Don't know specifics about who hired you to retrieve the painting for them, mind you, just that it was successful."

"You know enough."

"Maybe there's a reason I had to pick you for this job, Zen."

Cozen straightened her back a bit on the reclining lounger. "Excuse me?"

"You're a very specialized thief being that you … integrate into a mark's life, and leave quietly. You gain a mark's trust, and then most times when an item is stolen, they don't even look at you. Not even after you're gone."

"Fair," she said.

It wasn't a lie.

"The Astors needed a specific thief—one that could do this kind of job without the fanfare of making a scene, and causing trouble in the underground world, if you get what I mean."

Cozen lifted a single brow because this was the first she heard of this. "And how does that Van Gogh job come in to play?"

Ace sucked air through his teeth, and glanced away. "I got video of the party that night from a friend of a friend when I went asking about the job—you know who hired you, so put it together."

Anger flitted through Cozen.

She somehow hid it well.

"You know that's dangerous for someone like me," she said quietly. "To go around *asking* about a thief like that, especially one like me."

"As I said," Ace murmured, "this is a special job. They need a certain kind of thief that will integrate into the mark's life, and extract what they want without cause for concern or issue. They don't want a scene. They know it might take some time, and so, they sent me looking for the right thief. I knew it was you."

"Don't ever go asking about me to other brokers again," she warned.

Ace nodded. "Yeah, I got it. I am curious, though."

"About what?"

"The Van Gogh heist. One of the few paintings I know you've stolen."

"The owner sold it during a rough patch."

Ace shot her a look.

Cozen shrugged. "Basically, the bastard sold it to keep it out of his wife's hands during a nasty divorce."

"Ah. And what, he couldn't get it back afterward?"

"No." Cozen smiled, sly and slow. "The wife wanted it back. A gift from her father, apparently. Three million for a successful heist on a painting the size of my head, Ace. I *was* done after that one. I should have stayed done."

"Then why aren't you? I could have offered the job to someone else had you refused. I am *the broker*, Zen. I know other thieves who could have figured this out, and successfully got the job done."

Tension curled around her shoulders.

Unease settled in her gut.

Longing burrowed into her heart.

"Maybe it's me," she murmured.

"You?"

"I like the chase. I get a high from the thrill. I should say no, and be satisfied with the security I have in my life, but I can't. I need the next challenge."

"Ah, I see."

Before the two could talk more, a ring broke their attention away. Sitting higher on the reclined wicker lounger, the Blackberry vibrated and rang until it slid down to Cozen's waiting hand on the fourth ring.

It wasn't a call.

Just a message.

The Astors will see you now, it read.

"The Astors call," Cozen said heavily.

Ace was already standing and discarding his unfinished whiskey. "Never make that family wait. I swear there's nothing they hate more."

"I've only met them once, and that was at a third-party event. Are they as excessive and extravagant as everyone says?"

"Yes."

Ace didn't even bother to explain more of his confirmation. Her curious look did nothing to urge him on, either.

Just a simple *yes*.

"You know, Zen," Ace said as they navigated their way down the beach, "I do like that you went back to your natural hair color. The russet makes you stand out in a sea full of blondes here."

His hand came up to touch one of her free waves, but she was quick to react with a swing of her hand. She caught the side of his hand with her own, twisted his arm back, and yanked it down to his side without ever breaking stride beside him.

"Shit," Ace hissed.

Cozen let him go. "Don't touch me."

"I meant no harm. And damn, I can't give you a compliment, either?"

He rubbed his hand, and his eyes burned with fire.

Cozen smiled, and looked over the pretty, colorful streaks in the sky. "I don't need your compliments, Ace."

"You know what, better I don't even act friendly with you."

"Why is that?"

"You know why, Cozen."

Yeah, she did.

"You were warned once, Ace," was all she said.

He didn't even reply.

Excessive and extravagant did not do the Astor mansion justice, as far as Cozen was concerned. Tucked away on Tahiti Beach Island Road of Coral Cables, the three-level, two-wing monster of an estate looked to be the largest home in the area. And the most private, considering the carefully placed shrubbery and towering trees looming all around the property.

"We're not going in?" Cozen asked as Ace directed her down a pathway along the side of the east wing. "What, they don't want people to see the inside of their home?"

"This place is nearly thirty-thousand square feet," Ace muttered. "They almost always hold their meetings in the back where they can overlook the ocean. Sure, we could go through the house, but it'll take twice as long to navigate."

Windows looking inside the Astor mansion covered the east wing. Cozen caught sight of crystal chandeliers the size of small cars, and displays of wealth in every corner.

"Has no one told them that showcasing their wealth is a bad thing in a world like ours?" she asked.

Ace chuckled, and his gaze drifted to the right. "I don't think the Astors are very concerned, all things considered. They are the largest gun trafficking family in the world at the moment. It would be stupid of anyone—even a thief like you—to assume they go without protection."

Cozen followed his gaze. "Damn."

Walking the length of the east wing of the property was a man dressed entirely in black. Even his face was covered with a black bandana imprinted with the image of a skull. The crisscrossed belt around his chest showcased an assortment of weapons. In his hands, he kept a firm grip on an assault rifle.

"One of many," Ace murmured. "And always assume one is looking at you—even if you are inside the house."

"Noted."

Cozen wondered if the Astors would keep a better eye on her because she was a known thief. Of course, she didn't steal just to steal, and certainly not from a client. Sure, it was her job to steal, but there was the whole *don't bite the hand that feeds you* thing, too.

It was never good to betray those you worked for. No thief wanted their last job to go sour in that kind of way because it was unlikely they would ever get another job.

Not that it mattered.

This would be her last one.

It had to be.

It wasn't long before Cozen and Ace rounded the back of the east wing only to come face to face with another man dressed in black. He swung the assault rifle in his hand over his shoulder, and without saying a word, twirled a single finger at them.

"You should tell Fourth that his people need to start recognizing my face," Ace bitched under his breath as the man patted him down. First his front, and then after a quick spin, his back, too. "Fucking ridiculous."

The man in black came for Cozen next.

She cocked a brow at him. "Touch me, and I'll use one of your pretty knives to bleed you out on this walkway. It's a little dull with all the white marble—I'll bet it'll look far better with a bit of red on it, too."

All she could see of the man's face behind his skull bandana were his eyes. A flash of challenge and irritation answered her back, but he still didn't speak. She thought he was going to test her threat out—a threat she would have followed through on—but someone else saved them.

A dark, low laugh echoed from around the terrace.

The man who came around the corner wore an amused grin on his handsome face, and yet, he still managed to look severe. As though his amusement could just as easily be replaced with violence. His straight, thick eyebrows gave him a disinterested expression. It was a bright contrast to the smugness of his grin. He couldn't be any older than her, and if he was, then it wasn't by very much.

Dark brown eyes looked Cozen over as the man dressed in black Armani came to stand beside the guard. He waved one finger—showing off a black Rolex incrusted with diamonds around the face—and the guard was gone without a word.

"Cozen, is it?" he asked.

"Who's asking?"

The man smirked. "Fourth Astor. My great-grandmother has a fondness for white marble—please don't ruin it for her."

Cozen lifted a single brow. "I would appreciate your men keeping their distance, then."

"Fine." Fourth tipped his chin up, and looked her over with a keen eye. A look that felt almost … dismissive. "She's not much to see, is she?"

Her back straightened. "I beg your pardon?"

Fourth waved a hand, saying, "Don't take offence, Cozen. I mean, you're certainly something to look at as a *woman*. As a thief, though … I don't know, I can't see it."

"Well, you're looking at it."

And she didn't appreciate being disregarded, either. In fact, Cozen took that as a challenge.

"How long have you been in this business?" Fourth asked.

"Long enough."

"How many jobs?"

"More than you are old," she returned.

Fourth's gaze narrowed, and he took a step closer to Cozen. "And what makes you think a thief like you can handle a job like this?"

Easy.

"It's the same as any other job, but with a different face on the mark, a new location, and something else to extract. Logistics come in to play later, as I'm sure you understand."

Fourth passed Ace a look. "She certainly seems full of herself, doesn't she?"

"*She* is right here, and she is confident, not arrogant."

"Yes, well … we shall see."

Cozen smiled.

Fine.

"You will need to be checked before you can greet anyone else. Astor house rules, sorry."

"Why don't you check me, Fourth?" Cozen offered, simpering him with a smile that all men liked to be dazzled by. "Instead of your scary man there with his big gun, I am sure *you* could do the job."

Fourth's gaze flashed with something Cozen didn't recognize, but he didn't seem to sense anything off in her words. In fact, he didn't say anything at all as he came closer, and waved a hand for her to lift her arms.

Cozen did just that, and allowed Fourth to pat her down. He didn't tell her to put her arms back up when she dropped them down after he finished patting down her back. He didn't notice the way her hands lingered on his when he grabbed her waist to turn her around, and he didn't feel her fingers slip into his pocket, either.

Finally, Fourth straightened, and nodded. "You're fine."

Cozen shifted the cardigan hanging over her arm, and reached out to brush an invisible piece of lint from Fourth's shoulder before letting her hand move higher on his throat, and then back to his ear.

The man smiled at her.

And he thought *she* was arrogant.

"Shame that for such a handsome man, Fourth," Cozen murmured, "your attitude is a little hard to bear."

She kept her palm on his cheek, and her fingers at his ear.

Fourth shrugged. "As they say, nothing good comes easy."

Cozen dropped her hand back to her side, and closed her fingers into a tight fist. "No one said anything about you being good, though. Sorry."

"Cute."

Ace clapped his hands together, bringing them back to the man who had been silent during their entire exchange. "Where's your father, Fourth?"

"Around the back with Pearl." Fourth waved a hand. "Come, and we'll sit with them."

Cozen took in the immaculate estate as the three of them continued on the pathway. Ace chatted with Fourth just a few paces ahead. Something prickled at the back of her neck—she had never been very good at pretending like she could hold back her curiosity.

Maybe that was why she had a knack for stealing shiny, interesting things.

Who knew?

"Fourth is a strange name," Cozen noted.

Fourth glanced over his shoulder. "And *Cozen* isn't? Appropriate, though, considering the meaning."

Cozen shrugged. "Do you think you're the first to use that line, or what?"

The man barked out a laugh, and gave Ace a look. "Fuck, she's a good one."

"And her bark is just as bad as her bite," Ace said shaking his head.

Fourth slowed in his walk a bit, allowing Cozen to catch up and walk in stride. "The name is actually Remington Valor Astor the *Fourth*."

"How many Remingtons are still alive in your family?"

"Three at the moment. This is how we distinguish."

Cozen nodded. "I see."

"Care to share your story, too?"

She gave him a look. "About my name?"

"Mmm, exactly that."

Cozen smiled sweetly, but then turned her gaze back on the pathway ahead of them. "There's no story to tell, and not one that I know."

"Pardon?"

"Even if it has a story, I don't know it. Ask the woman who left me on the doorstep of a fire department in Vermont with nothing more than my name and age written on a card. And you know, if you find said woman, let me know her name. I have questions that need answers."

Fourth didn't reply.

No one ever did.

"Rem," Ace said, thrusting his hands into the waiting grasp of a man whose black hair was peppered with white. The two shook hands with wide smiles, and glinting eyes. As though they had shared all kinds of stories and secrets with more yet to come. "How are you?"

"Quite well," the older gentleman said before turning his gaze on Cozen. Dark eyes that looked her over, but quickly went to her face before he offered her a smile. "And you must be the *thief*."

At least he had the decency to say it with more respect than Fourth had. Cozen was still a little sour over that.

Cozen simpered him with a smile. "I prefer my name, actually."

"Yes. Cozen, right?"

"It is."

"Remington," the man said, moving closer with a hand out.

Cozen took the handshake, and then allowed him to kiss her knuckles before he dropped her hand. Normally she wouldn't allow that kind of thing, but she was trying to simply get the details of her job at the moment, and nothing more. "The third, or the second?"

A grin lit up Remington's face, and it spoke to his more youthful years. Before age had come in and wrote lines around his eyes, and left history on his face. She could definitely see the similarities between Fourth, and this man. Strong, square-cut jaws. Dark eyes. Black hair. She suspected he was Fourth's father, and his next words confirmed it.

"Do I look old enough to be a *second* to you?" he asked, and then just as quickly added, "Actually, never mind. Don't answer that question. I probably will not like the answer. My son gives me enough shit about my age as it is, don't you, Fourth?"

Fourth shrugged as he dropped into a large outdoor sectional beside a quiet, old woman. Her dark eyes—matched by the father and son—looked Cozen over with little interest before she went back to petting the ball of white fur on her lap.

A Persian cat.

It did not look like a nice cat, really. In fact, when it saw that Cozen was looking at it, the Persian hissed and bared its sharp teeth.

Yikes.

"Someone has to keep you in line," Fourth said.

The old woman had not looked away from Cozen yet. Her gaze would probably be unsettling to some, but Cozen was accustomed to people trying to figure her out. Like she was some kind of prize to be unwrapped if they could manage to get through her many layers.

"Tell me, girl," the woman said, her wrinkles being all the more prominent as her gaze narrowed on Cozen. "Do you genuinely believe you are the best thief on this continent?"

Cozen didn't even think about it. "I think I am one of the best, ma'am."

"But not *the* best."

"I was taught by the best. It would be incredibly rude of me to be so arrogant as to say I am better than them because they taught me. Isn't that how it should work?"

"Grandmamma, be nice," Remington told the woman as he slipped the cat from her lap, and put it to the ground. But not before the ball of white hell hissed and tried to bite the man on his arm. "There is a reason Ace suggested he take this job to Cozen."

"She'll get it done for you, Pearl," Ace agreed. "Cozen is golden. Never had a failed job, yet."

Wait.

This old woman was the one who called her for the job?

Seriously?

Damn.

It really did take all kinds of people to make the fucking world go around.

Fourth's gaze slipped in Cozen's direction, and with the narrowing of his eyes, she felt his disbelief about her presence make itself known once more. Although this time, he chose to keep it silent and not open his mouth.

Nonetheless, Cozen felt it.

She knew it.

Pearl peered up at Cozen with a slow smile. It was as though she could read Cozen's mind, or maybe it was just the woman's age who gave her insight to the people around her. Who knew what it was?

It was still unsettling.

"How old do you think I am, girl?" Pearl asked.

Cozen pressed her lips together. It was not nice to guess a woman's age, and certainly not a woman whose face looked like weathered, pale leather. "I would say you have lived long enough to know it wouldn't be appropriate for me to answer that question, Mrs. Astor."

Pearl smiled. "You would be right. I am ninety-five. I have outlived my husband, three of my children, and six dogs. I am on my fourth Persian cat at the moment—you saw her. I call her *Sweetness.*"

"She did not look very sweet."

"Because she isn't. I like to surprise people."

"You're older than the Queen of England."

Pearl nodded. "And richer than the bitch, too, darling."

Cozen smiled widely, unable to stop herself. Laughter lit up the estate from the men. None of them seemed particularly surprised by Pearl's quick wit.

She learned something in that moment.

Age meant *nothing.*

"Shoo," Pearl said to the gathered men. She flicked a jewel-covered hand. "Leave us alone for a while."

"Grandmamma," Remington started to say.

"Oh, go, Rem. I can do this myself."

Fourth and Ace were already pushing out of their chairs without needed to be told. Pearl and Remington the Third passed another look between one another before the man followed behind his son, and the broker he called in for this deal.

Or rather, the broker Pearl called in.

"Sit," the old woman said, gesturing at the seat across from hers.

Cozen sat. "I hear you need a thief."

Pearl tapped a weathered finger against the side of her cheek. "I have needed one for two decades, darling."

"And you're only now calling one in?"

"I gave her the chance to return it."

"Her?"

Pearl sighed, leaned forward, and snatched up a yellow folder on the glass table in front of the sectional. Flipping it open, the old woman perused the contents of the folder before seemingly settling on one.

"*Her*," Pearl said, turning a photo over to show Cozen. The woman in the photograph was beautiful for her age. A dark haired, and brown-eyed beauty who looked to be closer to Remington's age. In her fifties, or so. "My granddaughter."

Cozen's brow furrowed. "She looks like—"

"She is Rem's sister—*was*."

"Was."

Pearl cleared her throat, and set the photo aside on the seat. "She died four months ago. Cancer in her blood, or so we were told. We only know what we hear through the grapevine, as she made her choices, and we were forced to make ours."

"What choices were those?"

The old woman's eyes hardened. "I will let you in on a little secret about the Astors, Cozen. We have rules—many rules. One of them is to never let our name fall. We never hand it over, and we never give it up."

"And she did that?"

Pearl waved jeweled fingers as if to dismiss the question. "She married Jett Griffin."

"I don't understand how that breaks the rule you mentioned."

"She took his name."

Cozen straightened a bit on the chair. "Really? Your family takes it *that* far?"

"Beyond, actually," Pearl murmured. "Even a woman's children must keep the family name. Her children didn't have our name, either. She knew the rules, and what would happen. I hadn't seen her in almost two decades before she died. No one in our family had."

Cozen's gaze traveled to the photograph again as Pearl started flipping through the folder's contents. "Do you regret not closing the distance?"

"Astors burn bridges. We do not fix them."

Well, then …

Pearl flipped over another photograph, and handed it to Cozen. She took it, and quickly found herself entranced by the beautiful square-cut ruby set atop a woven gold band. The ruby was at least fifteen carats in size. It did not look like anything remotely close to a modern piece.

"My great-grandmother brought that ring over from Germany," Pearl said, her gaze traveling to the nasty white cat waddling its way back to their spot. "It has been through a great deal—seen more than most. Wars, and immigration. Poverty, and wealth. It was once sold by my great-grandmother to pay for her husband's court charges, and used again as bribery a few decades later by my grandmother when her husband found himself in trouble with the law."

"It has great history."

To say the least ...

Cozen wanted to physically get her hands on the actual piece just to *touch* it.

"My mother chose to give Anabelle the ruby as a piece to pass on. It's not uncommon in our family to take pieces of our history, and give them to another Astor to keep it moving through the generations."

Cozen nodded. "Sure. I take it, you want this ring back, now."

"I wanted it back the day Anabelle married Jett. I wanted it back *before* then. She knew the rules."

The cold hardness in Pearl's old voice took Cozen by surprise. She glanced up from the photograph to find Pearl's hissy cat had climbed back into the woman's lap. The Persian all but glared with its strange ice-blue eyes in Cozen's direction.

"She's dead, though," Cozen pointed out.

"Jett—her husband—still has the ring."

Cozen's brow lifted. "And how do you know this?"

"He taunted us with it when we asked to have it returned."

"Taunted you," she echoed.

"Yes, with some pretty little thing he paid to have on his arm during a charity event he knew Rem and his wife would be attending with Fourth. It was quite a show. Lucky my great-grandson didn't slice his throat right then and there."

Pearl sighed heavily, and waved a hand again. "Fourth and his father handled it well, at the time. I cannot say I would have done the same."

"It's never good to make a scene."

"Mmm, no." Pearl's lips flattened into a grim line. "I want my family's property returned. Everything that belongs to the Astors must come back to the Astors."

"Another rule?" Cozen asked.

"No, a way of life." Pearl looked to Cozen. "How long do you think it will take for you to pull this off?"

"Every heist is a little different. Sometimes, I can get one done quicker than others. It really all depends on what a mark does and how easily accessible the item is once I get into their life. I assume Ace approached me for a reason …"

"Yes," Pearl murmured, "because our family is about to make major moves in the criminal world, and we cannot afford to cause more uproar elsewhere when we might need to return in that direction for help later."

Huh.

"And so I am …?"

"The kind of thief that can apparently do a job very quietly," Pearl said.

"I am," Cozen agreed. "Like I was never even there to begin with."

"Good. If you return it to me before the year is out, I will make sure you never need to even *think* about money for the rest of your life, Cozen. How much did your last job pay?"

"Three million."

"Add two zeroes to the end of that, darling."

"That's a lot of money," Cozen said quietly.

"It is change in our bank accounts."

"Richer than the Queen, huh?"

Pearl smiled—old, bitter, and yet still beautiful. "Far richer than the Queen."

"I'll get the ring."

She didn't know how.

Not yet.

That was part of the job.

"Make sure of it. I have waited long enough to finally get it back. And to make sure it is the real ring, and not some fabricated piece, there is an *A* inscribed on the bottom of the ruby."

Cozen straightened in the chair. "Doesn't inscribing the jewel make it somewhat … well, worthless?"

"It may be worthless to everyone else, but not to an Astor."

Huh.

Three hundred million for a ruby only valuable to someone with a particular surname.

This was going to be interesting.

"I noticed something," Cozen hedged.

Pearl's sharp gaze drifted back to her again. "And what was that?"

"Your great-grandson—Fourth—he doesn't seem to think I am the right person for this job."

"If this were up to him, you would not be the thief he picked for this job, no. He is more a … well, he would just go ahead and blow the side of Jett Griffin's home off to get my ring back. And while I appreciate the sentiment, I know in the long run that it won't do us any good."

"He doesn't think I can steal," Cozen added.

Pearl lifted her brow. "Oh?"

"I can tell."

With that said, Cozen moved the cardigan that had been keeping one of her hands, and her arm hidden from view. She opened up her palm, and showcased the items hidden inside.

A signet ring with a cursive *A* decorated by plumage. A diamond earring. And a Rolex watch incrusted with diamonds.

All it had taken for her to steal from Fourth was a distraction of his attention, and quick, soft movements of her hands and fingers. Did it take time and patience to learn how to thieve quickly, and without notice? Yes, but it also took talent.

A thief was nothing without talent.

She would not allow someone—not even an Astor—to slight her. No good thief could let something like that go.

Cozen set Fourth's items in Pearl's hands and quietly said, "Do be sure to tell Fourth that appearances are deceiving, and the next thief he insults might not be so kind as to return what they take. It's a good lesson to learn when you're dabbling in this business."

Cozen stepped closer to the waiting town car. Her drive to the airstrip where she would be picked up by a private jet. Ace leaned against the back passenger door of the town car. They would be saying goodbye now, as his job in this whole thing was over.

He was the broker.

He made the deals.

Or he made them work.

Nothing more.

Cozen pressed the phone to her ear, and eyed the colors in the early morning sky. Miami was just as beautiful in the morning as it was at night.

"Hello?"

The voice on the other end of the phone was both comforting and familiar.

"Mama," Cozen greeted.

Well, the closest thing Cozen had ever had to a mother seeing as how she moved from foster home to foster home for the majority of her childhood years. She would give up her very heartbeat for her.

"Zen, baby, where are you? I thought you would be home already."

"A job came up," Cozen said.

"Ah."

Her mother didn't even sound surprised.

"I need some information, though. Mostly on the target. Think you could help me?"

"We'll *all* help," her mother said. "More so with some of us than others. I know how you work, Cozen."

Cozen smiled.

She hadn't expected anything different.

After all, she learned from the best.

April 2nd, 2013

Sargon Makri didn't know how to stay in one place for very long. It just wasn't in his nature. His father, William, liked to blame it on Sargon's Persian roots—the nomadic need to constantly move was just in his blood; he couldn't help it.

The one good thing about constantly bouncing from place to place, and never quite settling for long in any one, was that Sargon made a lot of friends.

And a lot of enemies, too.

A hand came up to clap his cheek before he could dodge it—not that he would, being it was his boss of the moment. He had a lot of those, too, over the years. His life had never had one clear path or goal, but rather, many winding roads.

He never managed to stay on one side of the tracks, either. Not good, or bad. Rather, he straddled the line, and occasionally jumped back and forth depending on his preference or need at the moment.

Sargon sometimes wondered if that was because of his roots, too.

He knew it wasn't.

Life made him this way.

The man who clapped his cheek filled his vision in front of the restaurant. Sargon closed the door of the black town car before giving his new boss the attention the man thought he deserved. It was not about respect why Sargon didn't care to indulge the man, but about the fact he didn't particularly like this guy.

"You good, Sargon?" Kale asked.

Kale Tompkins—small time coke smuggler, and big time gambler—had offered him a job two months ago when Sargon first rolled into New York. He'd overheard the man discussing an upcoming drug run he was taking down through Florida to get to the Keys.

Getting himself a new job was as easy as pointing out a safer route for Kale to take for the run. A route that didn't include going through territory that didn't belong to the guy. Things like that could get messy, and it wasn't any fucking skin off Sargon's back to speak up.

So, he got himself a job.

How long this job would last was another story. Maybe until he felt the restless need to get up and move again, or even once he became bored with his current surroundings.

It all depended …

Today, though, he was the muscle.

"I'm good," Sargon told Kale.

Being small time in a world full of big times meant Kale didn't have a lot of clout to back him up. A few men scattered between different jobs, or responsibilities. Certainly not enough to carve him out a respectful berth of space when it came to other people in the underground criminal world.

Sargon had been around all kinds of people in his lifetime.

Cartel leaders.

Cosa Nostra bosses.

Gun traffickers.

Thieves.

A Madame or two …

It took all fucking kinds of people to make this damn world go around, and Sargon was lucky—or unlucky—enough to have met quite a few of them over his twenty-eight years of life. He could tell a man who had made his mark in the criminal world simply by taking five seconds to talk to him.

Kale Tompkins was small fish.

Small time.

But the guy paid well, and let Sargon do his own thing when it came to a job. He appreciated that, so he watched the guy's back.

For the most part.

Sargon's tenure as Kale's man could end as easily as it begun, too. With something like a second job offer, or the dangling promise of something better.

"Looks like the subject of your meeting is already here," Sargon noted.

He nodded at the front door of the restaurant, and Kale's gaze followed. Behind the clear glass, a man stood waiting to open the door for them. He looked in their direction, and nodded before pressing the Bluetooth in his ear, and speaking something they couldn't hear.

Sargon was decent at lip reading, though.

They're here, boss.

"Gotta appreciate a fucker who doesn't make a guy wait," Kale muttered.

Despite the unbothered inflection in Kale's tone, Sargon knew the guy was worried about this meet with Jett Griffin.

As he should be, Sargon supposed.

Small time coke smuggler.

Big time gambler.

Someone had come to collect a debt they took over for someone else, and Kale needed to somehow convince the guy to let him extend the payment deadline. Sargon didn't see that happening. No one let a debt go unpaid for too long because it set a bad fucking example.

"Let's go," Kale said with a wave of his hand.

A bustling upper east side Manhattan restaurant greeted them, and so did a woman in a black dress with a botox smile.

"Kale Tompkins," his boss said to the woman.

She looked over her tablet, and then glanced up with guarded eyes.

Bad sign.

Sargon took note.

"You'll be dining in the private room with Mr. Griffin," the woman said as she stepped out from behind her podium. Setting the tablet aside, and gesturing with one hand at the men, she added, "Follow me, please."

Bad sign number two.

A private section meant no witnesses. Sargon didn't like that, either.

Soon, the two men had been guided through the main floor of the restaurant, and situated closer to the back. The woman in black stepped forward to open the door of the private dining area, and then gave Kale a wide berth to move ahead of her.

"Enjoy your meal," she said quietly.

She didn't meet his gaze.

Bad sign number three.

"Kale—"

Sargon thought to warn the man that he didn't think going into this meeting was a good idea just based on his own instincts. That shit had never let him down before, and he was not about to start ignoring it now.

Kale gave Sargon a look, and interrupted his warning with, "Just stay outside the door. It'll be fine."

Kale thought he could charm his way out of this. And sure, Sargon had seen the man do it before. He'd also seen him make a successful smuggle run, and then blow every bit of the profits made at an underground poker match instead of paying off his debt.

Bad news.

"Understood?" Kale asked.

Well …

"Suit yourself," Sargon murmured, and he turned his back to the wall directly beside the door. "Can't save you from yourself, man."

Kale didn't hear that last comment. He was already heading inside the private area. The woman closed the door behind him, and then shot Sargon a too-wide smile. Her blue eyes looked him over without shame.

Another time in his life, and he might have given her the time of day. Not now, though.

Her look said, *I'm interested.* He gave her a blank look in return. One that said, *fuck off.*

She fucked off.

Sargon waited for what he figured was going to be the inevitable outcome for Kale, but time continued to drag on. The thick door provided a bit of privacy for the meeting because he could only hear the occasional murmur sliding out from the crack at the bottom.

Across from Sargon rested a decorative mirror cut into six inch squares. He hadn't noticed it before, but now his gaze was drawn to the man reflected back.

Him.

It wasn't often he stared into a mirror. Not for too long, anyway. Sometimes, he didn't recognize the golden-skinned, brown-eyed, black-haired man looking back at him. Sometimes, he was too busy being someone else to remember where he came from.

Scrubbing a hand down his jaw, Sargon watched the man in the mirror mimic the action. He kept a short, well-trimmed beard, but he liked a clean throat. His throat needed a shave, according to the reflection.

His mother liked to tell Sargon that he looked like his father. That he'd taken the strong, prominent jaw, russet eyes, and thick, straight brows from his dad. His nose, and lips came from his mother, though.

For all purposes, on paper it looked as though Sargon was adopted by his parents, although that was just their way of muddying a paper trail so that they could not be found. They changed their clearly *un*-American names to something more fitting of the country they decided to run and hide in, and it was here in America that Sargon was born.

Although, if anyone looked for his parents, it would simply appear on paper as though they died shortly after coming to the States from Iran.

Sargon's gaze drifted to the mirror again, and the man staring back at him. Seeing his reflection reminded him of his mother and father, and that he missed them. That tug deep in his heart was painful in that way.

This was why he didn't like mirrors.

Sargon straightened a bit when the man in black from the front of the restaurant appeared at the end of the hallway. The guy pressed his finger to the Bluetooth in his ear, and nodded once as his gaze traveled to Sargon.

"Easy to handle," he heard the man say. "No worries—it'll be done before you are."

A thump echoed from inside the private room, followed by a loud *pop*. The kind of sound a bullet made going through a shitty homemade silencer.

Yeah, he knew this was going to go bad. Kale should have kept the fuck up with the program when Sargon tried to voice his concerns. Look at them now.

Shit.

Sargon glanced up at the ceiling, and wondered why nothing in his fucking life could be *easy*. The man in black strolled closer in his direction, while Sargon slid his hand into the pocket of his slacks. In a sheath he kept hidden in the pocket, he wrapped his fingers around the curved handle of the Obsidian. It was protected for now in its cocoon of leather. At least, until he brought it out to play.

He didn't like guns.

Heavy fucking things.

A knife was *far* easier.

An Obsidian blade was the *best*.

"Sorry to tell you, man," the guy started to say, "but your boss isn't going to be needing your services anymore."

Sargon looked to the right at the guy. "That so?"

The man's jacket opened a bit—a purposeful move—to showcase the gun resting at the guy's hip. He gave Sargon a pointed look, and then nodded down the hall.

"I think you should probably come with me, and let's not make it a fucking hassle, all right?"

Sargon lifted one thick brow. "I think not, no."

"*No?*"

"I don't stutter."

Or repeat himself.

A haughtiness flashed in the guy's eyes which just made Sargon roll his own. Everybody working for anybody in this world all thought they were some kind of hot shit. As though they were the very best, and the only one made for the job.

This guy wasn't different.

"You got it, fucker," the guy muttered.

The man reached for his gun.

Sargon slipped the blade from the leather sheath.

This was exactly why he preferred knives to any other kind of weapon. Jett Griffin's man barely even had time to yank his gun from the holster before Sargon was already reacting. The guy took his gaze away from Sargon for a half of a second, *at most*, and he signed his death warrant with the action.

Spinning away from the wall, Sargon's Obsidian blade struck out with a simple flick of his arm. First, he nicked the guy up under his jaw, and then a second slice under his ear.

The cuts were so fast, and so incredibly clean, that the man didn't even feel it until the blood was already starting to pour down onto the collar of his shirt. It was painful spots, though, and with a single touch of his fingers to the cuts, the fool hissed.

His eyes flashed with rage when they met Sargon's.

Too late.

He reached for Sargon, and grabbed his forearm. Sargon let him, but only long enough to grab the man by his forearm, too, and yank him forward.

Off-balance, the man stumbled.

He was spun around, and smashed into the wall before he had even gotten a chance to say a thing, or blink, for that matter. Paintings on the wall shuddered from the impact.

Sargon rolled his eyes upward, and cursed in his head. He likely just notified the fucking idiots inside the private area that something was happening out in the hallway. That wasn't a problem he needed, to be honest.

He didn't need to be causing himself problems in New York. That was not a part of his deal at the moment.

"You're going to fucking *die*," the guy said.

Sargon pressed the edge of the Obsidian blade against the lower portion of the back of the guy's neck. Right against his spine. "I *was* going to just finish this."

"You cocksucker—"

"I like pussy, actually."

The guy raged and spluttered on. Sargon simply continued to hold him against the wall with his blade driving into his skin. Already, the sharp edge had sliced paper thin lines over the man's flesh, and if he kept struggling like he was, it would only get worse.

"What are you doing to my man?"

The new voice made Sargon look to the side. He didn't need to be told who he was looking at. Jett Griffin, a fifty-something with his distinguished features, and salt and pepper hair, was a rather common sight in New York.

A broker for all things underground, and black market.

He was a business man.

Both legal, and illegal.

New York elite.

"He was going to kill me," Sargon offered.

Jett's gaze narrowed as another man in black slipped out behind him from the private area. "Clearly not, as you're very much alive."

"Because he is foolish, and I am not."

That seemed to prickle the man's amusement as his lips twitched, though he held back the smile. "Is that so?"

The man under Sargon's hold struggled, and the blade made more paper thin cuts. "I take it you're not interested in collecting the debt from Kale Tompkins?"

Jett's amusement was gone in a blink. "He will never pay, as his previous collector made clear to me."

"I could have told you that."

"He was your boss, wasn't he?"

Was.

Sargon did not miss that choice in words. "So to speak."

"What does that mean?" Jett asked. "He either was, or he was not. There is no gray area."

"There is gray everywhere," Sargon replied, smirking just a bit. "My boss is whoever pays me enough, and keeps my attention focused for the time being."

"So your loyalty ...?"

"Is flimsy."

And fickle.

Non-existent, practically.

Jett's gaze darted to the man Sargon was still keeping pinned to the wall. "Really, Gerald, you couldn't even handle removing this issue for me, so I didn't have to come out to it? You had *one* job."

"He took me by—"

"He tried to make a show of it, and gave me an opening," Sargon interrupted the man. "Someone else, and it probably would have been fine. I am not someone else, and I pay attention more so than others."

"Fucking idiot ... kill you!"

"You do realize the back of your neck looks like shredded steak right now, don't you?" Sargon asked the man. "This is an Obsidian blade, but I don't suspect you understand what that even means. Let me tell you. It means that this blade is so thin and sharp that on a cellular level, it slices through your cells rather than tear through them like steel. The more you move against the edge of this knife, the worse it cuts you."

Instantly, the man stopped struggling.

Sargon rolled his gaze upwards, and then looked to Jett. "Finally, he fucking gets it. Little late, though."

"What—"

Tilting his knife up so the tip rested against the bloody spot on the back of the man's neck, Sargon only needed to put the slightest bit of pressure against the hilt. First, though, he looked to the man's boss—Jett.

"I hope you're not very fond of this man," Sargon said.

Jett sighed. "I was … once."

"Shame."

It was a mantra of sorts for Sargon. Shame could be found in every corner of life, regardless of who carried the burden. Shame was not always obvious, either.

Sargon put pressure against the hilt of the knife. It sliced right through the man's skin and into his spine like a hot blade cutting through butter. He never once took his gaze away from Jett as he pulled the knife back out, and the man fell to the floor.

A morbid thump.

It echoed, even.

The hallway had turned that silent all around them. Sargon much preferred silence to anything else. He found it comforting.

"Shame," Jett murmured.

"Sorry, but you didn't exactly seem like you particularly liked the man," Sargon pointed out.

The man in black behind Jett had eyes so wide, they could be fucking saucers. He looked from the body on the floor, to Sargon, and then to his boss. Anger and disbelief colored up his features as he took a step forward like he was going to come at Sargon.

Welcome to try, asshole.

Jett stopped the man with a single hand held high. "Don't move."

"But, boss—"

"You have a mess to clean in the dining area, don't you?" Jett asked. "Get on that before someone comes back here. Oh," he added, waving a finger at the bleeding body on the floor, "and this one, too. Make some calls, if you need help."

The guy glared at Sargon.

Sargon smiled back.

"Where do you come from?" Jett asked once the man was gone.

Sargon leaned a shoulder against the wall. "Born in America."

"Mmm."

"My family came over from Iran."

"Ah, I see." Jett's white brows lifted high. "You do not sound like—"

"Raised out west."

"Ah."

Sargon shrugged. "I like surprising people."

Jett passed a look at the body on the floor. "So I see. Shame you killed my man."

"Shame you killed my boss."

"Yes, seems you need a job, don't you?"

"Seems I will."

Jett sighed. "Lucky for you, a spot with my men just opened up. If you're interested."

"That depends on the pay."

"I will pay you quite well if you assure me you'll protect me, and only me, for as long as I deem fit. Then, you can safely assume I will not also ask you to answer for ... well, this little mess here."

"Nice trade," Sargon said. "Being it's my life, and all."

"I suppose. And what is your life worth?"

"That would depend on who you ask."

"I asked *you*."

Fair enough.

He pretended like he was weighing his options. He really didn't care as long as he got the job done.

"My life is worth, well enough, I guess."

"Your name?" Jett asked.

"Sargon."

"Last name?"

"Makri," Sargon murmured.

He knew why Jett asked. The gentleman would crawl through any and all of Sargon's history to make sure he was who he said he was. That was one thing a person could count on when it came to people in this world— they did their fucking homework, or tried to.

Otherwise, it was just plain foolish not to look into someone's past. No one needed that kind of trouble at the end of the day.

Jett was welcomed to try to find whatever he wanted where Sargon and his life was concerned. There was nothing to find on this continent, really. His parents made sure of that, and it had served him well over the years.

Sargon Makri did not exist in any official capacity. Supposedly dead like his Iranian parents, or something like that. Sometimes he went by the name he had been given at birth, and other times, he used the name his parents gave him to help him blend in.

What did it matter?

He didn't exist.

Mostly empty floors and bare walls stared back at Cozen. The lower Manhattan apartment was going to cost her a pretty penny every month, but it was still considered *affordable* given New York rental rates.

It wasn't the kind of apartment—she didn't even like apartments—that Cozen would typically go for personally, but this wasn't personal. It was a job. She needed a place right in the city because she knew that was where Jett Griffin spent most of his days, and did the vast majority of his business.

She intended to, over time or sooner, put herself directly in his path, and work her way closer from there. It could be quick, or it could take time.

In between, Cozen didn't necessarily need to like or love the place she would call home. No, she simply needed a decent roof over her head that would not draw suspicion. This wasn't her first rodeo—not even her tenth.

The apartment wasn't anything particularly good to look at, but a person couldn't scoff at it, either. Light-toned hardwood floors, and beige walls. Freshly painted a week ago, according to the landlord. The one-bedroom apartment had been cleaned at some point. Bleach and lemon still clung to the air.

Cozen gave them points for that.

Not for much else, though.

Other than a basic kitchen table with two chairs, a small loveseat sitting in front of a nineteen-inch flat screen, and a box spring and mattress resting on metal rails in the bedroom, this place had no furniture. There wasn't even a cheap piece of art on the walls, and one of the taps in the bathroom had made an awful creak when Cozen checked it.

Apparently, this was considered *furnished*.

And up-to-date.

Cozen made a noise under her breath, and dismissed that notion. This place was not even close to being furnished, and it definitely needed some work. She couldn't see herself putting much time in to the place by way of fixing things, but she did have a taste for spaces that comforted her.

She might decorate.

Depending on how long she stayed, that was.

"Black and white, I think," Cozen murmured to herself.

She loved that style.

The little bungalow in California sitting on a private beach property overlooking the ocean where she called home came to mind. With its black and white interior, and simplistic bohemian inspired pieces scattered throughout the small rooms, it was the picture of peace and Zen. Cozen was always trying to mimic that style wherever she had to stay, even if only in little ways.

"Black and white?"

The unexpected—yet not unfamiliar—voice made Cozen spin on her heel with the intention of protecting herself. She was already reaching for the knife she had tucked into a sheath and hidden beneath her black lace bralette.

At the sight of the old landlord leaning in the apartment's front door, Cozen let her arm fall back to her side. In his late fifties, a little too round in his middle, and always wearing a wide, warm smile, the landlord of the building was harmless. He lived on the bottom floor—Cozen was on the second at the far end with an escape ladder right outside the living room window—and according to other tenants she spoke to, he liked to make his rounds.

A little too friendly, sure.

But harmless.

Cozen could handle the rest.

"How're you liking the place?" Ronald asked.

Cozen shrugged, and turned back to look at the apartment. "It's a little lonely looking."

"Mmm, I thought so, too. Last tenants snuck out a lot of shit."

"Furniture, you mean?"

"And some things we had on the walls. No worries—I have them in for a civil case in two months."

"I thought this was a little bare for being fully furnished."

"Never thought to change the ad for the place," Ronald said. "I just told the wife to put it back to active online. Sorry about that."

Cozen shrugged. "Maybe you'll have some things to keep for the next tenant."

"Why's that?"

Because she wouldn't be staying once this job was finished, and New York was not her home. Even if she wanted to stay in the city after she did what she needed to do, it would be incredibly dangerous.

And stupid.

Cozen disappeared after a job. She went back underground, and hid from anyone who might be able to find her. It made things easier. She did not take things back with her once she was done as they were *just* things.

Replaceable things.

Nothing she got attached to.

The ringing of Cozen's phone saved her from having to deflect the landlord's question. She gave him an apologetic look over her shoulder as she dug out the cell phone. He gave her another one of his too-wide smiles, and backed out of the apartment as he closed the door at the same time.

Cozen only answered the call once she was alone. "Cozen here."

"Pearl would like an update, Zen."

Ace's voice instantly grated on Cozen's nerves, and she didn't particularly have a reason why.

"Isn't your job done where this deal is concerned?" Cozen asked.

"It *should* be."

"And yet, you're calling me, Ace."

"It's the Astors. I *have* to call. Or they keep calling me. Make of that what you need or want to make of it, Zen."

Fuck.

"I've been in New York for an entire three days."

"Yes, and it's already the second week of April. Three months since Pearl transferred a quarter of your payment. She's getting antsy now for good news from you. You haven't updated them."

"I made it clear this job might take a while. Any heist like this takes time to do it properly."

"Anyone can go in and steal something if they know what they're doing, Cozen."

She took great offense to that.

She didn't even try to hide it.

"Anyone, really?"

"Well—"

"Why don't I transfer that money to you, and then you can make your way to this city. We'll let *you* do this job, Ace. How about that?"

"I just meant—"

"You're right," she interjected sharply. "Any *thief* can steal, but not every thief is like me. I have my own way of doing a job like this, and it is not the flash and dash kind of thing. I might like to work again someday. That's kind of hard to do when you make a fucking scene."

"My apologies."

Cozen played with the gold ring on her left thumb. She twisted the thick band around and around to let it calm her as much as possible. The small piece of jewelry gave her a sense of peace and security whenever she touched it.

That's why she wore it.

"It has been three months," he reminded her.

"I told her six at the most," Cozen returned.

"Might it be more?"

"Depends on how much people piss me off. And you know, how much Pearl Astor wants her ring back."

"Noted."

"Why is she all of the sudden concerned about how long this job takes, Ace? Pearl was well aware that it would take me time to integrate into Jett's life, and work on extracting the ring. They didn't want fanfare, *remember?*"

Ace cleared his throat. "Maybe it isn't so much Pearl as someone else."

Cozen's gaze narrowed. "Who is this someone else?"

"Fourth."

Really, again?

Didn't her little lesson with him teach the man *anything?*

"Fuck him—Fourth didn't hire me."

"True. Have you got eyes on the target?"

"Depends on what you mean by eyes."

"*Your* eyes?"

"I've seen him," Cozen replied, offering nothing else. "I plan on seeing more of him very soon."

"How soon?"

"Listen, I have to go. A job to do, and get, you know."

"And get? What in the hell does that mean?"

"It means the set up around a heist is just as important as the final scene, Ace," Cozen murmured, already done with this conversation. "Don't call me again. Be sure to pass the message along to anyone else who needs it."

She hung up the phone without saying goodbye.

April in New York was not like April in California.

Cozen was never more aware of that fact than right now. She was not used to this wet, cold weather. The dampness wouldn't let up, and she swore it soaked right into her bones no matter what she did.

Tightening the bomber jacket around her frame, she was grateful she opted for skinny jeans and knee-high boots instead of the dress and ankle boots she waffled over. Sometimes, showing off a little leg got her further when she was on a mission to get shit done, but she could do anything with just her smile, too.

Smile it was.

Today, anyway.

"Thirteen, twenty-five," the vendor said.

Cozen handed over the cash for the random paperback novel she had picked up from the vendor stand. The guy had tucked his cart in under an eave as to save anything from getting wet. She needed the book as a prop.

Of sorts …

"Thanks," the guy said, "and enjoy your book."

Cozen smiled. "I will."

But probably not.

She checked out the cover as she headed further down the street. A house loomed on a dark background surrounded by overgrowth and mist. Big, block letters gave the title, and in a bigger size font, gave the author's name, too.

How self-entitled did an author have to be to demand their name be the biggest thing on a book cover?

Cozen didn't get it.

She wasn't all that interested in the thriller, but it would make for a good distraction. Or rather, it would make people think she was just another New Yorker lost in her own space should anyone look her way.

Soon enough, she had grabbed a seat on a bench in upper Manhattan. People blew around her, bustling from one thing to the next, and never paying her much mind. A half a block down, Cozen could see someone shooting video of a guy stopping random people on the street, and asking them questions in front of the camera.

Her gaze drifted between the book in her hands, and the restaurant across the street.

The Kingdom.

Heavy, cursive font spelled the business's name above the door. The large windows covering the front were darkened enough that she couldn't see inside, except for the occasional shadow that passed behind one.

Four days after Cozen had settled into her apartment, and she already had her eyes on Jett Griffin. It took a while, and a couple of phone calls. A favor or two called in, just because. As much information as she could gather about the man, she needed it.

But she had it.

Now.

The Kingdom was a favorite haunt of Jett's. Not a business he owned, but rather, one he liked to frequent at least four times a week for lunch. A friend of a friend of a friend said the man knew the owner, and thus, could discuss business safely.

That business being ... many things.

Seemed the New York man was not just a king in the legal business sense, as Jett also had a heavy hand in the black market. He was sort of like Ace in the way some might call him a broker. A man who came in as the middle man to make deals, and sign them in blood.

But where Ace did his best work with *people*, Jett seemed to work with *things*.

Anything.

Drugs.

Guns.

Skin.

That told Cozen quite a few things all at once, and she didn't need them to be confirmed, either. The man likely didn't have a lot of morals if he didn't particularly care what he was selling. That also made him dangerous. And if he could sell just about anything to just about anyone, that meant he was a damn good talker.

Likely a charmer.

Sell ice to a Snowman.

Cozen kept that information in the back of her mind as a *just-in-case*. Just in case she forgot, and found herself in trouble. Just in case she needed it.

Checking her watch, Cozen noted the time as she tried to pretend like her ass *wasn't* frozen to the fucking bench.

Two minutes to go.

Four days of watching Jett Griffin told Cozen the man kept a firm schedule, and ran a tight ship. Maybe it was because the man was anal about his days, and spent the time wisely. Or maybe it was something else entirely. Like the fact he was so busy between his legal, illegal, and other ventures that he didn't have time to mess around.

Cozen counted down the seconds while she pretended to read her book. The large, black sunglasses she wore kept her eyes and more hidden from view. She was just another fashionably dressed, brown-haired New Yorker, as far as anyone else was concerned.

Easily looked over.

Sure enough, at twelve-thirty sharp, Jett Griffin stepped out of The Kingdom with his entourage in tow. A tail of four men, one of which opened the door of the restaurant for him so that his hands never had to touch the handle, and another who rushed to the still running town car on the side of the street to open the back door.

The two other men flanked Jett.

As fast as Cozen had gotten her eyes on the target, he and his men were gone. They never wasted any time between leaving a business, and getting the hell out of dodge. The longest she had ever seen Jett take from exit to entrance into a vehicle was, at most, fifteen seconds.

For some reason, he did not like to linger.

Safety, perhaps.

Who knew?

She filed that information away, too.

Cozen waited a few more minutes, and watched people begin to flood the restaurant for the afternoon rush. Done with her pretense of doing nothing, she tossed the paperback aside on the bench as she stood.

Someone else could find it and enjoy.

Thrillers weren't her thing.

Her whole life was a thrill.

Crossing the street when she had a chance, Cozen took the steps to the restaurant two at a time. She pulled the sunglasses from her face as she stepped inside to get a better look at the joint. While she had been watching it for a while, this was the first time she actually went as far as to come inside and look around.

She bypassed the woman chatting at a podium to people waiting to be seated. High-class, and upscale, the restaurant catered to those with deep pockets. Rich colors filled the business, and gleaming hardwood floors made her boots clack as she made a beeline for the bar. Patrons took comfort between tables with silk coverings and modern lights overhead, or tucked in booths closest to the walls.

She recognized the man standing behind the cherry oak, built-in bar with inverted lights shining down on a wall of top shelf liquor bottles. He was the same man who regularly was the last to leave the business at night, and lock the doors.

Either a manager, or the owner.

It didn't matter.

He had the say so.

That's what Cozen figured, anyway.

The closer she came to the bar, the more voices filtered in from the kitchen just to the left.

"He wants *what?*"

"Listen, Rowena, he's not asking for a lot. So you have to smile a little more, and be pleasant."

"I am fucking pleasant!"

"Could you say that without the cussing, too?"

Seemed not all was well in The Kingdom.

The man behind the bar sighed as his gaze drifted toward the kitchen, and then narrowed with irritation. As quickly as his frustration came on, it bled away when the girl working behind the bar handed him over a sheet to peruse.

"Thanks, Marissa."

"Everything checks out, right?" the redhead asked.

She was pretty with dainty features and blue eyes that made her look doe-eyed. Men had a habit of going for that kind of thing.

"So far. Get back to me on the second order, though."

"Will do, Chase."

Chase.

Such a fuck-boy name.

Cozen plastered on a smile as she came up to the bar, and *Chase* finally looked her way.

"Can I help you?"

His short tone told her that Miss Rowena in the kitchen wasn't the only person here with a fucking attitude problem.

"Maybe you can help me," Cozen said. "I was told The Kingdom was looking for new hires. Something behind the bar, or someone to work the floor."

She hadn't been told that.

It didn't matter.

Chase lifted one well-manicured eyebrow. Yeah, fuck-boy was a guy who groomed his eyebrows, apparently. Cozen was the type of woman who appreciated a little ruggedness in a man, but that was just her preference.

He pointed at the girl down the way with far too much concentration in her face as she chewed on the tip of a pen, and looked over the sheet. "Bar position has been filled."

"Twelve times twelve is one-twenty-four, right?" the girl asked.

Cozen cleared her throat, and clicked her tongue before saying, "One-forty-four, actually."

"Oh, okay, thanks!"

Chase stared blankly at Cozen. "And I haven't needed a server in a long time."

Shame.

"You sure? They were pretty specific—"

"Chase, you're a fucking asshole, and I don't give a shit what you want!"

The blonde that came rushing out of the kitchen from the right looked crazy as hell as she slipped around the bar where Cozen was still standing. She had a glinting, silver serving tray in her hand, and in her haste, stumbled over one of the barstools.

The woman went flying.

Cozen stepped out of the way of the falling woman, but managed to catch the serving tray in one hand, and the pen and pad that slipped off it with the other. She straightened up, and handed it over to a very frustrated looking fuck-boy manager behind the bar.

"Here you go," Cozen said. "I suspect these are a bit too expensive to be dropping all over the place, right?"

Chase scowled. "You know what, keep it. Your first day starts now."

"You haven't even asked my name."

"Although I don't care as long as you know how to work a table and not be a bitch every day you show up to work, do tell," he said dryly.

She could pretend not to be a bitch.

"Cozen."

"Got a last name?"

"Taylor," she returned. "I'm not exactly dressed for work, am I?"

All the other girls were done up in the same black bodycon dresses and silver heels.

"Just smile a lot," Chase said, shaking his head as he peered over the bar at Rowena on the floor. "Anything is an improvement over that one at the moment. I suspect the patrons won't even notice you're not in uniform as long as you treat them well."

As the man said those words, Rowena was still trying to get her legs untangled from the barstool.

Sometimes, shit just worked out.

Cozen was lucky like that.

Cozen handed over the drink orders to Marissa who—at least for the three days Cozen had been working at The Kingdom—was still struggling to figure out how to do proper liquor orders. It wasn't that the girl was stupid, or even a little bit flaky.

She was actually sweet, and nice.

And damn, she could make a good drink.

Marissa just wasn't good with numbers. Or as she liked to say, she didn't do *math*. Cozen figured the girl was skating along by the skin of her teeth because Chase had eyes for the bartender. Cozen saw him looking at Marissa one too many times when he thought nobody saw him do it.

"Need help?" Cozen asked the girl.

Marissa shook her head. "It's okay. I'll get used to it."

"You do know you have a calculator right in your phone, right?"

"Not supposed to have it on me while I'm working."

"Chase wants proper numbers on his orders, too. I think he'd suck it the fuck up."

Marissa smiled a little bit. "Yeah, maybe."

"Use your phone, hon. It'll be easier."

And less stressful, too.

Cozen didn't point that fact out, though.

Turning away from the bar, Cozen balanced the silver serving tray on her palm as she headed for the kitchen. For whatever reason, Jett Griffin had not yet came to the restaurant since she started working there.

Maybe some switch in his schedule.

A vacation, possibly.

Cozen didn't worry because men were creatures of habit. He would come back eventually, and she would get her chance. That was all she needed. Just one single chance to put herself into his path, and find a way to insert her presence into his life.

An opening.

All good thieves found their openings.

In the kitchen, Chase was doing his rounds. The manager—she had come to find he *wasn't* the owner of the restaurant—clapped his hands to speed up an already rushing crew. She figured a lot of the stress in the place was caused by his high-intensity nonsense.

Cozen didn't care.

She did her thing.

"Dinner rush is coming, so hurry it the hell up, guys! Herald, get that prep work finished! Courtney, go fix your hair before you get back on the floor! Cozen—"

"What?" Cozen asked.

She slid the food order over the kitchen rack to one of the men working behind it—a helper to the one chef working the stoves, and making the food. The chef was another one in the place causing all kinds of chaos whenever he could with his ridiculous demands and loud demeanor.

Another man Cozen didn't care about.

"I need you in the private room today," Chase said.

"I think you need more people on the floor, actually," she returned dryly. "It's busy, and the girls need all the help they can get."

"Yeah, well, you replaced Jett's favorite girl, and my only job when that man comes through the front doors is to make him happy. So guess what, sweetheart? It's *your* job now."

Cozen cocked a brow.

Jett, huh?

She knew he would be back.

"You got it, Chase."

Cozen didn't wait to hear what the manager had to say, as she was already leaving the busy kitchen, and heading for the private area to prep it. She didn't need to be told what to do—she already knew.

Jett wanted to be happy.

Cozen found her opening.

"Sir."

"Sir."

"Jett," Sargon greeted.

Jett gave Sargon a cutting smile as he stopped at the back passenger door held open for him. In the gated, circular driveway of the Griffin estate, Jett truly was a king in his kingdom, and typically expected to be addressed with the same respect.

Sargon was not typical, though.

"Sarg," Jett replied.

Sargon's upper lip curled back a bit in his disgust. It was an automatic reaction he wasn't very good at hiding whenever someone tried to use that nickname on him. For his new boss, the nickname had come after a conversation about shortening Sargon's name to something less ... strange and unique.

He quite liked his name.

"Still not a fan, huh?" Jett asked.

"Will never be a fan, Jett."

Jett's gaze drifted over the waiting men standing at the ready in the driveway. One would drive Jett while Sargon stayed close to the boss in the backseat, and another would follow close behind in a nondescript vehicle.

Depending on what Jett had planned for the day, he was known to take less or more men accordingly. He always had a small army guarding his four acre Long Island estate. Sargon, for the last two weeks, was ever present at Jett's side.

Maybe because Jett found him mildly amusing and interesting. Or perhaps because he thought Sargon was capable of protecting him far better than the rest of his men should something happen.

Sargon didn't know what it was. He did, however, know that the rest of Jett's men—all of them being friends of the man he had killed in a back hallway of a restaurant—were not at all fond of his presence, or Jett's preference to have him closer than the rest of them.

During the men's downtime, Sargon often found himself excluded from the group in whatever way they could shun him. The others had no qualms about making changes in schedules or the way they handled their boss without first letting Sargon know.

They thought it bothered him.

Offended him.

Sargon found it all amusing.

Like small children trying to punish him on the playground because the mommies and daddies paid him a little bit more attention than they got. It was nothing more than petty jealously, and he didn't entertain that sort of nonsense.

He had better things to do.

Foolish fuckers.

Sargon was there to do a job and get paid.

Nothing else.

"Are you enjoying your work?" Jett asked Sargon.

Sargon shrugged, and put a little more of his weight against the opened passenger door as if to seem relaxed. "It's been fine."

"The rest of the men have welcomed you, then?"

He looked over the other men—they dressed in black, while he kept his usual silk dress shirt, and black slacks—and then went back to Jett. He gave a nod, unwilling to say much else. He also wasn't the type to tattle. The men would either step the fuck up, or back the fuck off.

Either of which, Sargon could and would handle.

Alone.

Sargon didn't miss the way the men's gazes darted in his direction after he spoke. They likely believed he would have taken his opening to get them in shit with their boss, as that was probably what they would have done to him.

Predictable.

"Good to hear," Jett said.

Not saying another thing, Jett slid into the waiting car without a look back at Sargon or the other men. Sargon quickly closed the door behind the boss, and passed a look over his shoulder at the men. He cocked an eyebrow at them, still chewing on the piece of mint gum that helped to keep his mouth occupied instead of running more often than not.

The other two men didn't speak.

Sargon was grateful.

Soon, he was in the backseat with the boss while Jett finished up a phone call, and one of the two men from outside slipped into the front seat to drive. Leaning forward, Jett muttered orders to the driver, and then slammed the partition between the front and back seats closed. It allowed for some privacy, but not a lot if the voices raised more than a murmur.

"You lied," Jett said.

Sargon did not show the way his heart thundered at those two, seemingly simple words. Jett seemed harmless on the outside, and he was quite charming to those around him. Still, Sargon knew that was for show. Jett was as dangerous as the Obsidian blade Sargon liked.

"I beg your pardon?"

Jett's dark eyes looked him over, and then he lifted a white eyebrow. "About my men—you lied."

Calm settled back in Sargon.

"They're a little sour over their lost comrade," Sargon said, hoping to dismiss any concerns Jett may have. "I don't blame them, really."

"You know they run to me about every little thing you do," Jett added.

Sargon chuckled, and looked out the window to hide his grin. "Oh, they do?"

"He won't dress appropriately."

"I dress fine."

"Not like them," Jett returned. "But frankly, I prefer you as you are because it makes you seem less like them, if you get my drift. No one suspects you are part of my protection, and it gives you another upper hand, Sarg."

"You really need to stop using that nickname."

"Not yet."

Sargon sighed, and looked back at Jett. "What else do they whine about?"

"Nothing important, but I've let you know, so now you can do with it what you want."

"Keep my eye on them, but that's about it."

Jett nodded once. "Petty grievances can sometimes make the bloodiest problems. Oh, and I have something for you."

Sargon took the file Jett pulled from the black, leather case he always toted around. Flipping it open as the car finally pulled away from the Griffin estate, Sargon was surprised at the amount of information he found staring back at him.

Information about *himself*.

"You've found information even I didn't know," Sargon murmured as he looked over details of the supposed crash that killed his parents. Visa information that had allowed them travel into and semi-permanently stay in the United States. Details about their family in Iran, and who was left to contact from that group. "I don't suppose this helped you, though, did it?"

Jett gave him a look. "No."

The word was so dry, Sargon felt it scrape across his skin.

"I was adopted—not legally—by Mia and William Jones. They worried that should they file properly for me, I would be taken from them, or even my biological parents' families would come for me."

Sargon repeated the elaborate lie his parents had drummed into his skull over the years.

"Mmm."

Sargon thumbed through another paper. "Problem?"

"Those names—Mia, William, and Jones—are some of the most common in the United States, I suppose. It makes it hard to dig in to their details, that's all."

Which was the point.

Or so his parents always told him.

Sargon handed back the file. "I welcome you to go ahead and look in to them all you want, Jett. There's nothing to find. I am, and have always been since I was old enough to go out on my own, a transient. Nothing ties me down, and I don't put roots very far into the ground in case I find myself stuck there. I don't like to be *stuck*. I keep moving, and I only rest for so long before I go on again."

"And that's what this is to you?"

"This job with you?" Sargon asked.

Jett nodded.

"Yes, that's what it is. I haven't hidden that."

"You're right," Jett said, "you haven't."

Sargon smirked. "So, do I get to stay to work another day?"

Jett laughed darkly. "For now. And lunch, too."

"Hmm?"

"You will have lunch with me today, too."

Sargon lifted a brow high. "Why?"

"I find you interesting."

One of Sargon's many blessings.

And curses.

Jett pointed at the small golden ring hanging from the leather cord around Sargon's neck. The one and only piece of jewelry he wore, and never took off. He liked to have it close, but more so, the nearest to his heart that he could get it.

"I wondered about your … necklace there, if you could call it that," the man said. "Should I assume it comes from your lost parents?"

"Sure," Sargon said.

The man could *assume*.

Assumptions meant nothing.

"What would you do," Jett asked, "in the case where you had two organizations battling against each other—a decades long feud that has never been close to over—and both wish to work with you?"

Sargon glanced across the table where Jett seemed to be fully engrossed in a file he had pulled from his bag. Yet, there was no one else at the table, and it was only Sargon he could be conversing with.

Another man was stationed outside the private dining area, and the other one was guarding Jett's vehicle. One more had a seat at one of the tables on the main floor.

"It depends," Sargon hedged.

"On what?"

"Do they know you would be working for both of them?"

Jett grinned, but never looked up from the paperwork. "No, and they both have vastly different needs in the deals they want to put forth. One being a government bribe that is far more intricate than it appears, and another is a new drug connection."

"And I take it the separate organizations would not be pleased to find out you were working for both sides, even if it was not against the other one, per say?"

Jett's brow lifted. "To them, working with one is automatically working against the other. What do you say, now?"

"I say it still depends."

His boss did finally look up at him, then. "Are you one of the types with a constant death wish, Sargon?"

Sargon grinned. "No, I just have the mindset that if I can get away with it, and cleanly, then why not go for it?"

"Dangerous game."

"It can be. What types of organizations? That would be one thing I would weigh to make my choice. I would not risk putting myself between an Irish and Italian feud, for starters. The Irish and the Italians have long had volatile issues, and Irish are known for having little care or concern for the fodder used in their wars. Russians are another one that tend to be quite extreme and violent."

"Two Italians."

"Cosa Nostra, Camorra, or otherwise?" Sargon asked.

"You know a lot about criminal organizations, don't you?"

Sargon shrugged, and went back to gazing out the window. "I have lived many lives."

That was not a lie.

"Have you left many enemies behind, too?" Jett asked.

"Don't we all?"

"Fair enough. My issue in taking these two offers lie in the fact I don't like to shit where I eat or sleep."

Sargon's gaze cut back to Jett in an instant. "What in the hell does that mean?"

"One is Camorra based, one is Cosa Nostra based. Both are based here in the state, and most business is done in the city. One controls Queens, Brooklyn, and in there. The other manages Manhattan—across the bridge, basically. There is no buffer zone between them and I, should I take the deal. We are all in very close quarters."

"I advise you not to take it," Sargon settled on saying.

Because that would be the smart choice.

Jett sighed heavily. "I have to take at least one."

"And what, hope the other side doesn't find out?"

"Essentially."

"Who is the one playing dangerous games now, Jett?"

His boss didn't answer because his attention was now captured by something else entirely. Sargon chanced a look over his shoulder to see what it was that had Jett so moved he was willing to drop an entire conversation.

A woman, apparently.

A very *beautiful* woman.

At least five foot nine, the russet brunette with the same shade eyes simpered a smile. Her bow-shaped lips curved at the edges as she entered the private dining area.

First, Sargon noticed the perfect cupid's bow on her top lip, and then the way her dainty features set off the rest of her face. High cheekbones, and perfectly arched brows. She swayed a little when she walked—some women *learned* how to do that, and others were just born with the ability to look sensual when they moved.

This woman was clearly in the latter group.

Her sway drew his gaze down over her body—a trim waist, hips with enough curve to grab onto, and legs for days. All covered by a tight, black bodycon dress. The silver shoes, ones that matched the color of the serving plate in her hand, set the entire ensemble off for her.

It was not the first time Sargon had seen the girls in the restaurant wearing their uniform. It was the first time Sargon had seen *this* woman wearing it, and she looked far better than any of them, frankly.

To him, anyway.

Sargon was not the type to be silenced by a woman, or the look of her. He was not a boy who got his cock tied up over a woman.

Shit.

He might enjoy letting this one do it to him, though.

"Where is Rowena?" Jett asked.

The woman's gaze lingered on Sargon's face for a moment, and then jumped back to Jett. Her voice sounded like a melody when she spoke. "Rowena and Chase had a bit of a falling out. I am here to serve you today, sir."

"Jett."

The woman smiled. "I know your name. I thought it appropriate to address you respectfully unless you wished for me to do differently."

Jett smiled widely—clearly pleased with the woman. "Call me Jett."

"Sure, Jett."

Jett cocked a brow. "And what's your name?"

"Cozen, but you may address me with Zen, if you prefer. I don't mind either."

"Cozen," Sargon said.

All eyes drifted in his direction. He couldn't help himself but to look up at the woman. For the first time since she had walked into the room and looked at him, her eyes were back on his face. Piercing within their russet pools. Pinning him in place.

"To obtain by deception," Sargon added. "That's what the word means."

Cozen nodded. "So I have been told, although all the name has given me is a lot of strange stares when people ask me about it."

Jett laughed, drawing the attention back to him for the moment. "Interesting."

"I'm glad you like it, Jett."

Sargon's throat felt damn tight for a reason he couldn't name. This woman carefully chose her words with every single sentence. He didn't miss it. She offered Jett something the man liked in women—submission. The ability to be the person in control, and above everyone else around him.

"It is a strange name, though," Jett murmured. "Seems that's a common theme in my life lately. Meeting people with strange names, I mean."

Cozen laughed.

It too was a musical sound.

Like wind chimes, really.

"I don't understand," Cozen said.

Jett gestured in Sargon's direction, saying, "His name is Sargon. Sargon Makri. But don't call him Sarg, as he doesn't like it."

Cozen laughed again, and her hand came down to brush against Jett's shoulder over his suit jacket. Her loose, wavy hair fell over her shoulder and exposed the delicate line of her throat. Her skin looked soft, and sweet.

He bet it would taste just like that, too.

It was in that moment that Sargon finally understood the strange burst of heat radiating through his bloodstream.

Anger.

Possessiveness.

Jealousy.

He was jealous over this woman.

He had no reason to be.

Yet, there he was.

Jealous.

"You're not hungry, or what?" Jett asked him.

Sargon's gaze drifted away from the curve of Cozen's ass just as she disappeared out of the room. "Pardon?"

Jett gestured at his plate. "You've barely touched your steak. It's good food—the best on this side of Manhattan."

That was debatable, and not a debate Sargon wanted to get in to.

"No, I'm—"

"Distracted by that woman's backside, I would guess," Jett interjected.

Sargon swallowed thickly.

He hadn't even tried to hide it.

"I don't blame you," Jett said, raising one brow salaciously with a smile. "I was looking, too."

"Seems she was quite focused on you, though, wasn't she?"

Jett's smile deepened. "She was."

"My apologies."

The laugh that burst from Jett's lips took Sargon by surprise for a brief moment. His boss leaned back in his seat at the table, and tossed his napkin aside. Jett pointed a finger at Sargon, and waved it almost chidingly.

"There is something about you, Sargon, and I don't know what it is. You're too polite, but you're rough around your edges. You charm and grin and go it, yet you kill a man without blinking. A beautiful young woman catches your eye—she has to be far closer to your age than mine—and you apologize because she was sweet to me."

Sargon shrugged. "Manners are good for the soul."

Not that he had one of those.

Manners, sure.

His mother and father taught him those for a reason.

A soul, though?

That was another one of those unworthy debates.

Jett's gaze drifted to the doorway of the private dining area again. "Are you interested in her?"

"She's quite beautiful."

"That's not what I asked."

"That's what I noticed, Jett."

His boss nodded once. "Well, *I* am interested in her."

That tight feeing closed around Sargon's throat again—weighted and thick, and refusing to let up for even a single breath. His stomach pained as though someone had kicked him there, but he ignored that feeling, too.

"And what would you like me to do about that?" Sargon asked.

He meant it sarcastically, but Jett took it seriously.

Shit.

"My wife has been dead a while," Jett said. "What would you say the appropriate grieving period is before pursuing someone new?"

"You want to *pursue* her."

Sargon didn't even ask it.

Jett's eyes darted back to Sargon's, and glinted with the unbidden lust of a man who had a libido far more youthful than his actual age. "I liked Rowena—the woman who served me before this one. I once had a thing with her. Nothing more than her sucking me off in the back of my Benz, but it suited me well on stressful days. This girl, though, she doesn't seem like the type."

Sargon swallowed hard again. Jesus. Where had that lump in his throat come from, anyway?

"A quick blow or fuck is one thing," Jett continued, "but pursuing someone is something else entirely when you're a widower of my status. I wouldn't want to *offend*, you know."

Sargon doubted Jett was in any way concerned with offending anyone. "I suppose you're not the only person in the equation, though, are you?"

Jett chuckled and waved his finger at Sargon again. "Right you are, Sarg."

Stop calling me that.

"And so, I will leave that up to you," Jett added. "Approach her, and see if she is interested in something. Tell her I would like to see her again."

"Me?"

Why me?

"Yes, you," Jett said, scowling. "She will recognize you, and she's new here. One of my other men might scare her off, and you seem more relaxed. So yes, *you*."

Wonderful.

"Go," Jett said when Sargon didn't move.

Well, fuck.

Eyes on the fucking target, Cozen. Eyes on the—

"Is there a story behind your name?"

Cozen straightened up from the bar faster than she thought was possible. Her internal mantra interrupted by the sound of sin whispering in her ear.

Sargon.

Her heart thundered hard in her chest as she turned to find the man in question standing just a foot away in the shadows created by the hallway and lights. The man who put her entirely off balance from the first second she stepped into the private dining area. His dark amber gaze had landed on her, and from that moment, she found it a little harder to breathe.

Then, she remembered her task.

Jett Griffin.

Putting herself in his path.

Gaining his attention.

Going from there.

Well, Cozen figured she did that, but the only way she could was by practically ignoring the beautifully unsettling man sitting across from Jett.

It was going to be impossible for her to ignore Sargon right now. In fact, having him this close to her with the illusion of privacy from Jett and his men, Cozen found her skin heating under his gaze, and her heart would not calm down no matter how hard she tried to make it relax.

"I'm sorry, what did you say?" she asked.

Cozen kept her gaze on the bill she was writing out for Jett's dinner. She couldn't stop her eyes from traveling to the side, and catching a glimpse of the carved-from-stone God standing next to her.

"Your name," Sargon murmured.

The words fell from his lips, and he never moved an inch. Yet, Cozen still felt him far too close for her comfort.

Mostly because she wanted him closer.

Attraction could be a bitch.

"Is there a story behind it?" he asked again.

Broad shoulders framed his body, and the silk dress shirt he wore was just tight enough to show off a chest and arms full of hard lines, and firm muscles. His lips were shaped in such a way that he looked as though he was perpetually smirking, although she had seen him scowl. And damn him, because he was looking mighty fucking good doing that, too.

Cozen looked over at him fully. "Not that I know of."

Sargon's lips curved at the edges, and formed a wicked smile. The kind of grin that might make weaker women throw themselves at him. The sad thing was, Cozen knew she wasn't a weak woman, but she'd be a lying bitch if she said she wasn't tempted to throw *something* at him for that look.

"No one just picks a name like that with no reason behind it," he said, cocking a brow.

Thick, dark brows arched over those amber eyes of his. His brows were straight, and it gave him a look of disinterest until he arched them like that. It didn't matter—straight or not, it only made him look like something that walked out of a magazine.

"I was never told if there was a story," Cozen said.

She offered nothing else because she wasn't about to out the story of her past. She doubted this man would be very interested—at least, not at the moment—in listening to her regale him for hours about her life in the foster care system until her later teenage years.

Nobody liked that story.

It wasn't a fun one.

Sargon inched closer to Cozen, and as those few inches of space closed between them, he never once removed his gaze from her. No, he simply glided over her, taking in the way her dress covered her body, and the amount of leg the skirt provided for him to stare at. He lingered on the heels, and his eyebrow edged up fast again as his lips curved in that sexy way once more.

The guy was interested.

He didn't hide it.

Cozen would be stupid to say she didn't notice his interest in the dining room—the way he followed her with his eyes, and how his gaze had narrowed when she put more emphasis on her attention to Jett.

Sure, Sargon hid it well.

The man still took notice of her.

This was unsettling.

"I should apologize," he said.

Cozen, surprised at that statement, turned to face him fully. It closed practically all and any distance between them. If she breathed too hard, her breasts would brush against his chest. His gorgeous lines and intoxicating scent were all the more apparent like this, too.

"For what?" she asked.

He smiled—softer, yet still sexy. "For frightening you when I came up on you just now."

"You didn't—"

"You jumped."

He offered the words as though he didn't intend for her to argue with him, and without any challenge at all. She knew then that this man was not as simple as he may seem. His silk shirt—the top two buttons undone, hinting at a light dusting of dark hair on his chest, and the leather cord hanging down from his neck—and slacks were a ruse.

He was not a friend or associate of Jett's. He took notice of too many things; he *watched*. And carefully.

"You jumped," he repeated, "and that frightened you. My intentions with beautiful women are never to frighten them. Challenge them, maybe. Never frighten."

Cozen's throat thickened with a lump of desire. One she couldn't swallow no matter how hard she tried.

He called her beautiful. How many men called her beautiful, and she brushed the compliment off? Too many.

Yet, she wanted his.

"You startled me a little," she admitted.

Something else she wasn't used to …

"My apologies," Sargon murmured.

His skin was a light shade of russet with a golden tint, and his hair, a short-cropped, dark black. The straight nose, and strong, square jaw gave him that all-man appearance. Add in the fact he looked like he hadn't shaved for a good week, and Sargon had all the trappings of a man.

Even the scent he wore—a strong musk with overtones of amber and spice, and hints of pine—made Cozen want to get a little closer to him.

She did not have this problem.

Not during jobs!

That's what Sargon was.

A fucking *problem*.

Sargon's tongue peeked out to wet his bottom lip before he said,

"With that out of the way, I was told to deliver you an offer."

The warmth in his tone fled just like that. A clinical coldness took its place instead.

Cozen heard footsteps coming from the kitchen, and quickly put a few inches of space between her and Sargon. She had a goal in mind with Jett Griffin, and she did not need even the idea of something inappropriate with someone else to ruin her endgame.

Sure enough, Marissa came out from the kitchen and resumed her work behind the bar. Cozen slid the finished tab across to the girl, saying, "Would you mind giving that to Chase for me?"

"No problem, Zen."

"Thanks."

Once Marissa was out of sight again—although not for long, Cozen knew—she put her attention back on Sargon.

"What offer is that?" she asked.

Sargon didn't close the distance between them, either. It was like a switch had flipped in him, and his direction had altogether changed because of it.

She didn't mind.

Much.

"Can my boss assume your attention in the private dining area was not in some way … misguided?" he asked.

Cozen cocked a brow. "In what way would my attention be misguided?"

"Maybe for a bigger tip, who knows?"

Ah.

"He can assume my attention was very well intended," she returned.

Sargon's gaze hardened the same way his jaw did at her words.

Jealous, she thought.

He was jealous.

Cozen pushed it away. "How old is Jett, anyway?"

She knew Jett's age. She was simply testing Sargon. It was a dangerous game to play, but she didn't know any better at the moment.

"Fifty-five, edging closer to fifty-six."

"And yet, he looks forty, at the most. Good genes, I guess."

Sargon sucked air through his teeth. "That offer—Jett would like to see you again. Outside of here, I assume. Dinner, likely. That is, if you're also interested."

"I would be."

It was her opening.

She didn't even have to think about it.

Sargon gave her one last piercing look, and then immediately spun on his heel, and left her presence. She was stuck staring at the way his back looked in tight silk, and how his muscles moved beneath the fabric before he disappeared entirely down the hall.

Instantly, she let out a breath.

Cozen turned to find Marissa was standing behind the bar again.

"Good day?" Marissa asked, her tone suggesting something else.

"Something like that," Cozen agreed.

It wasn't five minutes after Jett and his men had left the restaurant that Chase came to find Cozen. The wide smile on his face told her something good had happened, but she didn't know what exactly that was.

"Take the rest of the day off," he told her.

She was only half way through cleaning up the private dining area. "Pardon?"

Chase leaned over the table, and waved the bill from Jett's dinner at her. "I said, take the rest of the day off. You deserve it, because you girl, are a fucking *payday*."

Cozen blinked, unsure. "I don't—"

He slammed the tab down on the table, and tapped his finger against the note at the bottom. Written in bold handwriting, the words made Cozen's eyes widen.

A tip, Chase, and do make sure she gets it. Every single penny.

The added tip was three thousand dollars.

Chase pointed a finger at Cozen. "Also, he stays a half hour—*at most*—every day when he eats here. Do you know how long he stayed today?"

"No."

She had been too busy trying to ignore the sexy man sitting across from Jett while at the same time, catching Jett's eye.

Apparently, she had done both of those things, plus more.

What a fucking talent.

"He stayed for an hour and a half," Chase said, nodding. "Fucking unheard of for that man, Cozen. He is too strict with his schedule, and he never stays in one place for long because business always comes first for Jett Griffin."

"Okay."

What else did he want her to say?

"You get the rest of the day off. He'll be here tomorrow, too. I want you to do whatever you have to do tonight to be on your best game for tomorrow."

"All right," Cozen replied.

Chase had no idea. At least, not about how right he was. And this game was far from over.

Cozen moved from the small bathroom to her bedroom. With her hair still rolled up in curlers, she once more tried to decide between one dress, or an entirely different one. The red number was a bit sexier, and slightly shorter. The purple item was still tight, but with less of a plunge in the neckline, and fell to her knees.

Choosing an outfit wasn't typically such a struggle for Cozen, but tonight was not quite the same. She needed to pick the *right* dress. One that reminded whoever needed a reminder that she was very much a woman, but not every other woman, too.

And certainly not an easy woman.

Only a few days after stepping into Jett Griffin's path, and things were starting to come together. Tonight was just one more step forward for her plans. Another way to try and get even closer to the older gentleman, and inside his very private life.

Jett made no secret earlier that week when he came to the restaurant, and called Chase in at the same time Cozen was delivering the man's food. He wanted Cozen to have that Saturday off—demanded Chase give it to her, actually.

Unsurprisingly, and despite Saturdays being the busiest for the restaurant, Chase was quick to agree. Jett was pleased.

All the while, Sargon—still attached to Jett's side—had barely passed Cozen a glance. For that, she was grateful. She was not forced to make even more of an effort to keep her attention on Jett while he was in her presence when what she really wanted to do was feed in to the desire she felt to learn more about the dark-eyed God in the corner.

Small blessings.

Now, it was Saturday.

Cozen was left to pick a dress.

Quickly, she began to pull the curlers from her hair, and opted to settle on the purple dress. It was a bit too modest for her tastes—no low neckline, and no high slit in the skirt. It was still tight enough to say she was all woman, and with a killer pair of heels, it would do more than any other dress could have.

Her makeup was already done—a mixture of a deep maroon to accentuate her lips, and nude tones to compliment her eyes. Anything more, and she worried it might be a bit too much for a man like Jett who appeared to appreciate a more regal appearance when it came to himself.

She suspected—because men were predictable in that way—that he would also appreciate her to dress, and look, the same way. Classy, but not over the top. Stylish, but not like she walked off a goddamn runway. Simple and pretty, but not as though she could blend into the crowd with everyone else in New York.

She had to stand out, but not too much, of course. Just enough for people to appreciate. She knew all too well how men like Jett worked, and what they needed hanging off their arm.

Some people called those kinds of women arm candy.

Their men preferred *assets*.

Cozen wasn't keen on being called, or seen as, anyone's asset, but whatever. It was for the job—she would do damn near anything for the job.

As long as it got done.

She had just slipped on a pair of black peep-toe pumps with a six-inch heel when a knock echoed on the door of her apartment. She moved swiftly through the apartment, and ran her fingers through the loose curls to open them up a bit more along the way.

Cozen didn't bother to check the peephole—Jett had said he would send someone to pick her up, and according to the clock, they were right on time. She just pulled the door open, and then damn near tripped over her own feet at the sight of the man waiting behind it.

Sargon.

He wasn't looking at her at first, instead staring at the eighties carpet in the hallway that greatly needed to be replaced. But then he lifted his head, and those amber eyes burrowed into hers with some kind of hell waiting behind them.

Jesus.

He was still cut-from-stone.

Still bad for her body.

Still *distracting*.

"You look lovely," Sargon said, smiling crookedly.

"You haven't even looked at anything other than my face. How do you know I look *lovely*?"

Cozen should have just taken his compliment, and shut her fucking mouth. Instead, she gave him an opening to peruse her dress and body without concern of being ashamed that he was doing so. And Sargon did just that, too.

His gaze traveled down her bare throat, over her dress, lingering on her breasts, and hips, and then down her legs to her heels. He didn't hide the way he lingered there, either.

Definitely a leg man.

It made a shiver crawl up her spine with damning intent. Devastating and wonderful, it coated her nerves with a lustful need, and threatened to derail everything she was working for.

Goddamn him.

As fast as he had looked her over, Sargon came back to meet her gaze with a slow, sensual smile. "As I said, Cozen, you look lovely."

"Thank you," she managed to say.

She mentally patted herself on the back because fuck her, this was going to go downhill fast if she couldn't get this shit under control.

"Jett didn't say he was going to be sending you," she said.

Sargon lifted one brow, and nodded. "Yes, well, he figured I would be the better choice to pick you up, and whatever else was needed."

"Why?"

"He thinks I don't scare you, and he's very concerned about keeping you happy and pleasant while he … pursues you."

Cozen cleared her throat.

Sargon just gave her a lot of information without realizing he had done so. Or shit, maybe he did realize it. Who knew?

"Oh."

She offered nothing else. Sargon didn't press for more, either.

Then, he held out a black velvet box. It was the size of his palm with two tiny hinges on the other side. She didn't immediately reach out to take the box, instead letting Sargon decide what she was supposed to do with it.

"A gift," he said.

"From Jett."

She didn't even pose it as a question.

Sargon tried to smile, but it just ended up looking like a half sneer. "Yes, from *Jett*. Open it."

Cozen flipped the top open on the velvet box, and eyed the golden piece resting inside on crushed velvet. Two thin ropes of gold connected by dangling gold bars. It was a simple design, but still beautiful. A piece that could be layered, or worn by itself.

"He thought," Sargon said, "that it would match the ring on your thumb."

Instantly, Cozen withdrew her hands from the necklace in the box, and covered the ring on her thumb to hide it.

"He notices everything," Sargon added, "and he found that you don't take the ring off. He figured you might like something to accentuate the ring, and compliment it at the same time."

Well …

Shit.

"It's beautiful," she said.

That wasn't a lie.

"Would you like me to help you put it on?" Sargon asked.

The last thing Cozen needed was this man's hands on her body. Her stupid desire spoke up before the rational part of her brain could.

"Yes, I would," she said.

Cozen got a nice show of Sargon's fast reflexes as he yanked the jewelry out with one hand, snapped the lid closed on the box at the same time, and in a blink, had discarded the box to his back pocket. Never once did he take his eyes off her.

Stepping closer, he moved behind Cozen, and allowed the necklace to dangle over her throat. At the first graze of his fingertips along her skin, she sucked in a fast breath. Her best bet was to talk while he worked as to keep her libido in fucking check.

"Sargon—where does that come from?" she asked. "The name, I mean."

"Persian, mostly, and my bloodline comes from Iran."

"Huh. And how did you come to work for Jett?"

Talking wasn't really helping all that much. She could still feel his fingers sliding over the side of her neck where her pulse raced in her throat.

Sargon's fingertips pressed softly into the spot, showcasing her traitorous emotions to him. To his credit, he didn't mention a thing.

"He stumbled upon me, you could say," Sargon murmured in her ear. "As most of my bosses do. I am—sort of—a jack of all trades. I never settle in one place for long, and there's always something new on the horizon. It keeps me entertained and never bored, anyway."

Cozen closed her eyes, and briefly sucked in a deep breath. She hoped it would help to settle her. It really didn't. She was still just as turned on and unsettled by Sargon's close proximity has she had been seconds before.

This man was going to be a problem for her.

A big one.

"Relax," Sargon said behind her. "Calm your heart."

"Perhaps you should stop touching me, then."

"Ask me to, and I will."

Cozen didn't.

It was Sargon's phone ringing that sent them two of the moving feet apart, but it was the caller who sent them out of the apartment.

Jett was waiting.

Cozen nearly forgot.

Sargon was dangerous, she knew.

In more ways than one.

Sargon had been silent for the entire drive across Manhattan. He never even looked into the rearview mirror, and Cozen kept checking.

He pulled the car to a stop outside a restaurant—one even fancier than the place she worked for—and still said nothing. He only spoke once he had opened up her door, and helped her from the car.

What he said?

"Enjoy your evening, Cozen."

This man was an enigma.

Cozen couldn't think on it, or Sargon, for very long. Jett was waiting. Dressed in a black suit with a silver vest and tie, he waited at the entrance of the restaurant with a welcoming smile. He didn't hide how he looked her over as he offered his hand for her to take.

"You look quite beautiful," Jett said, bringing her closer to his side as they started the walk up the steps. "Not that I expected anything different."

His fingers grazed the necklace at her throat, but she didn't feel the same sparks and shivers she had felt with Sargon at the touch.

"The necklace looks beautiful, too. I'm happy to see you wearing it."

"I liked it."

"Wonderful."

"I waffled a bit."

"I hope not on coming tonight."

Cozen gave him a look, and laughed. "No, on the dress. I couldn't decide."

She was testing the waters.

Giving him an opening.

Jett took it like a gaping-mouthed fish—hook, line, and sinker. "I like this dress, actually. Not too much, but just enough. It suits you."

Good to know.

"You'll enjoy this restaurant. They make the best Italian food. Owned by an associate of mine," Jett continued.

He prattled on.

Cozen acted entertained.

She chanced a look over her shoulder just before they entered the restaurant. Sargon had not left the side of the vehicle where he remained standing with his hands clasped at his back. He had barely spoke or looked at her before.

He was looking at her now.

Unashamed.

Yeah.

Bad all over.

Especially for her.

Cozen shook off the odd feeling, and went back to her date, and main target for the foreseeable future. Jett, that was.

"Jett," she murmured.

His dark eyes looked her over, and he smiled. "What, darling?"

"I was wondering …"

"Mmm, keep going."

"What your plans are for tonight? With me, I mean."

Jett's smile deepened a bit—a look some women might consider sexy, or suggestive. He was not a bad looking man, and she had not lied when she said he appeared in his forties. He was fit, tall, dark, and handsome.

Any woman would be quite lucky to catch Jett's eye, and keep his attention.

Cozen, however, was just using him. He was a means to an end. Her attraction and affections for him would only last for as long as it took to get the Astor's ring back, and not one second longer.

"That would depend," Jett said.

"On what?"

"Well, you, I suppose. And of course, what *you* want, Cozen."

"I would like to have a good time here, but you should know that I am not the kind of woman who is quick to get on my back for a good looking man."

Jett chuckled as they waited for the woman at the podium to finish with other patrons. His hand on Cozen's arm tightened a bit—not a hurtful squeeze, but one that said he heard her unspoken words loud and clear.

"What about a rich one?" he asked.

"Not even for that."

"Good—never let a fancy man demean you … unless, of course, you're ready and willing to be demeaned. Then by all means, do what you wish." Jett passed her a look, and winked. "I like you, Cozen. You're an interesting one."

"And what does that mean?"

"It means you should remain interesting to me. Otherwise, my patience runs thin, and my expectations change."

Duly noted.

Duly fucking noted.

6

Sargon did not drink spirits when he worked. It was a rule that tended to serve him well over the years. When everyone else around him was drunk from consuming too much liquor, his mind was still fairly sound. He was still capable of handling whatever was thrown his way without falling over like a fool.

And yet, there he sat at the bar inside the Reverie Manhattan, tossing back his fourth shot in an hour. The whiskey burned his throat on the way down, but he reveled in that harsh sting. He needed it at the moment.

Waving two fingers at the male bartender, Sargon then pointed down at his empty glass. "One more, thanks."

"You got it, man." Spinning the bottle in a way that Sargon supposed was interesting—if playing dangerously with top shelf liquor was amusing to some people—the bartender came his way. Once his next drink was poured, the guy said, "You drinking something away, or what?"

Sargon muttered, "Or something."

A blonde woman with a short red dress came up to the other end of the bar, and just like that, the bartender's attention was gone from Sargon. Something better—prettier—had come along to catch his attention.

Not that Sargon minded.

He wasn't in the mood to be sharing his *troubles*, anyway. Not with some random stranger behind a bar pouring his drinks. Besides, he didn't even have a fucking reason to be troubled, considering.

Except he did …

Chancing a glance over his shoulder, Sargon's gaze narrowed in on where he was supposed to be watching. He hadn't been watching them since they came into the restaurant, actually. Who the fuck was going to bother them in here?

Sargon found Jett and Cozen tucked away in the far corner of the restaurant. Shadowed by dim lights, and blocked partially by a partition wall. Still, he could see enough.

Of *her*, that was.

He could only see Jett from the shoulders up.

Cozen, however, was mostly in full view but for the dim lighting. Sargon could see her smile, though, and the purple dress that hugged her young curves. Those black heels on her feet did a real number for her legs.

Smooth legs. Her skin was a shade lighter than olive, but fuck him if he didn't think they still had that creamy quality, too. Had it been him with that woman, the last thing he would have done was hide her away in a dimly lit corner where she couldn't be properly seen by those around them.

No.

He would show her off.

On *his* arm.

It's what a beauty like her deserved.

Nothing less.

Sargon wasn't entirely sure what it was about Cozen that got to him. Something about her had claws—they'd dug into his skin, and burrowed inside his body with a few passing words, and one too many lingering looks.

The woman couldn't be older than her mid-twenties—*at most*. What was she doing with a man in his fifties?

Sargon wasn't foolish. He knew all too well that there were women willing to forgo their preferences in men simply to get a hand into a bank account. He didn't think that was the case with Cozen because she genuinely seemed interested in Jett.

And then, in their quick moments alone, she had also seemed struck and caught by Sargon. He was not a dumb man. He saw the way she looked at him, and felt how her heart picked up at nothing more than his *touch*.

He wondered how fast he might get her heart racing if he could get the chance to sink his teeth in her neck while he fucked her from—

"Sorry about that, man," said the bartender.

Sargon blinked out of his less than innocent thoughts to find the bartender was back. This time, the man had no bottle or fancy trick to show. Instead, the guy wiped the bar top down with a rag as he talked.

About Sargon.

"Anyway, don't think I forgot because a lady came up," the guy said. "Men have to look out for each other, huh? What's up?"

Great.

Now Sargon's life was being condensed to cliché moments.

The weary barkeep, and the drunk he entertained.

The rich man, and the girl he couldn't have.

Sargon shook his head, and pushed the shot glass across the bar to the man. "Not in the mood to talk, now, but thank you anyway."

The bartender shrugged his shoulders. "Up to you, man."

Frankly, Sargon needed to take his place again before Jett noticed he had left it. Not that the older man would mind, really. Jett tended to be pretty laid back as long as he wasn't outside when one of his men wandered off for a few minutes.

Sargon was still new.

He figured—why push it?

Right, that's what you figured. It's not the pretty piece of ass with the interestingly strange name, killer smile, russet eyes, and legs for days that's making you want to get back there. Not at all.

Sargon ignored his taunting inner voice, and turned around on the barstool. He didn't get up right away, instead choosing to look back at the table, and see if he even was needed over there. It didn't look like it, considering Jett and Cozen were still chatting away.

Actually, laughing about something.

Jett reached across the table, and stroked Cozen's cheek with two fingers. Sargon had no doubt the man was complimenting her, then. Women loved their compliments, and they craved the feeling of being wanted by someone amazing.

Was Jett *amazing?*

Not really.

A dime a dozen in New York.

Minus the criminal thing, of course.

Still, at the sight of Cozen's demure smile from the touch—and whatever words Jett had told her—that burning feeling was back in Sargon's gut. Hot, heavy, and fast. Devastating, really, like a punch hard enough to his gut that it made him bleed from the inside.

Jealous.

Again.

Jesus.

He really needed to get this shit under control somehow. This was bad for him—bad for the job. He didn't need to find himself dead and in a makeshift grave because he couldn't control his baser urges.

Sargon's attention snapped back to the spot it was supposed to be as Cozen stood from the table. She smoothed down her dress, and nodded at Jett before simpering him with another one of those sweet smiles. Then, she quickly turned and headed in the direction of the bathrooms.

Jett didn't wait more than two seconds before his gaze swept the restaurant. Once he found Sargon sitting at the bar, Jett waved his hand subtly.

A silent order to come his way.

At the moment, going to Jett was the last thing Sargon wanted to do, but he forced himself off the stool. It was the longest ten seconds of his life to cross the floor before he leaned over the partition wall keeping his boss mildly protected.

"Yes?" Sargon asked.

Jett pointed in the direction Cozen had gone. "Twenty-five. Cozen Grace Taylor. Born in Vermont."

Sargon blinked.

That's what Jett had been doing?

Plying information from her all night?

"What do you want me to do with that information?" Sargon asked.

"I have a busy couple of weeks. I will give you the name of my contacts who pull information for me, and you can call this in for me, and handle it. I want you to get information on the woman. Whatever you can find, bring it to me."

Sargon cleared his throat, and his gaze drifted in the direction Cozen had left. "What, do you not trust her, or something?"

"I don't trust *anyone*," Jett muttered, chuckling. "But no, mostly, I like her. And so, I have to know about her."

"Like her," Sargon echoed.

"She's fascinating."

To say the least …

Sargon stayed a few paces behind Jett and Cozen as the two took a stroll down Fifth Avenue. He was far enough behind them that he couldn't hear their conversation, yet still close enough that he could step in should he need to.

Cozen kept her hand tucked into Jett's arm as he pointed at a statue they passed, and she laughed.

For the nearly three weeks that Sargon had worked for Jett, he did not know the man to casually take walks in the middle of the city. He much preferred to be chauffeured to and from wherever he was going.

Personal preference.

Safety, too.

Sargon was lost to his thoughts, and starting to wish he was anywhere but there, when a ringing phone brought him back to reality with a bang. He damn near slammed into Jett and Cozen before he realized the two had stopped walking.

It only took a quick look from Jett for Sargon to put the distance back between them once more, but not the same amount as before. He could now hear what Jett was saying on the phone, and it sounded like this *date* was going to be cut short.

Thank God for small miracles.

"Right now?" Jett asked.

Cozen passed a look to Sargon—questioning. He only shrugged, and looked across the street to give the two some semblance of privacy.

Not that it mattered.

"Really, Silas?" Jett snapped.

Silas—Jett's oldest son—was a lot like his father in many ways. In too deep with bad people, and distrustful of everyone around him. Sargon spent less than ten minutes in the man's presence, and wished it had been less.

Some people just had that effect on others.

"Fine, yes," Jett said after a few seconds, "I will be there in thirty minutes. No, no … tell him to stay where he is. I will handle it. I told you not to put your opinion in on this. That deal is going to be a big one for us."

Jett wasted no time hanging up on his oldest son, and Sargon brought his attention back to his boss for the moment.

"I'm sorry," Jett told Cozen, "but this is where I have to say goodbye for the night."

Cozen frowned.

It was genuine—or it looked like it.

In her eyes, though, Sargon swore he saw relief.

Or was he wishing to see that?

"Shame," Cozen said, smiling a little. "I thought you were going to show me around a little more. I was looking forward to it."

Jett laughed, and reached out to stroke Cozen's cheek like he had back at the restaurant. This time, she used her hand to cover his, and wrap her fingers around his hand. Jett's gaze never left Cozen as he spoke, and she didn't seem to mind keeping her attention entirely on him, either.

Christ.

That strange jealousy burned inside Sargon again. This shit was getting out of control. What was wrong with him?

"I promise I will show you around another evening," Jett promised. "And you, too. I will show *you* off on another evening."

Cozen's smile widened to show off teeth. "Sounds like a plan."

Jett nodded, and then looked to Sargon with a wave in his direction. "I will have Sargon take you home, and I will have my other men come with me. I have no doubt Sargon will look after you, and make sure you get home safe and sound."

She gazed at Sargon for the briefest second before going back to Jett. "Whatever you like, Jett."

As fast as the evening had begun, it seemed like it was now over. Jett moved closer to Cozen, and gave her a quick kiss on her cheek. She didn't turn her head to offer anything more, and Jett didn't try for something else, either.

Still, the jealousy raged.

Sargon seethed.

And he had no idea why.

"Have a good evening," Jett murmured to Cozen, "and thank you for keeping me company."

"I will see you on Monday at the restaurant, right?"

"Twelve sharp."

Cozen winked. "Sounds like a plan."

Jett took a large step back from Cozen, and raised his hand toward the street. Within seconds, a black town car had pulled up next to the man, and he slipped inside without a word. But not before he gave Sargon a pointed look.

A silent order.

Sargon heard it loud and clear.

It was only once Jett was gone that Cozen finally turned to him with her face a mask of nothingness. The smiles and twinkling eyes she had been wearing all night were now gone, and instead, an expressionless doll stared back at him.

"Exhausting, is it?" Sargon asked.

He had no business doing so.

Cozen's mask slipped as she cocked a brow. "What is?"

"Pretending."

Fire flashed in her sharp gaze, but just as quick as it came on, it was gone. She didn't entertain his question or statement, but he didn't really need her to. That glint in her eye had been more than enough to tell him what he needed to know.

The girl was pretending.

Just enough, apparently.

But for what?

"I guess you're the one stuck with taking me home, Sargon," Cozen muttered.

Sargon smirked, and for the first time all night, he didn't mind being close to this woman. At least, not now that it was just them alone. "I wouldn't describe it as being stuck, no."

"Hmm."

He gestured back the way they had come. "The car left for me is this way."

"Great."

Sargon let Cozen move in to step with him before he snagged her arm, and tucked her hand into his elbow. At first, she tried to tug her hand back, but he held firm and refused to let her go.

"What are you doing?" she asked, eyes flashing with indignation.

"Keeping you safe. It's what Jett wants."

Her lips flattened from their pretty bow-shape into a grim line. "I don't think he means this close, actually."

Sargon glanced down at her—she wasn't very much shorter than his six foot three in her heels—and lifted a brow. The sweet pink flush had colored up her neck just beneath the collar of her trench coat, and he could see her pulse racing in her throat just below her skin.

"He's going to look in to your history," Sargon murmured.

Cozen stiffened a bit. "Is he?"

"Do you have something to hide, Cozen?"

Her laughter came out musical as people blew by them on the street. "Don't we all have skeletons in our closet?"

"Some bones are harder to find than others."

"Only if there's bones left behind."

Sargon smiled—she had a damn good point. "I'll be the one tasked with looking in to your history. You could save me a bit of trouble, and let me know what I'm going to find here and now."

"Is that your way of trying to pry personal information out of me?"

"Perhaps."

Cozen gave him a look, but he saw the amusement dancing in her eyes. "I'll take my chances, Sargon."

"Your call, woman."

The two walked in silence until Sargon had found his vehicle from earlier. He helped Cozen into the back seat, but before he closed the door, he once again caught her staring at him.

Not in distain.

Not in irritation.

No, in *interest*.

He smiled. "Something on your mind?"

"Should there be, Sargon?"

"You tell me."

Cozen shook her head, and then glanced away. "I don't think so."

"Shame. I know I told you this already, but it deserves a second mention. You really do look beautiful, Cozen. The most beautiful woman in New York at the moment. It's too bad you spent your night with a man who didn't understand you deserved to be showcased first, and not a promise of more."

Her head snapped back in his direction, and the interest in her eyes had changed to something else entirely. Something that looked a hell of a lot like *lust*.

"Is that so?" she whispered.

"I never say things I don't mean."

Sargon closed the passenger door before he said something else. Or rather ... did something else.

"You don't have to walk me right to my door," Cozen grumbled half-heartedly over her shoulder.

Sargon simply lifted a brow, but said nothing else in response. He lingered a step behind her as she climbed the flights of stairs to her apartment. All the while, occasionally throwing words at him like she wanted him to respond.

Or maybe to see if he would.

Sargon was trying to control his nonsense. Nothing more. That meant keeping his mouth shut, regardless of what he was screaming inside.

Sargon stepped up to the door for Cozen's hallway as she reached for the handle, and quickly pulled the door open before she could.

"Thanks," she said, strolling past him.

"It's what a gentleman does—or so someone told me once."

That caught her attention.

He was not good at this keeping quiet thing, clearly.

"Who is this *someone?*"

"My mother," he admitted. "She once told me that even men who are not entirely good in everything they do can still be gentlemen at the end of the day."

Cozen came to a stop in front of an apartment with a brass 7 on the door. "And does that mean you're not an entirely good man, Sargon?"

"I am a lot of things."

"Is good one of them?"

"Depends on who you ask," he murmured.

Cozen took her time unlocking the door of her apartment, and once it was opened, she turned to him again. "Thank you for seeing me to my door."

"My pleasure."

"Was it?"

He smiled, and caught himself getting lost in memorizing the soft lines of her heart-shaped face. He swore that depending on the moment or situation, Cozen changed in subtle ways. Like a chameleon, he wondered what her true colors were.

"Very much so," he confessed.

Cozen glanced away before saying, "I think had Jett gotten his way tonight, you would not have needed to see me home at all."

"I'm sorry?"

"He asked if I would like to spend the night with him. I could pick any hotel in the city, he said, and we would have a room until I was ready to leave."

Instantly, that burning tightness was back in Sargon's chest and gut again. Like fire ravaging his insides, and a noose had suddenly tightened around his neck.

Jealousy was a monster.

He did not particularly wear it well.

It seemed Cozen also didn't miss the heat that flashed in Sargon's eyes, never mind the sneer that worked its way over his lips. Her soft, almost *knowing*, smile reflected back at him.

"Do you enjoy that?" he asked.

Cozen's tongue peeked out to wet her lips. "Enjoy what, Sargon?"

"Poking at a monster."

"You have a monster to poke?"

"Seems so."

"Jealousy is not a good look on a handsome man," she told him. "And by the way, I told him no."

Sargon glanced down the hallway seeing that it was still empty. He was a mess of confusion and chaos. Struck stupid over a woman he had no business being anything over, and currently working for a man he held no loyalty to at the end of the day.

This was not the kind of mess he got himself caught up in. He didn't know what it was about Cozen that had seemed to get under his skin so easily.

It didn't help that she clearly knew, too.

"I won't say I'm sad that you refused him," Sargon said. "But you also agreed to see him again."

"I have to."

Sargon's gaze darted back to meet hers. "And why is that?"

Cozen didn't answer his question, instead moving closer until her sweet floral scent was soaking into Sargon's lungs with every breath he took. The scent of her perfume was familiar to him—comforting for reasons he couldn't explain. She crowded his personal space. Something he took great pride in keeping closed to others. Her pretty features and sexy little grin all but clouded his vision.

Sargon saw nothing but her.

He liked that a little too much.

"What would you have done had I agreed to spend the night with him tonight?"

Her question whispered across his skin, yet it still stung like a slap. His first reaction was to curl his lip up at the corner in another sneer, and then his second instinct was to take what he wanted from her while she was this close, and he had the chance.

So, he did just that.

Sargon kissed her. He closed the small bit of distance between him and Cozen, and let his lips crash down on hers. The force was enough to bruise, and yet, she didn't shy away from his kiss at all. If anything, she urged him on and silently challenged when her tongue snaked out to strike against his bottom lip.

He gave her what she wanted—deepening the kiss to tangle their tongues together as she started to walk backward. He went with her, backing her into the apartment until they couldn't be seen from the hallway.

Her fingernails dug into his jaw, and his hand enclosed her throat. She tasted like red wine, and cherries. The heat of her mouth, and the way her tongue clashed against his was enough to get his dick straining in his pants.

Then, she bit his lip.

Sargon gave a little growl from the shock, and snapped back from her. Cozen stood just a few inches away with blazing eyes, and swollen pink lips. He bet the only way she could look hotter than she did right then was if he put her on her knees, and stuffed his cock down her throat.

Jesus.

What was he doing?

"I don't think I asked you to stop."

Sargon nodded, and took a couple of steps backward toward the door. "Be careful, Cozen. I don't know what game you're playing, but it's a dangerous one."

She needed to be careful with more than just her games …

With her life …

With him.

"I didn't ask you to stop," she repeated.

Sargon took one more step backward. Just enough to grab hold of the door, and slam it shut.

Cozen was not a stupid woman, and she was not the type to take risks that may land her in a heap of shit. Especially not when she was on a damn job. Yet, when Sargon slammed the apartment door and took a step closer to her, her heart thundered so hard, she could feel it throughout her entire body.

Not with fear, no.

With *anticipation*.

The what ifs, and all her traitorous desires.

See, she wasn't stupid—she felt his eyes on her from the moment he placed her in the back of the town car, and his gaze didn't leave all night. Not at the restaurant, and not when she was hanging off Jett's arm to charm the older man with every talent she had.

How did she know that?

Because she had been looking at Sargon, too. Whenever he thought she wasn't looking, Cozen saw him. He was too beautiful of a man not to look at, honestly. And one look was not nearly enough to satisfy her. He was not very good at being subtle, she had found, and the way he watched her was a palpable feeling.

Like something soft caressing her skin from afar. Silk roving over her body, wrapping skin-tight around her, and taking every inch of her in. She would have to be stupid not to notice, and she definitely was not that.

She wasn't risky on a job, either. She loved a thrill—her entire life was one thrill after another. She was paid to steal things from people, after all. She lived to do dangerous things that other people feared.

Still, Cozen never put her foot too deep into something if she didn't think she could pull it back out afterward. She worried that Sargon might be exactly that kind of problem for her. Something she was not in control of when a successful job demanded she have control of everything around her.

And yet …

Here she still was.

Watching him come closer.

"Tell me something about you," Sargon said.

"What kind of thing?"

"Something."

"Anything?"

"A *truthful* thing."

"Anything?" she countered again.

Sargon's dark eyes traveled down the length of her body, and he wasn't the least bit ashamed to be doing so. His pupils widened—a sure sign that he liked what he saw standing there waiting for him. That silky sensation washed over Cozen's nerves again.

How he did that, she couldn't begin to understand. She wanted more of it, though.

So much more.

"Something he doesn't know," Sargon returned, looking back up at her once more. "Tell me something he doesn't know."

Dangerous territory.

The warning bells rang in her head.

Cozen ignored them.

"I'll do just about anything to get what I want, but I won't sleep with him for it," she said, letting the words slip past her barely moving lips. Maybe then, she could pretend like she hadn't actually said them at all. "Your turn."

"This isn't a tit for tat."

Cozen pouted.

The pout was quickly erased when Sargon came close enough to grab her face, and yank her toward him. His fingertips dug into the sensitive skin of her jaw as he brought her close enough for his warm breath to wash over her lips. She had found earlier that his mouth tasted like whiskey, and mint.

Quite a combo.

Two of her favorite things.

Sargon's gaze pinned her in place, and she let out a shuddering breath. "I don't ever give more than I *want* to—I always make the rules, and control how they are executed."

Cozen blinked. "I see."

He had told her something, after all.

In more ways than one.

"Do you understand?" he asked.

"Well enough."

"Do you have a problem with that—do you have a problem with me controlling how I use you, fuck you, or otherwise?"

"I have a problem with ropes, but not much else."

Sargon's eyes flashed with something unknown as his gaze dropped to her lips for a brief second. "Why ropes?"

"I simply prefer something less bulky."

He let out a strangled sound that came off like both a groan, and a growl. "Jesus Christ, woman."

Cozen let out a breathy laugh, but Sargon quickly quieted her by slamming his mouth down on hers. He was all teeth and lips and tongue when he kissed her, then. A war started between them with that kiss, one that she was sure she could not win. She didn't mind surrendering to the way his tongue struck against hers, and wore what was left of her control down.

The spots where his fingertips dug into her skin sung with a sting that she was sure would linger for days. She didn't mind a bruise or two; she knew how to cover them.

Sargon bit her bottom lip hard enough to make Cozen whine before he pulled away from her kiss. Like the first time, he took a step back. Far enough that there was a good foot or two of space between them where she could not reach out to touch or grab him. Certainly not to bring him closer.

He waved a finger at her. "Remove your clothes."

The order—it didn't even come off like a demand—washed over her senses with a devastating intent. She was the type of woman who always needed to be in some kind of control, and maybe that was why during sex, she liked to give it up.

Be wild.

Free.

Unrestricted.

"And then get on your knees," Sargon added.

Cozen's fingers hesitated on the zipper of the dress, and she glanced up at Sargon. The edges of his lips had curved in the most sinful smirk she had ever seen. The kind of grin that likely melted panties, and broke hearts.

She wondered if she would be immune.

"Backing out?" he asked.

"No."

"Then hurry up, Cozen."

She tugged the zipper on the side of the dress down, and then shimmied out of the piece until it fell to the floor. Just like that, it was forgotten. Sargon's gaze traveled over the red and black lace bra and panty set she had on underneath. He lingered on the junction where her panties met her inner thighs.

"Waxed, bare, or trimmed?" he asked.

As he spoke, he undid the buttons on his shirt, and tugged the article down his arms. Discarding it to the floor with her dress, he still didn't come any closer than he already was.

Cozen unsnapped her bra, and let it fall down her arms before dropping it to the floor. "All three, actually. Waxed where it matters, bare all over my pussy, and trimmed short on my pubis."

Sargon let out another one of those sexy noises. "That sounds like a lot of upkeep."

"I aim to please."

His eyes found hers in a blink. "And who exactly are you doing that to *please*, Cozen?"

"Does it please you?" she asked instead of answering his question.

She tugged her panties down, and let them fall to the floor. That left her standing in nothing but the black peep-toe pumps, and for the first time, Sargon's carefully managed mask slipped as she stood naked before him. His eyebrow cocked, and he flashed his teeth as he looked her over. He didn't even have to answer her—she knew what he would say before the words came out of his mouth.

"Yes," he murmured, "it pleases me."

"Then that's what matters."

"Is that tiger lilies on your thigh?"

Cozen peered down at the bright red bushel of tiger lilies tattooed on her thigh. "It is."

"Any particular reason why?"

"They're my favorite flower."

She didn't say why, and he didn't ask for more information.

"Any other tattoos I can't see yet?"

"No."

With that said, Cozen lowered to her knees.

As she had been told to do.

Staring down at her, Sargon said nothing as he unbuckled his belt, and pulled the leather from the loopholes on the pants. Cozen's eager gaze never left his as he tossed the item away, and unsnapped the buttons on his pants.

He opened his fly, and she grinned a little.

"What?" he asked.

"Commando," she said, shrugging. "I'm not surprised."

"Do I seem like the type, or something?"

He fisted his length, and stroked his already-hard cock with firm, long strokes. Cut, thick, and long, his cock was a beautiful sight to lay her eyes on. She was pretty sure just the sight alone made her even wetter between her thighs.

"I wouldn't say there's a type," she replied, "but I had a *feeling*."

Sargon wet his lips as he came closer. "I bet you did. I liked the way your lips looked after I kissed you."

Her gaze jumped from his cock to his eyes as he came to stand directly in front of her. "Did you?"

"Very much. Why were you so willing to get on your knees for me like this?"

"Maybe I like it here."

"Oh, a sassy one."

Cozen grinned. "I *do* like it here."

"Like what, exactly—being a man's slut? Letting him use you? Wearing his marks and his cum? Which one?"

"All of it."

Sargon chuckled darkly. "All I want to know now is what your mouth looks like after I fuck it. Open up, beautiful girl."

His hand stuck out like a flash of lightning, and grabbed her throat to tilt her head up even higher. Cozen's natural instinct kicked in at having someone's hand on her throat, and she opened her mouth.

Sargon took the opportunity to slide the thick head of his cock between her parted lips. He kept the one hand on her throat, but his other wrapped tightly in her hair, and tugged hard enough to sting. He worked his length in her mouth—a brutal pace that had her eyes watering, and her pussy wet.

He had a distinct taste—like salt and sin in her mouth. His cock was a smooth velvet against the roughness of her tongue. He didn't slow for a second as he fucked her mouth harder, and grinned up above her.

Cozen tried to smile around his length, but it didn't quite work. Instead, she settled on flicking her tongue against the underside of his shaft where she could feel his heart racing. He must have liked that considering he grabbed hold of her hair a little bit harder.

"Don't you choke," he taunted.

Cozen let her teeth graze the skin of his dick.

Sargon grunted hard. "*Fuck*, watch it."

She bet he liked that, too.

"Are you going to take it all?" Sargon asked. "Every last drop, Cozen?"

She couldn't speak like this, but her gaze flicked upward to meet his. It was apparently all the answer he needed. His hand closed around her throat, damn near taking what was left of her air away, and he tugged firmly on her hair on the next thrust. His cock hit the back of her throat, and she swallowed at the feeling of his length jerking. His cum hit the back of her tongue in spurts, and he didn't release his hold.

She took it all.

Just like he wanted.

"Jesus Christ," Sargon snarled, his hands shaking against her. "*That* would kill me."

He pulled out of her mouth, and Cozen took the chance to suck in a deeper breath than she had been getting using just her nose. He didn't waste any time to pull her up from the floor, and spin her around.

Cozen's chest slammed in to the wall, and all she could do was laugh. A breathless, pleased laugh that only seemed to urge Sargon on a little more.

"You like this, don't you?" he asked in her ear. "I've got a special trick—make me come once, and I can fuck you for hours before I can come again."

His hands drove up her body, and then down again. Fingertips raking her skin, and leaving lines behind. Or … she hoped.

"You like it rough, beautiful girl?" he asked.

"Love it when it hurts."

As if to check if she was lying, his hand slipped between her thighs. Two long, teasing fingers swept through the folds of her pussy, and then thrust in deep. It wasn't enough to give her what she really wanted because just as fast, he pulled those fingers back out.

"I bet you fucking like it," he said. "Your cunt is wet enough to drown me. Be a good girl, and I'll let you ride my face when I'm done filling you up."

Oh, God.

She heard the shuffle of foil, and then Sargon's hand was back in her hair, and pushing her head against the wall. Her cheek scraped against the paint as she let out another one of those taunting laughs. His hand slapped her ass, and she knew he was looking at a pretty, red handprint now.

"Just *fuck me*," she whispered.

He didn't need to tell her to widen her legs—she was already spread for him. He didn't give her any warning either before he took her from behind. His cock split her open with one brutal thrust that sent Cozen up on her toes in her heels.

It ached.

It filled her full.

It stretched her open.

It hurt, and it was so good, too.

Sargon gave her no time to catch a breath, or get used to the feeling of his thickness inside of her cunt. He just pulled out, and thrust right back in. Fucked her hard enough that her body slammed in to the wall again and again.

He pulled her hair, and then he spanked her ass. Those two fingers he used to tease her pussy were shoved into her mouth, and then quickly taken away to be shoved up her ass once he felt they were wet enough.

"Come for me," he urged in her ear. "And then I'll let you show me how good of a slut you can really be."

All dark, and sinful.

Like his eyes.

Like his taste.

Like him.

"Fucking come for me, Cozen. I want it—it's mine tonight."

Her orgasm crashed down on her body like a tsunami. What started in her womb quickly spread out, and drowned her in nothing but sensation.

Sargon fucked her through it.

And then he did it again.

The sky was beginning to lighten with the rising sun, and the oncoming morning. It was only then that Sargon finally pulled away from Cozen, and began to get dressed. He barely looked at her sparse apartment, and he didn't mention a thing about the fact she was using a mound of blankets and pillows on the floor of the living room as a bed.

Cozen sipped from a glass of red wine—she needed a drink after a night like that—and watched Sargon button his silk dress shirt. "You're not very loyal to your boss, are you?"

His gaze darted to her, but then quickly went back to the task of rolling up the sleeves of his shirt. "He's a job—not a friend."

"Still, don't you think you should draw clearer lines in the sand when it comes to things he has interest in?"

Sargon chuckled, and his lips curved sardonically. "Says the woman who sucked my dick like it was a straw, and water was going to come out of it."

Pink colored Cozen's cheeks.

She didn't let his words bother her, though.

"Nice deflection," she murmured.

Taking another sip of her wine, the two of them locked gazes, and she cocked her brow as if to challenge him.

Sargon sighed. "I take what I want—I don't know how to do things differently than how I have always done them."

A lump formed in Cozen's throat at his suggestion. She somehow forced it down.

"And you wanted me," she stated.

"There is no past tense. I learned that last night." He came closer to her as he said, "He's going to continue to pursue you, Cozen."

"Let him."

Sargon gaze darkened. "Let him?"

"It's what I need."

"And what else do you need, woman?"

Cozen smiled. "I'm not here to hurt him."

Only take from him …

Sargon stiffened, and then murmured, "He will only wait so long before whatever game you're playing with him becomes boring, or worse, he figures it out."

"I will take that risk."

Cozen leaned over, and pulled an item from its hidden place. She had kept it there all night … maybe she should have been the one to make sure it got back to its owner, but the possibility that she would have to wait to see Jett again meant she couldn't take that risk.

Besides, she had someone here who could likely return it without Jett noticing. Sargon watched Cozen with a keen eye as she brought her hand up high. She opened her palm, and resting there was a ring.

One Sargon seemed to recognize if the raising of his brow was any indication. Cozen might have laughed at the look on his face if she didn't think he would get offended.

She held Jett's ring from his index finger a little higher—a large gold band protected a rather large ruby. She turned the ring over, and examined it for any sign it was the Astor ring, but unfortunately found nothing. No cursive *A* or nothing to say this ruby had come from another ring and was placed in a new setting.

That's why she had taken it in the first place because she had the opportunity, and it wasn't unusual for people to repurpose their jewels into new pieces.

It wasn't the right ring, though.

Shame.

This whole thing could have been done before it even got started.

No job was ever that easy.

"Would you mind returning this for me?" Cozen asked.

"Where did you get that?" Sargon asked. "Did he take it off or something?"

Cozen arched a brow. "Or *something.*"

Just the way Sargon's gaze widened a bit, Cozen knew he then understood where she had gotten the ring from. He remembered, then. She smiled at the way the realization flitted over Sargon's handsome features.

On the street before Jett left. His hand on her face. Hers covering his.

"You took it? Just like that with me standing *right there* to watch?"

"Will you return it?" she asked, instead of answering him. "Jett will probably want it back, and I would hate if he thought he lost it. Just slip it anywhere he might find it. I think it's only fair after our little … time together."

Sargon's throat bobbed, and his jaw tightened. "Blackmail?"

"I wouldn't call it that."

"I would, woman."

"So be it," Cozen returned.

Sargon still took the stolen ring.

Cozen smiled. "Thank you."

He answered that by moving across her floor, yanking open her apartment door, stepping out, and slamming it behind him as he left. He didn't even say goodbye.

Cozen didn't blame him.

She waited just long enough to watch the sun fill the sky before she finally moved away from the window to find her phone. Turning the device on, she hit the number three key, and held it. It automatically dialed, and she put the phone to her ear.

The ring echoed.

Once, then twice.

Someone picked up on the third ring.

"Mathieu here," the man said. "What can I do for you?"

"Put me through to Pearl Astor, please."

The butler—Cozen only knew that because the man barked it at her when she called the last time—sighed. "Mrs. Astor is currently sleeping."

"Wake her up. Tell her it's the thief, and I have good news."

"She does not want to be—"

"*Wake her up.*"

"Fine," the man snapped.

She heard muttering, and the phone clacked as it was dropped on something hard. It took a few minutes, and she heard a click on the line before Pearl Astor's voice filled the receiver.

"Cozen, you better have a good reason for waking me up, child," Pearl said with a gravelly tone.

"You sound unwell."

"I am *fine*." Pearl's voice—despite being low—was still sharp enough to cut glass. Cozen got the point; personal shit was not on the table, apparently. "Why did you call?"

"Contact was made. I am in. The job is in play. It won't be long now before I'm closer."

Pearl was quiet for a long while before she asked in a whisper, "How long until the end?"

"That, I can't say."

"Then do not call me again until you have an answer."
Pearl hung up the phone.
Cozen downed the rest of her wine.
What else could she do?

Sargon was not the kind of man who might find himself pining over a woman—especially not if said woman was entirely off-limits to him in a big way. And really, he would not consider his current position to be *pining*.

More like obsessing.

Which was *far* worse.

He barely blinked, and two weeks had passed him by. Two weeks since he had Cozen Taylor alone, and gotten a taste of her. One taste was not nearly enough to satisfy him, and now he found himself like this.

Watching her.

Checking on her.

Wanting to be around her.

Because he was fucked like that.

He blamed her.

To be fair, Jett wanted this. The man all but demanded someone keep an eye on Cozen occasionally, and was quick to tell Sargon to do the job because she was not put off by him.

Fuck.

That woman was so far from being put off when it came to Sargon, really. He put that into the what-Jett-didn't-know-wouldn't-kill-him category. For now, anyway. Although who was he to say. It very well might kill the man at the end of the day.

Cozen was playing games.

Sargon just didn't know what.

He knew for a fact Jett had not been around the restaurant to ask for Cozen on her off hours. Actually, it had been a good week since Jett had even gone to eat at The Kingdom at all. Jett didn't like the idea of Cozen being ... left alone.

His boss had shit coming up—the Italian deal. Jett was trying to get things nailed down for that, and left Sargon to be the babysitter.

So to speak ...

He should be annoyed.

Irritated, at the very least.

Who wanted to watch someone for hours and hours, sometimes?

Sargon, apparently.

Sure enough, at exactly three minutes past seven in the evening, Cozen came out of the restaurant. She covered up her all black attire with a long tweed coat she left opened at the middle. She had let her hair down loose and free today. Her face was nearly free of all makeup but for a red lipstick that contrasted brightly against her black clothes.

The messenger bag she always carried was thrown over her shoulder. For a brief second, Cozen stood on the stoop of the restaurant, and glanced around at her surroundings. Her gaze traveled but didn't linger on any particular thing, and so he figured she was still unaware of his presence.

She actually didn't live very far away from the restaurant. Four blocks or so. Although frankly, Sargon wasn't quite sure if he would call her apartment a place that she actually lived in. He hadn't been so caught up in her pussy that he didn't take a second to look around.

There was barely anything there.

No pictures.

No knickknacks.

A few pieces of furniture.

Not much else. Nothing to say she had any attachment to the place. She could easily up and leave, and not feel as though she had left something important behind.

Cozen took the steps of the restaurant two at a time, and then started down the sidewalk. Something else Sargon noticed about her after watching her for two weeks—she didn't like cabs, and she walked *everywhere*. Even in those goddamn silver heels.

She could run in them, too.

He figured that took some kind of skill.

Sargon readied to pull the car—a vehicle he had been given by Jett to use—from the spot keeping him shadowed, but the ringing of his cell phone stopped him. He cussed under his breath, kept one eye on Cozen as she headed further into the crowd of people coming her way, and snatched his phone up from the seat.

Goddamn.

He was going to lose her.

"What?" Sargon barked into the phone.

"Is that anyway to greet your boss?" Jett asked.

Sargon glanced up at the roof of the car, taking his gaze away from Cozen's swaying—and *disappearing*—backside. She looked good walking in heels, too. A natural sway to her body that could memorize a man.

Fuck.

That's exactly what Sargon was.

So fucked.

"I'm currently a little busy here," Sargon said.

Fuck the risk of a fine.

He pulled the car out of the shaded parking spot, and onto the road. A little too fast, probably, considering his tires squealed a bit on the wet pavement. He even flipped the bird at the guy in the shitty white Toyota behind him when the asshole honked at him for cutting him off.

He probably shouldn't have done that, either.

Sargon was not supposed to draw attention to himself—Jett's orders. Or rather, *Cozen* was not supposed to notice he was following her.

Jett didn't want his possible toy to run off, or some nonsense like that.

"She's off now, isn't she?" Jett asked.

Sargon checked the clock. "For about four minutes now, yeah."

"Then, she's fine."

"She walks home." Sargon thought he might have caught sight of Cozen's wavy, russet-brown hair as he slowed his car behind a cab. He couldn't be sure, though. "In the middle of Manhattan, Jett. She doesn't even take a cab."

"Mmm, I know. I would send a car for her, but—"

"Wouldn't want her to know you're spying on her, huh?"

Jett chuckled. "Well, something like that."

"What did you need?"

Because Sargon really *was* kind of busy. Honestly, he just didn't like to obsess over Cozen while having Jett in the same vicinity. Even talking on the phone was a little too close for comfort as far as Sargon was concerned.

Did his voice change when he talked about her? Was it obvious his dick was tied in a knot over her?

He did not think Jett would appreciate Sargon's interest in Cozen, never mind the fact he had slept with the woman. Disrespect was one thing, but this was an all-out betrayal. Not to mention, if Jett did find out, he was liable to come back on Cozen for it, too.

Sargon wasn't willing to risk something like that simply because he didn't have more self-control, and slipped up. Yeah, a slip up. That was a good way to describe what the two of them had done together. He had fucked her for hours, tasted her pussy, and left his marks all over her body before he left the next morning.

Sargon *did* like to leave a mark of possession. Cozen's body was a blank canvas, and he couldn't help himself but mark it up.

Not a blank canvas anymore.

It made his dick hard to think about it.

Jesus Christ.

He was going to get himself killed.

Sargon felt foolish.

Absolutely fucking foolish.

"It's been, what, three weeks?" Jett asked. "Time to hand over whatever you have for me, I think."

Sargon was almost grateful for the man's interruption into his thoughts. "Three weeks for what, Jett?"

"Since I gave you the contacts to find information on Cozen. What is up with you, Sargon? You're usually quicker on the ball than this."

Shit.

"Yeah, three weeks."

"Bring me what you found, and brief me."

Without another word, Jett hung up the phone. Sargon was left staring blankly out the windshield as his car became gridlocked in Manhattan traffic. He wasn't going anywhere for a while, it seemed.

Jett was going to have to wait until traffic thinned out a bit. Not that the man would be pleased with the excuse—even if it wasn't technically a lie.

Nothing fucking new.

This was why he hated the city. He much preferred the beach.

Sargon peered in to the crowd again as his hands tightened around the leather-wrapped steering wheel. So tight, in fact, that his knuckles turned white from the pressure. Stress was eating at him all the time now.

He had lost Cozen. She was nowhere to be seen in the crowd.

Not that it mattered, now.

The boss calls.

Sargon stepped out of the car at a little past ten. The dark, inky sky hovered high above his head, and for a moment, he took the time to count the stars he could see. It was one of the things he missed the most.

Stars, that was.

In the city, the stars were not as visible. All the bright lights and pollution made a haze of sorts that kept them clouded from view. Whenever he did get the chance to appreciate the sky and stars, he took a minute or two to do just that.

"Took you long enough."

Sargon closed his eyes, and sucked in a deep breath. Counting back from five to settle the sudden jolt of irritation he felt at being interrupted, it only helped a minuscule amount. He opened his eyes again to find one of Jett's other bodyguards approaching him.

"He knew where I was," Sargon said. "I can't help that he sends me into Manhattan, and then calls me back during rush hour. I am not fucking Houdini. I'm not magic, and I don't work miracles just because someone demands I do."

So the counting thing probably didn't work.

Jean didn't look like he cared, either. "Whatever. Boss is inside waiting for you. In the dining room, I guess."

Sargon didn't bother to reply to the man. Things were still a bit tense for him with Jett's men, although the less time Sargon spent with them, the nicer they seemed to be. Not that he blamed them, really.

He wasn't particularly open to them, either.

Tucking the folder under his arm, Sargon headed for the entrance of the Griffin mansion. The estate rested on a few acres of land that was heavily guarded, but also allowed Jett privacy. Not that it really mattered.

Jett spent as much time away from his home as he did inside of it. The guy had penthouses and luxury apartments scattered all over the city. He wasn't overly fond of hotels—would use one if he absolutely had to—so he preferred to keep his options open.

A man opened the large French doors to allow Sargon in before he could even reach for the handle. He passed the black-dressed man a nod, and headed in the direction of the dining room on the bottom floor of the three-wing monster.

Jett rarely allowed his men beyond certain areas in his home, and if he did let them go further, it was with supervision. Sargon had seen most of the bottom floor plan, and the back of the house where a large in-ground pool rested around a white marble setting.

The whole mansion dripped in wealth. From the gold plated decals on the trim around the doorways, to the overly large chandeliers hanging from the cathedral-style ceilings. Jett did not make any effort to hide his riches inside his home.

Every which way someone turned, there was something more expensive to look at. A person could get lost simply going from one thing to the next.

It took Sargon a couple of minutes to get to the dining room. The voices filtering out from the space made him slow in his walk a bit. He wasn't one to eavesdrop, but Jett's relationship—or sometimes, lack thereof—with his two sons was a source of interest for Sargon.

The man had two grown sons.

Silas—twenty-eight.

And the youngest at twenty-five, Dash.

Apparently born to Jett's now-dead wife, Anabelle. Sargon didn't know much about the dead woman, and it wasn't a topic that was open for discussion. Jett didn't allow people to talk about her, not even his own sons.

"You should do the deal with the—"

"Both," Dash interjected. "Dad should do it with both of them."

"That's called signing your own death warrant," Silas returned.

Sargon rolled his eyes upward, and stepped into the entrance. If all they were discussing was business, he had no interest in spying. Jett's business dealings with various crime organizations held little interest to him.

The moment Sargon stepped into the entryway, all eyes in the room turned on him. He found Jett's sons—younger mirrors of their father in appearance—to be slightly more tolerable than the men he was forced to work with.

"Finally," Jett grumbled as he slammed his laptop shut. "Go find something to do, Silas, and take Dash with you. I will be around later."

Silas passed Sargon a look, and then glanced at his father's closed laptop. "But—"

"I am doing both deals. *End of discussion.*"

A deep scowl etched into Silas' face before he nodded once. "Fine."

Dash looked all too smug as he patted his father on the back, and then made a beeline for the doorway. "You're making the right choice, Dad."

Silas followed behind. "A choice that's going to either kill him, or ruin this operation, sure."

"Don't think I didn't hear that!"

The two men passed Sargon by in the entryway, and gave him a polite nod. Their three-piece suits were cut and tailored perfectly for their tall heights, and wide shoulders. He knew some people found the Griffin sons to be a bit … intimidating.

Sargon wasn't one of those people.

Barely anyone intimidated him.

Sure, the Griffin sons were arrogant, far too rich for their own good, and a little difficult to deal with, but that all came with the territory of their lives. It was partly how they were raised, and more so, what their lifestyles demanded from them.

Like their father, they too worked as brokers on the black market. A weaker man would not be able to face some of the most dangerous and vile humans on the earth and walk out with a deal the way they did on a regular basis. And no worse for wear, too. They always seemed to walk out alive.

That demanded some kind of respect at the end of the day.

"Come in," Jett said, waving a hand. "Stop standing there and making me wait longer than you already have. I am not getting any goddamn younger here, Sargon."

"Traffic was bad."

The excuse—as he figured it would—rolled right off Jett's shoulders like it didn't even matter in the first place.

"I gave you a fast car for a reason," Jett muttered before pointing at a chair. "Sit, and give me what you've got."

Sargon approached the left side of the table, and pulled out a chair closest to Jett's at the head seat. Unceremoniously dropping into the seat— an action that raised an eyebrow from Jett—he could only shrug.

"It's been a long day," Sargon muttered.

"I bet. Sitting in a car all day long can be tiring."

"It is when you sit and wait for nothing."

Jett's amusement faded fast. "I beg your pardon?"

"Nothing is happening. So I sit and wait for nothing."

"But you do it incredibly well."

Good for me.

Sargon almost felt like Jett's patronizing could have been helped along with a pat on the back, too. He didn't say that out loud.

Instead, he tossed the folder he'd been holding over to his boss. The manila file slid across the shiny oak tabletop, and skidded to a stop under Jett's waiting hand.

Sargon leaned back in the chair as Jett opened up the file, and waited the man out. He figured if Jett wanted his opinion, or needed to know more information, then he would ask. He didn't have anything to offer.

Not that he hadn't looked at the information in the folder. He *had.* He knew every little detail about Cozen's life that could be found because he had been obsessing over the contents of the folder from the moment he got the information two days ago.

He wasn't going to tell Jett that he had the information for that long, however.

A good fifteen minutes passed. Fifteen minutes of shuffling papers, and the occasional murmur or mutter from Jett. None of which were directed right at Sargon.

Finally, Jett closed the folder, and gave Sargon a look.

"What?" he asked.

Jett leaned back in his chair, and steepled his fingers. "Seems she has lived a rather difficult life."

Sargon nodded. "Dropped off at a fire station as a young infant, and then passed from foster home to foster home. One of which—because your guy looked in to that—was closed down for legal reasons. The husband and wife were quite abusive. Some of the minors in their care suggested sexual molestation, too, but that was never confirmed."

His boss cleared his throat. "I saw that, too. She would have been what, thirteen or so when she was at that particular home?"

"According to the documents found."

"Ran away, apparently," Jett added.

"Maybe she had a reason to."

"Mmm." Jett's gaze drifted to the folder before he said, "She was moved to another foster home before running away after a couple of years of living at that one, too."

"Sixteen," Sargon said, glancing up at the ceiling. "She would have been just shy of sixteen, then."

"Not much is on record for her after that. Why do you think that is?"

"Probably because like all runaways, she did what she could do. Worked where she could work, or did whatever she had to do to stay alive. Slept wherever there was shelter. Who knows? People don't mind taking advantage of that sort of thing—a worker they don't have to pay health insurance or taxes for, you know."

"She showed up at nineteen in California to get a license," Jett noted. "And some other documents, apparently."

"The address used checked out to a mid-list apartment complex. I take it she was probably doing moderately okay in her life by that point."

"As in, maybe she found a decent job, or whatever else, and settled into a good space."

"Looks like it," Sargon agreed.

"So why New York?"

Sargon met Jett's gaze. "Maybe she was tired of the sun. Or maybe she's got a restless heart, and needed to move again. Look at the file again, Jett. The woman has spent the majority of her life on the run."

Jett smiled a little, and nodded. "Maybe she's looking for home."

A twinge panged in Sargon's chest.

Home.

Where was that?

Even he didn't know at the moment.

"Maybe I could give her one," Jett murmured.

Sargon cleared his throat. "She's looking for something."

He couldn't bring himself to say much else, really.

Jett drummed his fingertips to the table. "There's nothing in this information that perks my suspicions, or draws concern, anyway. I will consider that a good thing."

Or maybe you should dig deeper.

Sargon kept his mouth shut. He was already knee-deep into his own pile of shit where Cozen was concerned.

"I've been gone a while," Jett added.

Sargon gave him a look. "Pardon?"

"From her—Cozen. I haven't been around in a while. Business, you know."

"Quite aware, yeah."

Hence the reason Sargon was on babysitting duty.

"She seemed to take well to you, didn't she?" Jett asked.

Sargon lifted a brow. "She didn't run away screaming."

To say the least ...

"Good. I'll be busy over the next little while. I think I will send a gift with you to take to her. Remind her I am still around, so to speak."

Sargon's throat tightened.

His chest felt heavy.

He nodded. "Whatever you want, boss."

Cozen carefully balanced the silver serving tray on her palm as she weaved in and around tables filled with diners, and the other two servers working the floor. The Kingdom was a popular eatery, sure, but the place wasn't usually this busy. Today, the servers had extra slack to pick up because one of the girls called in sick.

"Sorry, be with you in just a moment," Cozen told a man who raised a hand to get her attention. "Just let me drop this order off—you're next, sir, I promise."

She kept her tone polite and sweet, but inside, she wanted to scream and run the hell away. Her life had afforded her certain luxuries. Things like a lot of money because she was a successful thief. A beautiful house on the beach. And even a vineyard gifted to her by her adoptive parents.

She could be walking through wine country, or resting on a beach right now. Instead, she was in cold New York City, working tables at a fucking Manhattan restaurant, wearing clothes she hated, and shoes that were cheap as hell despite how nice they looked. Oh, yeah, her toes could *really* feel the cheapness after a month working in them.

Sighing, Cozen shook her head to rid those thoughts. She wasn't frustrated with the restaurant, or the job she took on for appearance's sake, either. It was *the* job she was irritated with. The heist on Jett Griffin.

He'd all but up and disappeared on her for a good two weeks, or a little more. She was sure he had not been offended that she refused his offer to sleep with him after their date, but maybe she had been wrong.

It didn't matter.

Cozen would give up a lot of things for a good heist, but her body was not one of them. It was possible that Jett's life simply became too busy to be making his regular stops at the restaurant but she didn't know how likely that was. Some of the girls suggested he did occasionally go a week or so at a time randomly without coming to eat when she had asked.

Whatever it was, when or if Jett came back in to her presence, Cozen was going to have to do whatever she could—short of fucking the man—to gain his trust, and get him close. Whatever it took to make him let her in to his personal life a bit more so that she could finally get this done.

She had goals to obtain here: get in, find the ring, and get the hell out. That was all that mattered at the end of the day.

And if she couldn't steal the ring by means of getting close to Jett?

Well, then Cozen was just going to call in a favor or two, and see if they could take the ring by force. Of course, she didn't think the Astors would like that route very much considering Pearl hired her for a purpose.

Because of how she did a job.

They didn't want attention drawn to them, or the heist in general.

Cozen understood, but sometimes, a thief had to do what they had to do. It was rather simple. Did they want the ring, or not?

Maybe she was just panicking.

She slid up to the table who had been waiting far too long for their order to be delivered. She gave the man a quick smile, and offered the same to the scowling blonde who was likely his date. Neither of them seemed very pleased.

"We're swamped, and I'm sorry," Cozen said, sliding their plates in front of them. She offered the two nothing else, and suspected she wasn't going to get a tip, either. Not that she needed it, frankly. "Enjoy your meal."

That time, she didn't even bother to smile.

Cozen darted back to the table with the man sitting alone. He smiled at her—a genuine smile that was not at all irritated or showed a lack of patience. "So sorry, sir. What would you like?"

The man chuckled, and waved a hand. "Could I just start with some coffee, please?"

"Sure, I'll just—"

All at once, a feeling buzzed over her skin, and made the hair on the back of her neck prickle. A palpable feeling that had come on and off throughout her whole shift—like someone was watching her, and only her. The sensation drove over her skin like a sweet caress, and then burrowed beneath to swim through her bloodstream, too.

The man at the table gave her a curious look—seemingly having noticed her speech suddenly cut off—and smiled again. "Everything okay?"

Cozen nodded fast. "Yes, of course. Coffee?"

"Yes, thanks. I'll order after."

"Okay. I'll get it right now."

As she left the man and the table behind, Cozen's gaze slid over the patrons, and the booths and tables hidden in the shadows. This was not even the third time today that she had felt like someone was watching her.

Of course, there were diners giving her passing looks as she made her way across the floor. One of the girls working the floor rolled her eyes upward as Cozen looked her way as if to silently say, *kill me*—commiserating the busy day. And Marissa, behind the bar, flashed Cozen a smile as she moved behind it to make the coffee for her patron.

No one else, though.

Not that she could see.

Cozen worked on the coffee, and checked the floor again. Some tables the other girls had been working were in more private sections, and she hadn't even gone in those directions at all today. Her spot was the main floor for her shift.

A spot where she was visible to all.

"Oh, hey," Marissa said.

Cozen took her gaze away from the diners to look at her coworker. "Yeah?"

"Guess what Chase told me."

She lifted a brow—frankly, Chase could have told Marissa a lot of things. She still suspected Chase had a hard nut for Marissa, and the woman didn't mind indulging her manager because she needed her job. And she still wasn't all that great at math. Two screwed up liquor orders proved that big time.

"What did Chase tell you?" Cozen asked dryly.

She stirred the coffee, and went back to staring out at the crowd. She didn't believe for a second that Marissa would tell her anything very shocking, or noteworthy. And she was still trying to find the invisible person watching her.

"Someone sent word asking for you," the bartender said.

Cozen's hand froze overtop the coffee mug. "What?"

Marissa's eyes widened. "Yup."

"Who?"

"Who do you think?"

Cozen shook her head, and gave Marissa a look. "Listen, this isn't a game where I ask you a question, and then you answer with a question, too. I don't have time for that kind of nonsense. Just tell me who it was."

Marissa pouted. "You are not fun."

"It's been a long day."

Yes, let's use that excuse.

Whatever worked.

"Fine, whatever," Marissa said, still fake pouting. "I guess he sent word asking about your work, not asking about you. He already knows you, and that you work here, right? So, yeah."

Cozen's brow furrowed. "What?"

"Jett Griffin."

Now we're getting warmer.

"What did Jett want to know?" Cozen asked. "He hasn't been around the restaurant for a while."

"Apparently, he asked about your shift schedules for the next couple of weeks."

"My shifts," she echoed.

"Mmhmm. I think you have an admirer."

No shit.

"Well, good," Cozen said.

Marissa gave her a look. "Good?"

"That's what I said."

It was what she needed, after all.

She was the spider. Jett was the fly.

Cozen would keep spinning her web, and hoped it would catch him. It kind of seemed like maybe she had, now. All her worries were for naught.

"Let me get back on the floor, and get this guy his coffee," Cozen said, pointing a finger at Marissa. "But thanks for the info. I appreciate it."

More than the girl knew, too.

All the while, Cozen still felt someone's eyes on her.

It was harder to ignore, now.

Cozen rounded the bar and said to the man who had taken over after Marissa's shift was over to, "Make me a Long Island Iced Tea."

"Are you supposed to be drinking during your shift?"

Cozen froze.

That voice.

That fucking voice.

Spinning around, she found the owner of that voice sitting at the very far end of the bar. Sargon lifted a brow in her direction, and offered her a smile. If you could call it that. It was more like a smirk, of sorts.

Suddenly, that strange sensation that Cozen had been feeling all day— the one where someone was looking at her—disappeared. She had a sneaking suspicion that she knew exactly why it was gone, now, too.

Because she found her culprit.

She knew who it was.

Sargon.

"Well?" he asked again. "Are you supposed to be drinking on your shift, Cozen?"

"Not that it matters to you," she said, lifting her messenger bag higher in to view, and then dropping it on the bar, "but I am officially off the time clock."

Then, she turned to the male bartender again, "Seriously, make my drink."

"You got it, Cozen."

"Come and sit with me," Sargon murmured.

A flash of heat burst in Cozen's lower regions. Her muscles clenched at his demand, too. Like her body had no fucking control over what it did or wanted when he was close by. It was definitely a problem she was going to have to handle at some point.

Sargon stared at Cozen when she didn't move. "Well?"

She didn't move around the bar to sit, and instead, crossed her arms over her chest. "What do you want?"

He gave her a look, and then waved a finger at the item sitting in front of him on the bar. It was a large black velvet box. Possibly a jewelry box— Cozen had seen more than enough of those in her lifetime to know what they look like.

"You brought me a gift?" she asked.

She didn't mean for her tone to soften as much as it did, but it seemed she didn't have control of that, either.

Sargon chuckled deeply.

A rough, lovely sound that rocked Cozen to her very core. It didn't seem to matter what this man did—stand still, smile, or scowl; he looked like a fucking God regardless. All bronzed skin, dark eyes, and clothes that molded perfectly to his toned, fit frame.

They could make statues of him.

It was disgusting.

"No," he said, tilting his head to the side a bit, "I was sent to bring it to you. Seems you've *taken to me*, apparently. Or you don't run screaming from me."

Sargon flashed a sexy smile and added, "Well, not yet, anyway."

Jesus.

Bad all around.

This man was bad news.

Bad for her.

Bad, bad, *bad.*

"Sit," he demanded again.

This time, Cozen's legs worked without needing her permission. She moved around The Kingdom's bar, and took the open bar stool next to

Sargon. When she was this close to the man, it was much harder to ignore the way his muscles flexed under his red silk shirt, or the fact he looked like he hadn't shaved in a week or more.

Not to mention, the cologne he wore.

That in itself was a goddamn drug.

His gaze darted over to hers, and the edges of his lips curved upward sinfully. "You look tired, Cozen. Busy day?"

"Something like that."

Sargon hummed a noncommittal sound, and gazed at the bottles behind the bar. "Seems that's all this city does is give us days longer than we can handle."

"You don't like your days?" she asked.

"There's always something I like about them. I find the silver linings. Getting to keep an eye on beautiful things and keep them out of harm's way is certainly a good part."

He gave her a pointed look.

She heard his unspoken words.

He meant her. He had been looking after her.

"Jett sent a gift?" Cozen asked.

She greatly wanted to get off the topic they were currently on, and onto something else entirely. It wasn't Sargon's fault, really.

Not at all.

Cozen simply didn't trust herself around this man. When he murmured, her skin heated. When he looked at her, her heart picked up speed. When he was still and silent, she wanted to know what was running through that beautiful head of his.

She had a feeling that if he offered to take her out back to the dirty, damp alley behind the restaurant and fuck her, she would be all too happy to skip along with him to do the deed. Because he *demanded*, and she apparently couldn't tell him no.

She would probably get on her knees for him, too.

Dirt be damned.

Wasn't it bad enough that she had spent the last couple of weeks practically obsessing over this man?

Cozen couldn't afford the risks associated with being involved with Sargon Makri. Not at the moment, anyway. He was too close to Jett, and she was not willing to put the chance of a successful heist on the line just to get this man between her thighs again.

Oh, God.

Or was she willing to do exactly that?

Yeah.

Bad all over.

"He did send a gift," Sargon said.

Wordlessly, he pushed a finger against the edge of the black velvet box, and moved it in front of Cozen on the bar. It was maybe the size of his palm, or a little bigger. Two golden hinges on one side, and a golden clasp on the other.

"He thought you might like something to remind you of him," Sargon said quietly. "He worried that his lack of presence might have been concerning for you."

"It was," she admitted.

Sargon's gaze narrowed for a brief second, and something flashed across his handsome features. Something dark and hot—like jealousy.

"Open it," he said, his expression reverting back to a cool, cold nothingness.

This man was good.

Cozen reached for the box, and unhooked the golden latch on the front. Overturning the top, she was entirely unsurprised to find jewelry resting inside on crushed, black velvet. Not that it wasn't a beautiful piece, but still *expected.*

Princess-cut sapphires rested on top of crowns of white diamonds in a set of three to form a beautiful, sparkling cluster. The white-gold rope of the necklace was long enough to allow the cluster of sapphires and diamonds to fall likely at the top swells of her breasts.

Cozen took a moment to appreciate the beautiful piece. She ran her fingertips over the smooth surfaces of the deep blue sapphires, and then she traced the crown of diamonds around each one.

Pulling the necklace out, she rested the cluster against her palm, and brought it closer to her face to get a look good at all the gems. She took her time looking over each one—jewelry was her specialty, in a way.

"All real," she murmured.

"Did you expect anything less?" Sargon asked.

"I am not sure what I expected," Cozen returned. "Perhaps something a little less expensive, but still shocking enough to make me take a double look. A piece like this suggests Jett is …"

"Very interested in you, and intends to pursue you as much as he needs to in order to get what he wants from you," Sargon said, finishing her unspoken words.

"Exactly that."

Which was a *good thing.*

At least, it was good for her end game.

She could see from the darkness in Sargon's eyes that it was not at all good for him. She, too, found herself torn because of it.

Do the job, Cozen.

"Expect more."

With that said, Sargon stood from the barstool, and turned to walk away.

"More what?" she asked at his back.

He didn't stop walking, but he did say, "More gifts, Cozen."

Cozen barely shut her door when she finally got home before someone was knocking on it. She huffed hard, and tossed her messenger bag aside. She figured it was likely the landlord—he had a habit of checking up on every tenant in the building.

Usually, she didn't mind.

Today, she kind of did.

Cozen really just wanted to relax as much as possible after her busy day, and then Sargon showing up. Speaking of which ...

The black velvet jewelry box stuck out from the top of her messenger bag. She was going to have to do something with that necklace. Wear it, make sure Jett sees her with it, or something. She would figure that out in due time.

The knock on her door came again. More persistent the second time. Cozen grumbled under her breath, and kicked off her high heels as she closed in on the door. Grabbing the knob, she twisted it hard, and flung it open with far more force than was necessary.

It was not the landlord.

A guy dressed in white held a huge vase with at least three dozen red roses high, blocking his face. "Delivery for a Miss ... Cozen Taylor?"

Cozen took a step back just from the size of the bushel alone. It was a good two feet wide, and would probably graze the doorjamb when the guy brought it inside her place. The smell of the roses were heavenly.

"Is that you, ma'am?" the guy asked.

"That's me," Cozen replied.

"Do you have a place you might like me to sit these? They're kind of heavy."

Cozen laughed. "Well, I have a floor."

And not much else. She hadn't made much effort to fill the apartment with furniture, or otherwise. A good portion of her day was spent at the restaurant, and for the hours she was at home, she was planning, or meditating.

Who needed *things* to do any of that?

Not her.

"Just point and say," the guy muttered. "Getting heavier."

"Come on in."

Cozen stepped back, and waved a hand as the guy passed her to direct him further into the apartment. She directed him through the entry hallway, and into the main rooms of the apartment. She had him place the roses on the floor next to the large kitchen window.

"Thank you," she said.

The guy laughed. "Oh, I have ten more."

Cozen froze. "Ten more of *what*?"

He pointed at the roses. "Of those. And here, this is yours."

The guy whipped out a white envelope, and handed it over. Cozen took it as he turned his back, and headed for the front door. She opened up the envelope to find unfamiliar handwriting staring back at her.

All beautiful woman love their roses, don't they? I hope you liked my gift today, Cozen, and this one, too. Remember, I'm always thinking of you even if I am not around to see you. —Jett.

Cozen blinked at the note, and she didn't realize how long she had stayed like that until the guy came barreling into her apartment with yet another humongous bushel of roses. He had said ten, right?

Ten *more*.

Cozen's place was not that big. She did not like roses that much, really. The heavenly smell would soon turn into a little too much.

She couldn't very well tell the delivery man to remove the flowers, or take them away. She didn't want to say the two bushels were more than enough for her small place. Honestly, she found her voice was lost until the guy had heaved ten more bushels of those goddamn roses into her apartment.

"Uh … thank you?" Cozen said.

The guy put the last bushel in the middle of the floor. Her apartment was now a sea of red and white roses.

She had been right.

The smell was overwhelming.

"One last—"

"Does it look like I have room?" Cozen asked him.

Jesus Christ.

The guy laughed. "No … here, sorry."

He bent down, and pulled a single, fire-red tiger lily from within the bushel of red roses. Giving her a little smile and shrug, he handed the beautiful flower over to her.

Cozen held it tight.

Jett would not have sent this flower to her, considering all the roses in her place. He didn't know about her tattoo—she had not told him while naked in front of him that her favorite flower was a red tiger lily.

She fingered the petals with a careful touch.

"Same person?" she dared to ask.

The guy shook his head. "No—a second one called this in right after the first order was placed."

"No note, then?"
"No note," the man echoed.
Cozen didn't need a note.
She *knew*.
Sargon sent it.
Of course, he did.

Sargon looked up from the ground just in time to see a cab pull up to the sidewalk. A scene he had been watching play out for a while as the club he had come to was packed full, and seemed to be a popular spot.

The woman inside the cab—looking ten shades of disgusted and ready to get the hell out of the vehicle—was not entirely unexpected, either.

Sargon lifted an eyebrow, and took a drag off his smoke as Cozen threw a handful of bills over the seats in the cab. It was almost as if she didn't want to touch the cab, or anything inside it. Not even the money she was paying the guy.

"Keep the change, asshole," Sargon heard her say as she stepped out of the car.

Cozen didn't wait to hear the guy's response because she wasted no time slamming the passenger door closed. Her heels clicked against the wet pavement as she stepped onto the sidewalk.

The cool May air wrapped around Sargon, but he barely felt it at all beneath his silk dress shirt and slacks. He supposed the club had been hot enough to chase the Devil out from the heat. Cozen, on the other hand, shivered a bit.

All she had on was a long-sleeved, mid-thigh wool dress, and knee-high boots. Part of him was glad she hadn't thought to throw on a coat or something because that dress hugged all of her curves in the most sinful way. It draped along her body, sure, but moved with it, too. Each step closer to the club she took was damn near mesmerizing.

She was not used to the New York cold, he bet.

Neither was he, really.

The cab peeled away from the sidewalk with screeching tires, making Cozen shoot a look over her shoulder at the disappearing checkered black and yellow car. The narrowing of her eyes said she felt the same way he did about a lot of people in New York—some people in this city could really be something else sometimes.

Manners were nonexistent.

"Can't say I have seen you use a cab," he said before he could stop himself. "Why use one tonight?"

Cozen's head whipped back around, and she quickly found Sargon half tucked into the side alley next to the Little Odessa club. Sargon flashed her a smile when her russet eyes looked him over. Unashamed, and curious, her gaze drifted from his legs to his face before her tongue peeked out to wet her bottom lip.

His slacks tightened around his growing cock. She had no idea what she could do to him with just a look. She had no fucking idea how little control he had when it came to her. Especially if her pretty little mouth was involved.

Yeah, he had a fascination with her mouth. He blamed the way she let him fuck her mouth, and smiled when he was done with her, too. His fascination had turned to obsession just as fast, and now this woman was constantly playing on repeat during his late nights when he couldn't sleep.

Sargon was so fucked.

Entirely fucked.

"I guess you would know, wouldn't you?" Cozen asked.

Sargon took a hard drag from a mostly-gone cigarette, and eyed her curiously. "What do you mean, Zen?"

"You would know that I don't use cabs. Or at least, not very often. Considering you follow me around on a daily basis."

A husky chuckle escaped his lips. "Figured that out, did you?"

"I figured it out yesterday when you brought me Jett's gift. I knew he had someone tailing me—I can feel you watching me. I didn't know it was you until yesterday."

"You don't know that it was me, woman. It could have been any of his—"

"I *feel* you when you watch me, Sargon. I know it's you."

Did she?

Did she really *feel* him watching her?

He found that all too interesting. He found that little detail all too fucking appealing. This little game between them—whatever the hell it was—could get dangerous quick, fast, and in a real goddamn hurry.

He was starting to get worried that neither of them would realize the kind of danger they were in until it was far too late to do anything about it. And yet there he still was … kind of wishing she would come close enough to him so that he could drag her into the alley where no one would be able to see them.

Sargon cleared his throat, and steeled his mind to think about *anything* else for the moment. He shrugged one shoulder, and eyed the tip of his cigarette. "I do what I am told to do, Cozen, and when I am told to do it."

"Is the smoking a new thing?" she asked.

Sargon looked at the cigarette, and then pinged it from his fingertips to send the butt flying into the street. "I like a smoke whenever shit is piling up. I don't make it a habit, though. It's bad for your lungs."

"I bet that's only one bad habit of many when it comes to you, huh?"

Sargon's dark gaze jumped up to slam into hers. She froze on the spot—her gaze pinned to his, and her breaths picking up speed a bit the longer they stared at one another. He bet her little heart was just racing under her skin, too.

It was funny, really.

With everyone else, she seemed to be such a good actor. Her mask was always firmly in place. She could make any man around her think that he was her only one—her only interest. She could wrap them around her pinky finger with a smile, and reel them in closer with a wink and a few words.

She was a fucking master at it.

He knew.

He watched her do it.

And yet with him, it seemed like Cozen didn't have that ability at all. Not to hide her interest, or how her body reacted to his presence. He liked that far too much, too. He liked that he affected her.

Finally, Cozen tore her gaze away from his, and broke their staring contest. She peered down the dark street, and then gave the front of the club a once over, too. "You don't seem very surprised to see me here."

"I heard you were asking around about me," he returned. "Word travels when you know people, Cozen. I figured if you were asking, that must mean you were going to come looking for me, too."

She still wouldn't look at him. "Apparently, you come to this club quite often."

"I know the DJ."

With that said, Sargon pushed away from the wall he had been leaning against, and stepped out on the sidewalk. He tipped his head to the side, saying, "Are you coming in, or what?"

Cozen lifted a brow. "I don't know—should I?"

"I'm aware of your schedule, Cozen. Jett sent for it, and handed it off to me so I would know when you would be working. I know why you came tonight—it's your one night off before the weekend. And I think Jett sent word that he has plans for you this weekend."

"So?"

"So, I made this easy on you, sweetheart. Clubs aren't Jett Griffin's thing. He doesn't particularly like the music, and the lights give him a headache. That means if we go inside, we're going to be much less likely to be seen. If we stay out here, I can't help if someone drives by and sees us. Got it?"

Cozen looked to the club's front entrance. "Yeah, I got it."

Sargon watched as Cozen lifted a red martini to her lips, and took a small sip. Next to him at the bar, she looked like all kinds of sin and fun under the lights of the club. She didn't seem to want to dance, though, and she only agreed to one drink.

"You know, he's going to look further in to your history," Sargon said. "Jett, I mean. He's going to try, anyway. You've got him obsessed like nothing else."

A lot like Sargon, too.

Cozen's glass hesitated on the next lift to her painted-red lips. "Why, he didn't find anything worth looking at the first time?"

"No, he did."

For the briefest second, something unknown flashed in her eyes—fear, maybe, or just enough concern to make her do a double-take.

"What was that, then?" she asked. "That he found, I mean."

"Foster homes. Unknown parents. Runaway."

Cozen laughed, and almost smiled—if that bitter sneer could be considered a smile. "Oh, *that*."

"Yeah, that, Cozen."

"What, did my rough upbringing and shitty circumstances pull at Jett's heartstrings?"

"Yes."

Seemed his simple response did make her reassess his words for a second. Cozen passed him a look, and Sargon only shrugged his shoulders in response.

"One of the foster homes you ran away from … they were eventually shut down, and charged with a variety of things. Physical and sexual abuse amongst many allegations brought up in the documents I unfortunately read."

"They're not allegations when they pleaded guilty," she murmured.

Sargon nodded. "My mistake. How did you know they pleaded guilty if you were already long gone by then?"

Cozen grinned into her glass. "I'm sure *someone* helped evidence get into the right hands at one point or another."

"Did you go back for that?"

"Someone else helped," she offered, but her tone said she wasn't going to give him much else for details in that regard. "And in a way, you could say that helped me, too."

"Did it really?" he pressed.

"What?"

"Help, Cozen. Did it take away the pain, and the memories? Did it make you feel less dirty, and not as used? Did the nightmares go away?"

Her lips flattered in a thin line before she whispered, "Not right away."

"How long did it take?"

"Long enough to know that they wouldn't be able to do it to someone else, Sargon."

She looked over at him, and he didn't hide the fact he was staring at her. He had the slightest feeling this woman was by far one of the strongest and most beautiful people he had ever met in his life. A little broken, too, sure.

Who wasn't broken?

Who didn't have a story?

Jett would never be able to fully appreciate how entirely amazing this woman was, or how her history had probably shaped her into the person she was today. No, Jett was the type who would want to *save* Cozen from it all, and not let her save herself. He would be the kind of man who figured giving her nice things, and locking her away in a life full of wealth and wonders would erase a lifetime of horrible memories.

The idea made Sargon sick.

So disgusted.

"Why California?" Sargon asked.

He needed to get far away from his thoughts, so he moved onto something else entirely.

"Pardon?"

"You showed up in California at nineteen to get a proper license. Why?"

She smiled—softer and genuine this time. "Someone taught me how to drive. It was … a big thing for me to go and get my license. I never had a real piece of ID before that. It was all faked. Good enough to get me by, essentially. Certainly never under Cozen Taylor."

"And what were the other names you used?"

Cozen shot him a look. "Nice try."

Sargon laughed. "Worth a shot."

"The tiger lily was a nice touch."

He stiffened on the stool which earned him a light laugh from Cozen. Shooting her a look from the side, he asked, "Liked that, did you?"

"You even got the color right."

"Fire-red, like your tattoo."

"Mmhmm." Cozen used the tip of her finger to trace around the rim of the martini glass. "You never asked me that night why the tiger lily is my favorite flower."

"I had other things on my mind, Cozen."

Her grin turned suggestive in a blink. "I bet. Go on, ask me."

"Now?"

She took another drink. "Right now, yeah."

"Why the tiger lily?"

"A *fire-red* tiger lily."

"Why that flower, Cozen?"

She winked. "I always thought all women loved roses. It's the flower of romance and love, right? Petals spread out on the bed, or a trail leading a woman to the altar. They're in the backdrops of movies, and men shell out ungodly amounts of cash for a decent bouquet. On Valentine's Day, teenagers send out a single rose to their crushes all through high school. Roses are a *staple*."

"True."

"Someone once told me that roses were like women. All women were soft, beautiful, sweet, and could draw attention. All women were like roses—dangerous with their obvious thorns, but the surface beauty was a bit of trickery."

"But?"

"Only a few women could be the tiger lilies. Striking, different, strong, and resilient. Those kinds of women could not simply blend in with all the other roses. They stand out far too much. I was told once … well, I suppose what I was told taught me more than anyone else ever did."

"And what was it, Cozen?"

"Never aspire to be a rose when you have always been a tiger lily."

"They make a good point."

Cozen tipped her glass in his direction. "Is that enough talking for the night?"

"Have I reached my limit of questions?" he asked back.

"I really didn't come here to talk."

"I figured, Cozen."

She eyed him curiously. "Did you?"

"I'm not stupid or blind, woman. I know what you want."

"Are you playing games with me now, Sargon?"

He spun off the barstool with a laugh, grabbed her wrist, and tugged to make her follow him. "You're the queen of games, aren't you? You tell me if I'm playing games, Cozen."

The parking lot across from the club was dark, but not entirely empty. A few people lingered near cars twenty stalls away, but the thick cloud of weed seemed to keep the people distracted from the couple slipping into the back of the back town car.

"Jesus, you won't even shell out money for a hotel for me?" Cozen asked as she hiked up her skirt. "We can't even go to your place?"

Sargon slammed the door behind him. "First—I don't feel like fucking waiting that long. Second—my place is almost two hours away from here."

"Oh."

He reached out and snagged her jaw with his hand, and yanked her toward him. Her mouth crashed against his with a bruising kiss that left his lips numb in the best way.

"Open up and let me taste," he demanded.

She did just that, and parted her lips enough to let his tongue snake into her mouth. She tasted like that martini she had been drinking with hints of cherry and black licorice undertones. He controlled the kiss, and she let him.

Something else to make his dick rock-hard.

Cozen slid into his lap when his hand curved around her waist, and pulled her closer. He let go of her jaw just long enough to slide his hand between her thighs, and under the gusset of her panties.

A slick, hot pussy met his fingertips. Her cunt was still waxed bare along the soft folds but trimmed short at her pubis. He stroked his fingers through the folds, and teased her entrance with the tips of his digits just to make her whine.

Christ.

She sounded so good when she whined.

Even better when she begged.

"Someone is going to see us," she whispered in his ear.

Sargon kissed the underside of his jaw. "I bet you like that, too. Someone might see me eating or fucking your pussy—watch you come, and get hot. Shit, maybe they'll think you're my little slut, Cozen."

She shivered.

He grinned.

"Yeah, you like it," he murmured against her throat.

"I am, though."

"What?"

"Your little slut."

Sargon pulled back from her sweet-smelling skin just long enough to see her eyes lock on his. "And don't you fucking forget it, either."

"How can I? I'm here, aren't I?"

She was.

As crazy and stupid as it was, she was here.

With *him*.

No one else.

Sargon slipped down against the door until his back was flat against the seat, and Cozen hovered above him. He said nothing as his hands slid beneath the back of her skirt to grab tight to her ass.

"Keep your panties out of my fucking way, or I will rip them off," he told her.

"Jesus."

"No, try again."

Cozen let out a shaky breath. "Just let me ride your face."

"Say it *right*."

He punctuated that with a slap to her ass. The sweet pink that flushed her skin was addictive. He loved making her blush.

"Fine …" Her hand fell between her thighs to move her panties aside, and keep them like that. Less work for him. "*Sargon*, let me ride your smug face."

She didn't technically ask, but it was just as good. His name in her mouth was something else—he wasn't ever going to get tired of hearing it. He let his fingers dig into her soft skin roughly, and then yanked her down to meet his mouth.

He lapped at her cunt first, tunneling his tongue into her clenching pussy and taking in what sweet juices of hers had already slicked up her folds. He felt the way she grinded her hips against his mouth in an effort to get him to go higher, but he held firm to her ass, and kept her in place.

He would get there when *he* wanted to.

When he was ready to.

Not one second before.

Cozen's teasing little whines turned in to breathless moans when he did finally move up to her clit. There, he held nothing back. His tongue flicked hard against the throbbing nub relentlessly. With the taste of her sex in his mouth, and the smell of her pussy soaking into his lungs with every breath he took—this was heaven.

He didn't need or want to stop.

"Make me come," he heard her say.

A mantra, really.

Mixed in with her *please*, and *fuck, fuck, fuck*.

This woman was unashamed. He looked up to find her staring back— the most beautiful sight, really. She was wild like this. Amazing like this.

Perfect like this.

Soon, her legs were clenching tightly around his head, and her inner thighs shook. He felt the way her muscles clenched all over her body, and her pupils blew wide as his name fell from her parted lips one more time.

"*Sargon.*"

He fucked her pussy with his mouth through the orgasm, and didn't waste time to get what he wanted when she was finally done. Cozen lifted just enough to let him sit back up against the door, and then her hands worked at his groin to undo his belt and pants.

A soft, warm palm fished his cock from his pants.

Commando, as always.

It just made shit easier.

Her shaking thighs came around his waist, and she fit his hard cock between her legs. She came down on him *hard*. No hesitation, and no waiting. She was hot and wet all over, and fit him like a velvet glove.

Sucking him deep, filling her full, and making his lungs ache.

God.

It was good.

Something sinful.

Something wonderful.

Something so fucked up.

Sargon grabbed hold of her throat, and squeezed as he forced her head back. Cozen's wide eyes met his, and a sneer worked its way over her lips as she started rocking her hips back and forth in the slowest way.

Jesus.

She would *kill* him like this.

"Are you going to fuck me good?" she asked breathlessly.

His fingers tightened more on her throat. "Who else can fuck you like this, woman?"

Her throat bobbed under his hand with a swallow. "No one."

"You didn't even give me the chance to get a fucking condom, Cozen."

"I take the shot. I don't *need* one. I just needed you to fuck me."

His gaze drifted over her lax, red lips as she continued that teasing rocking motion. "I could be fucking someone else. You don't know."

"I *know*. You're not."

She was right.

Christ.

She was so right.

"And neither am I," she added. "So shut up, and *fuck me.*"

He did—diving his hands into her hair, and pulling on the strands close to the scalp. He dragged her closer to him. Close enough that he could bite her lips, and suck on her throat while he fucked them both to oblivion.

Her pretty little cries turned high-pitched, and then breathless in a blink. Sweat slicked up her back, and then she raked red lines down his chest.

She took every one of his thrusts no matter how hard to deep they came. She met him on every one. The slap of skin on skin echoing in the quiet car mingled in with her moans, and his grunts.

And even after she came again, she still wanted more.

"Fuck me, fuck me, *fuck me*," she begged again.

Bent over, ass high, and her arms pinned at her back that time.

"Fuck me, fuck me ... fuck me."

He heard more, though.

He heard so much more.

I'm yours, I'm yours ... I'm yours.

Fuck.

He wanted her to be his.

Maybe that's why he heard it.

Cozen paced the length of the living room in her small apartment. It wasn't a very big space, but gave enough room to move. When her mind was racing, all she wanted to do was let her restless legs walk it out.

Since someone seemed to be following her—Sargon, she now knew for sure—her options were limited. She didn't want anyone to see her in something they might consider a state to report back. She didn't need to give anyone any inkling that something was wrong with her.

Even if *everything* was wrong with her.

Well, not everything, no. Just a small part in the grand scheme of things. That small part, however, was a big complication for Cozen.

That part being Sargon.

She slowed in her pacing just long enough to watch early morning sunlight filter in through the crack in the curtains. Specks of dust danced in the yellow stream, and for a moment, took her attention away from her chaotic thoughts.

It didn't last long.

It couldn't.

The morning light only served to remind her that she had just gotten home an hour before. A single hour before the sun rose in the sky. And why was that?

Because she spent the night with a man she had no business spending the night with. Fucking in the backseat of a car, and then dancing in a club.

Coffee at a little shop down the street, and then a quick breakfast at a small, tucked away diner in Little Odessa.

Before she even realized how much time had passed, Sargon was the one who told her that he needed to get back to his place. He said goodbye with a kiss.

To her forehead.

A sweet, loving kiss.

This game was becoming dangerous. Far too dangerous, really.

Sargon had become a giant complication in Cozen's plans. Probably without meaning to, she knew. He had—without barely trying at all—taken her entirely off her game when it came to this goddamn job. Instead of focusing on getting closer to Jett, she was dreaming about a man with a Persian bloodline. Where she should have been getting Jett to trust her, she was looking for the dark eyes she knew would be watching her.

She was seeking Sargon out.

Already, she wanted him again.

To see him again.

To fuck him again.

Anything.

It wasn't like Cozen to get emotionally or physically invested in something—or *someone*, rather—during a job. She went in, did what she needed to do with a clear, clean conscience, and came back out successful.

Always.

Or … that's how it normally went.

That's how it should have went!

Frustrated, Cozen tossed herself into the pile of blankets and pillows in the middle of the living room. She still refused to buy a bed

Cozen settled herself on the things she knew for sure.

One—the job was the job, and it was all that mattered until it was done. She was going to have to do whatever she needed to fucking do to get this job done, and be successful. It didn't matter; the job was number one.

Two—she needed to screw her head back on straight, so to speak. Fucking Sargon once should have been enough, but apparently she needed a second go. The second time was nothing more than a mistake. She couldn't afford more of those. It was too dangerous. For her, and for her stupid heart that liked to play tricks on her.

Three—she didn't have time for anything else but getting this job done. No time to entertain the feelings she had for Sargon, or the way he kept drawing her in like a moth to the flame. She didn't have time to play games anymore.

No time.

After all, the deadline for the Astors was now almost up. Five more weeks.

She knew enough about the Astor family to know that if she wasn't successful in returning Pearl's ring, it was not going to end well for her.

The ringing of the cell phone broke Cozen from her thoughts. Reaching above her head, she snatched the device where she had tossed it to the big pillow when she got home. She was smart enough to check the caller ID before answering.

Good thing, too.

An Astor number stared back at Cozen. She chewed on her bottom lip, and glanced at the number in the left-hand corner of the screen. It showed a seven. Seven times they had called her in a couple of days. Seven times she had ignored them.

Cozen knew that didn't bode well for her, but she didn't have much of a choice. She had nothing good or new to tell them, and she had a feeling Pearl would not be amicable to allowing Cozen more time on this job.

She gave six months.

She was going to do it in *six months*.

Cozen tossed the phone back to the pillow, and buried her head into the blankets. She let the call ring until it stopped completely, and heard the beep that said there was a voice mail left behind. She would delete that later without even listening to it, too.

What did they want other than to make demands, or yell at her? Threaten her, maybe? All that could wait.

It wasn't just Sargon she needed to get out of her head. She needed to keep her mind clear. She was not adding angry Astors with their crazy demands to the mix, too.

Cozen would deal with them later.

Maybe.

Smooth, almost too-hot rocks rolled over the muscles in Cozen's back. From her shoulders down to the spot where a thin sheet rested over her ass to hide her nakedness, the hot rock massage took away the stress lingering in her body.

Hot rocks was a preference for her. That, and a damn good deep tissue massage. She also didn't mind the occasional soak in mud, or a stint in the steam room for long enough to draw the toxins out of her body. Whatever could remove the tension from her body, and take the stress from her mind, she was game to try it.

Cozen almost always came back to hot rocks, though.

"Your muscles are very tight," the woman said.

She hadn't even gotten the masseuse's name.

"Mmm," Cozen muttered into the hole on the massage table. "A lot going on lately."

"This will help."

Obviously.

That's why she came to the spa. Sometimes, Cozen just needed a single day to recharge her body and mind. That's what today was dedicated to. Herself, basically. Self-care was just as important as physical care.

Maybe that had been her problem.

She neglected herself.

All too often when doing a job, Cozen became lost in the person—the persona—she took on for a spell. This time, she was the waitress with a job that put her in high heels for a ridiculous amount of hours. A woman who lived in a tiny Manhattan apartment with barely any furniture. She had no friends, no social life, and very little to show for all of it.

But that was who she was.

This time.

In the process, she lost who she actually was until she could get back to that woman. Sometimes in the midst of a job, she needed to be reminded that she was someone else, and she would be getting back to that person soon enough.

The hot rocks rolled over the lines of her shoulders once more, and Cozen couldn't stop the sigh that escaped from her lax lips even if she tried. The masseuse even laughed lightly at the steady stream of soft air Cozen didn't try to hide.

"Yeah, that's … good," Cozen settled on saying.

"The lavender oils help in the air, too."

"They make me sleepy."

"Maybe you need to sleep more, child."

Maybe.

Or maybe she needed to finally call it quits with this life of hers. Stop chasing the next thrill. Find her peace in something else other than being a thief. Relax into stability. Something she felt was never really tangible to someone like her.

"Definitely sleep more," the woman said. "Sleep is—like laughter or sex—one of nature's best medicines for us humans."

Who was Cozen to argue?

"I will place hotter rocks on your pressure points, and down your spine. We will let them set for a half an hour—at least until they cool. I'll add a bit more oil to the diffuser as well. Do you want some sounds while you wait?"

"Rain," Cozen murmured.

"Rain is a good choice."

She loved the sound of soft rain pelting down to the ground, on windows, or even a roof. Hours and hours of rain when she was tucked away and warm could take away any stress Cozen might have been feeling.

"Do you want it on—"

A knock on the private room interrupted the woman from finishing her question. Cozen frowned because she wanted to get on with her massage, and the best part of it was still yet to come. Not to mention, there should be a sign on the door requesting quiet and privacy as all massage rooms had.

"Sorry, just give me a minute," the woman said. "We usually don't have our sessions interrupted, so it must be important."

"No problem."

Footsteps echoed as the woman approached the door when the knock echoed a second time—more persistently. She heard the creak of the door as it opened, and then the sound of it closing. Cozen suspected the woman stepped outside to chat because she couldn't even hear murmurings.

Despite being interrupted, Cozen was still pretty relaxed at the moment. So much so, that when she closed her eyes, she was sure that she fell asleep for a spell. Or as close to sleep as she could get. Long enough, anyway, that she jerked a bit when the sound of the door opening made her eyes fly wide again.

Cozen didn't bother to lift her head to check who it was that had come back into the room. She assumed it was the same woman who just left—the masseuse for her hot rock massage. The footsteps coming across the room weren't particularly lighter or heavier, but the woman didn't speak as she came closer to Cozen.

Rocks moved against steel.

The boiling pot, she knew.

The first smooth, circular rock to touch Cozen's lower spine almost made her hiss from the heat coming in contact with her flesh. It was hot— almost too hot, really. Still, the cool temperature of her skin helped to soothe the initial sting, and quickly, it felt like the rock was sinking deliciously into her spine.

Pushing into the stress.

Cutting through it.

Sucking toxins away.

Absorbing bad energy.

Taking it all away.

The next rock was placed slightly higher on her spine. And then again, and again until she had several rocks—all of varying sizes and weights—up her spine. The next rocks were placed on her shoulders, although they were far larger and heavier than the ones on her spine.

A beat of time passed, as though the woman was letting those rocks settle into Cozen's skin and muscles before she moved onto the next phase.

Two smaller rocks were then placed at the dimples on her lower back. Two larger ones were placed against the spot known to be where kidney pain often presented the strongest.

It was sometimes believed that rocks were like magnets. And when presented with heat, rocks could absorb many things from the human body. From stress, to illness, and otherwise. Cozen wasn't sure if she particularly believed any of that, but it certainly felt good enough for her to ask for one more rock on the back of her neck. A spot that had been particularly hard lately—like a knot had formed in the muscle.

"Right here," she said, lifting a hand and pointing at the spot. "Please."

A soft hum—one most definitely *not* belonging to a woman—answered Cozen's request before a rock came to rest on the back of her neck. Panic shot through her, as did the swell of rage when it quickly followed right behind.

Her first thought was to roll over and put the knife she had hidden under her stomach to the asshole's throat for coming in on her like this. It was the light touch of a single hand pressing to the back of her thigh, and his fingers digging into her skin that stopped her.

She knew it was him before he spoke.

She knew it by his touch.

Only his touch.

Sargon bent down near her head, and murmured in her ear, "I just paid that woman a lot of cash to get in this room to see you privately, not to mention, I lied a bit to assure her you would not be angry with me for surprising you. She thinks I am your *husband.*"

The admission passing his lips made her gasp.

He laughed darkly. "So be a good girl, huh? Do not get the cops called on me by screaming or some other nonsense."

"Jesus, you couldn't let me know when you first came in? That's a dangerous thing to do, you know. Sneaking up on me, I mean. It's a good way to get yourself killed."

Sargon's chuckles rocked her to the core. Like darts of delicious heat sliding through her veins, and shooting right down to her pussy. A day to recharge, and the attempt to set her mind back on the plan at hand was not going to help Cozen very much with how Sargon made her feel. It was not going to help her traitorous body.

Not at all.

"Where's the fun in that?" he asked.

"What do you want?"

"At the moment, to look at you."

His words wrapped around her like a silky caress as he stood. A lot like the tip of his fingertip sliding down her spine alongside the rocks. Cozen felt the goosebumps bloom along her flesh in the wake of his touch. The sensation raced after his touch everywhere he went, and more so where he lingered. It could kill her from the need—she swore it was true.

It would be a beautiful way to die, though.

"Quite a sight you are, Cozen. One of the *most* beautiful."

She swallowed hard. "Should I thank you, or ...?"

"Not necessary. Beautiful things should be admired. They do not, however, need to be gracious *because* they are beautiful. You owe nothing to anyone who notices your beauty. You neither need to thank someone for it, nor apologize for it."

He finished his statement by dragging his hands up the backs of her thighs. Cozen instantly sucked in a sharp breath when his fingertips edged beneath the sheet covering her backside. His fingers edged a little bit higher until they stroked the smooth skin where her thighs melded into the curve of her ass.

"May I touch you?" he asked.

Cozen wet her lips, and kept her gaze locked on the rug beneath the massage table. It was the first time he had *asked* for something from her. Mostly, in their sexual encounters, Sargon had simply took and took.

Not that she minded.

Oh, she loved it.

Still, it made her heart skip a beat, and her breath catch in her throat. She should have said no. She should have put a stop to this little cat and mouse game between them once and for all. It was her chance to finally put a barrier up, and draw the line.

She needed to get back to the job.

Still, she whispered, "Yes, you may touch me."

Because apparently she had no self-control whatsoever. And honestly, it only took a few deep presses of Sargon's talented, long fingers into the cheeks of her ass to remind her exactly why that was. The rock massage had nothing on the way his hands kneaded her muscles—deep, firm, and perfectly poised at just the right spots.

Cozen damn near closed her eyes at the feeling. She didn't, though, not when those hands of his slid down over her ass, and in between her thighs. His deft fingers slipped between her legs, and found her pussy without any hesitation. He glided his fingertip through her folds, stroked her awake, and then moved his position again.

Tight, quick circles roved over her clit again and again. A relentless, yet still sure pace that had her legs shaking, and her muscles tensing.

"Won't you come for me?" he asked.

"This was not supposed to be a happy ending massage, Sargon."

Sargon bent down to talk in her ear again. "Good thing. Do you know how irritated I was when I had to watch you walk in here *knowing* there were men who might touch you?"

Cozen's throat tightened. "It was a woman."

"But it might not have been."

"But it *was*."

His fingertips pressed harder against her clit, and then he gave the little nub a quick pinch before he went right back to massaging again. The jolt of pain mixed in heavily with Cozen's pleasure before it was gone again just as fast. He moved down from her clit to stuff two fingers deep into her pussy. Those knowing digits curved in just the right way, and he began to massage her G-spot with insistent strokes.

"Oh, my God," she whined.

"Lucky it was a woman," he told her. "Still, I had to come in and check."

"I bet."

"Come so I can taste you this morning."

Jesus.

"That's what you want to taste in the morning?"

Sargon chuckled, and she swore she could see his sinful smirk in her mind when he murmured, "Every morning, if you would let me."

Cozen came then.

Maybe it was his words.

Maybe the unspoken promise.

Maybe his fingers still working her crazy.

Who knew?

But it was glorious.

Sargon pulled his fingers from between her thighs before he quickly removed the rocks from Cozen's body. Once she was cleared of the rocks, she sat up straight on the table, and found him waiting for her with hard eyes.

She didn't like that.

Not after what he just did.

Still, he was close enough to her that she could reach out and touch him. So, she did just that. She fingered the gold band hanging from the thin cord of black leather around his neck for a moment, reveling in the silence instead of her crazy thoughts.

Sargon didn't seem to mind, as he didn't ask her to remove her hand. If anything, for the briefest second, his gaze softened at her touch. Finally, his hand did come up and cup around hers when she slid the tip of her index finger into the ring.

He sighed, and tugged her hand away from the leather cord. "Time to get back to reality, then."

"What?" she asked.

"Jett would like to see you today. Dinner, and maybe something else afterward. A trip to his mansion, if you would like."

Cozen's gaze locked with Sargon's, and didn't move even an inch. "Would he?"

"Yes."

"I suppose he must have known this was my only day off for the weekend since he has my schedule."

"Yes," Sargon repeated.

"Could you give me something more than one-word answers after you just had your fingers shoved up my cunt?"

Sargon's expression didn't change, and neither did the coldness in his eyes. How fast their moment had gone from something sweet to something entirely different was shocking to her. To say the least.

"Well, can you?"

"Not particularly," he murmured.

"I'm not dressed. And my makeup and hair isn't—"

"It will be taken care of," Sargon interjected. "He heard from a little bird that you were here today getting pampered, and thought he might add onto it with some of his own tricks. He would like you to stop by your place and grab the necklace he gave to you. Apparently, it will match something he had picked out for you."

"Which necklace?"

"Pardon?"

"The one with the gold bars, or the sapphire piece?"

"Sapphires."

"Oh, well ..."

"Yes."

Sargon stepped away from the table, and moved for the door. He just opened it up when he looked over his shoulder at her. Finally, that expression of his broke as his lips curved wickedly at the edges, and he lifted his two fingers to his mouth for a taste.

His digits disappeared between those lips of his, and his grin deepened even more as his eyebrow raised.

He had gotten that taste, after all.

Christ.

Every muscle in her body clenched—from her fingers clutching into the sheet at her waist, to her pussy—at the sight.

He was everything that was bad, sinful, and wonderful wrapped up in a gorgeous face, one hell of a body, and a mind so deep and enigmatic Cozen didn't know where to begin.

Who was playing games now?

Sargon took a place against the wall as Cozen made her way inside the hotel room. Instantly, she was greeted by several people. People who were there to either pamper her, or serve her in some way.

That's what Jett hired them for. He loved to spoil his women, apparently.

Sargon wasn't entirely sure how he felt about Cozen getting lumped into the category as one of Jett's women—how many there were, Sargon was unsure—but here he was. And there she was, too.

Looking entirely out of place, sure, but there she was.

"Miss Taylor, it's great to finally meet you!" the bubbly blonde said, stepping forward from the others. "I brought you a few things to look over, but I think—now that I finally have eyes on you—the navy blue piece will be the best."

Cozen blinked.

Sargon chuckled.

"Of course, you can look over everything. It's your choice in the end."

Cozen glanced his way, and Sargon offered her a smile. "Start with hello, hmm?"

She turned back to the people, still looking like she didn't know what was happening, or if she was entirely comfortable with it. Sargon knew that feeling all too well.

"Um, hello," Cozen said.

She waved an awkward hand.

Sargon almost smiled.

He didn't think he had ever seen her look so off-kilter than she did in that moment. Clearly, this was not what she had been expecting to be waiting for her inside the hotel room. He had to wonder if she was the type to let people fawn over her.

A massage was one thing.

This was different.

"They are here to serve at your pleasure," Sargon said when Cozen glanced his way. "Whatever you need or might want to make you feel wonderful, and get you ready for the evening. Should you need something, let one of them know."

Cozen looked back at the waiting people.

The bubbly blonde personal shopper who had spent the day in the city finding her the *perfect* dress for the evening. A woman to manage Cozen's russet waves into something pretty—not that he thought she didn't look wonderful with her hair loose and free. Another woman to make her face up, and someone else to let her look through jewelry that might match the sapphire necklace.

Quickly, she glanced back at him, asking, "And where will you be?"

"Right outside the door."

Trying not to think about tonight.

His mind was being a bitch today.

Nothing new.

It started the moment he knew she was going in a spa to get a massage. The idea of someone else touching her had felt like an icepick sticking inside his brain. He had told her the idea of a *man* touching her bothered him, but it hadn't really mattered.

Man.

Woman.

It all made him want to choke someone to fucking death, really. No one needed to be touching her but him. Not a masseuse, not the guy making her coffee in the mornings, and definitely not Jett Griffin.

Fuck.

Yeah, that's what Sargon was: fucked.

Cozen hugged the black velvet case belonging to the sapphire necklace to her chest. "And then what's going to happen?"

"Dinner at a very upscale place. More so than The Kingdom. It's why you need a proper outfit for it. Dress and black tie all the way."

"After that?"

"I believe Jett is having a drink with a few friends at the mansion."

"Oh," Cozen said.

"He intends to bring you along."

Cozen did perk up at that statement. "Does he?"

"As far as I know."

Which was the biggest reason for Sargon's discomfort. He did not know what would happen once the dinner date was over, and Cozen was led into the mansion. Once those doors were closed, she would be entirely out of his sight, and his reach.

He suspected Cozen could probably handle herself, if she needed to. Not to mention, he had not seen Jett act anything less than gentlemanly with a woman. Jett didn't seem like the type to get his rocks off by hurting females.

That wasn't the point, though.

The point was … *fucked.*

Sargon was tangled up with a woman he had no business entangling with. A woman who had some kind of secrets she was hiding, and likely a plan in the works, too. A woman whom his boss was courting, and *he* was fucking.

Nothing about this felt good or right.

It was all bad.

Sargon still hadn't found a reason to stop. Or even a reason to stay away from Cozen. It didn't help that Jett continued to put him in her path when all he wanted to do was have Jett's back during the day, and otherwise.

No …

That was a lie.

It was not *all* Sargon wanted to do.

Not now.

Not after Cozen.

He wasn't very loyal to Jett at all.

Frankly, he never had been.

"Enjoy yourself," Sargon said as he moved for the door. And just before he closed it, he added, "Do let me know if you need anything, Cozen."

"Anything?" she asked quietly.

Despite all the people around looking at them, he confirmed what he said. "Anything, sweetheart."

The sad thing was?

He did mean *anything.*

This woman was going to kill him.

It was another three hours—long enough for the sun to settle and darken the sky—before Sargon found himself on the next stop of the evening.

Or rather, delivering Cozen to her next stop. Of course, she got to take a limo. He had to take his town car, and arrive before her at the restaurant.

Sargon took his sweet time parking the black Mercedes sedan. He couldn't lie—he didn't want to be very involved in this evening.

Maybe he could fake it, though.

Even that was up for debate.

All too soon, Sargon found where his boss was waiting for him. Jett stood at the top of the stairs leading into what Sargon now knew to be his youngest son's restaurant. Quite the fancy place, Sargon assumed, considering the gold plated trim around the windows, the heavy, expensive-looking drapery hiding the inside from view, and not to mention the dress code to attend.

"Glad to see you threw on a suit," Jett muttered.

Sargon shrugged as he moved in beside the man. "I managed to get five minutes to do so."

Sometime in between checking on Cozen, and having a suit delivered to him, that was. He pulled the suit on, and took his sweet fucking time knotting the tie. Sargon was not a three-piece kind of man. He much preferred a good silk shirt, and properly pressed slacks.

This suit thing was Jett's demand.

Dress code policy, after all.

"Well?" Jett asked. "How did it go today?"

"Quite well."

"That tells me nothing."

Sargon glanced over at the man, but Jett wasn't even giving him any attention. He was too busy staring down at something on the screen of his phone. "She was pampered, like you wanted. Properly spoiled."

"And she liked it?"

That was up for debate.

Sargon figured Cozen had tolerated all the attention, not to mention having people constantly touching her. She put up with the one who ignored every suggestion she had about her clothes, and the other one who all but demanded she put her hair up into some kind of classic style instead of wearing it down.

Eventually, she just settled into the idea of letting them do whatever they wanted or needed to do so she could get it over with. Or, that was Sargon's perspective of how that all went down earlier.

He didn't think Jett wanted to know those details, though. The man would only care to know that Cozen appeared happy, and beautiful.

That's all Jett needed.

"I think," Sargon drawled, "you will be pleased to see her."

Jett did finally glance up from his phone at that statement. A wide smile spread over his features as he gave Sargon a nod. "That's all that matters."

As I figured …

Sargon had not been lying.

Jett *was* pleased when he finally saw Cozen.

How could he blame the man?

She was quite a sight.

Sargon had a hard time tearing his gaze away from the woman, actually. He stayed to the shadows of the restaurant. He moved along the walls, and occasionally found his way back to the bar when needed for a drink.

Still, he couldn't help but watch her.

She had settled on the navy silk gown. Or, the bitch pushed it on her. Either way, it looked damn good draped over her curves, and sweeping the floor. Low cut in the front, and dangerously opened in the back, it showed off all kinds of skin.

A slit up the leg showcased a peek of her tanned skin and smooth thighs every time turned to follow Jett to another table.

This restaurant was just as much about eating food as it was about mingling, and seeing people. People who were worth knowing, essentially. Rich fucks with pockets so deep, they might never find their way out again should they get lost.

Sargon didn't miss the way Cozen's gaze swept the room as though she was looking for something—or *someone*—when Jett's back was turned to talk to yet another three-piece. Him, probably. She knew he was there.

Hidden by the shadows of a hallway at the moment, she couldn't see him at all. He saw the way her gaze dropped, as did her smile briefly, before her mask came back in to place like it had never left at all.

She went back to the conversation at hand with a grin from Jett like she had never drifted from it in the first place. She stuck a hand out, and allowed the three-piece to kiss her knuckles as she was introduced and greeted.

Again.

And all over again, Sargon's gut burned.

Jealousy was a horrible feeling.

A monster, really.

As quickly as this meeting between Jett, Cozen, and the three-piece had started, they moved on to someone else. Another faceless suit to greet, and smile for. Someone else to admire a beauty they would never fully appreciate or understand.

Their dinner had been done over an hour ago, and then this whole charade started. Sargon wondered how long it was going to last because he was already growing tired of it.

This was exactly why he never lasted long in any one job. His patience was thin, and his heart was far too restless to stay put in one place for long.

Of course, this job was different.

Cozen was the biggest difference. Her presence was more than enough to put Sargon on an entirely different foot when it came to the job. If he were smart, he would consider backing off, and telling Jett he no longer wanted to work for the man. Take his feelings out of the equation entirely, and stop putting himself—and Cozen, likely—in danger with this game they were playing.

Apparently, Sargon was not a smart man because he didn't entertain the idea for long. Just long enough to get that heavy, burning sensation back in his gut that told him there was no fucking way he would let that woman out of his sights for very long. Certainly not long enough that he might lose her for good.

Sargon's gaze drifted to Cozen and Jett again.

Ah ...

Another three-piece, but this time, the faceless rich fuck had a too-young, very plastic wife on his arm. Fake all over from the extensions in her hair, to the slightly orange tan on her skin. That was before Sargon got to the tits, nails, and oddly proportioned hips.

Christ.

Sargon knew what Jett was doing.

He *knew*.

He could see it without needing confirmation.

This was a test for Cozen, in a way. Jett was testing her tonight. Seeing how she did as he moved her from table to table, and new person to new person. He was checking to see if she was malleable enough to fit in with these kinds of people. Could she blend in with their high-rolling society, and never look out of place?

Sargon had news for the man.

Cozen was far too unique to blend in.

She was always going to stand out.

Always outshine.

Goddamn.

Sargon really needed a drink at the moment. He pushed out of the shadows, and headed directly for the bar knowing that alcohol was the only thing that might make this night slightly more fucking bearable.

He didn't care that he was supposed to be keeping out of sight—from Cozen, and anyone else who Jett mingled with for the evening.

Soon, a bartender was pushing three shots of top-shelf whiskey across the bar. Sargon threw the first shot back, and relished in the harsh burn it provided as he swallowed it down. The second shot went down just as fucking easily.

There was something about whiskey …

It made all things better.

He grabbed the last shot, but hesitated to take it.

Sargon looked for his boss and Cozen again. He found them moving away from another couple, and closer to the dance floor. If you could call the small patch of hardwood floor in the middle of the place a dance floor.

People were dancing there. Jett and Cozen soon joined them.

Sargon's gaze was only on Cozen, though. On the way that dress of hers fell over her curves, and the deep plunges teasing him far too much. Not to mention, the slit in the leg that kept giving him peeks of heaven. A heaven *he* knew, and Jett did not.

The two of them moved quickly across the dance floor in a fast waltz, and on a turn, Cozen happened to finally lay eyes on Sargon for the first time that night. She had not seen him since he said goodbye to her at the hotel.

Oh, he had been watching her.

All night.

He didn't give a shit about Jett.

"You know," said a voice from Sargon's side, "I am not sure my father would appreciate the way you are looking at his date for the evening."

Yeah, whiskey made *everything* better.

Except for this night.

Sargon tossed back the third shot, turned his back to Jett and Cozen, and slammed the shot glass to the bar. "Another three, thanks."

The bartender's brow shot up, but he did as he was told.

Dash, however, laughed. "Did you not hear me, or what?"

"I heard you," Sargon muttered, passing Jett's youngest son—and the owner of the establishment—a look. "I just don't care what you have to say."

"Little unwise, isn't it? I might have useful things to say, Sarg."

Sargon sneered. "It's Sargon. Call me that again, and Jett or no Jett, I will feed you your fingertips after I slice them off your fingers."

"Touchy." The twenty-five year old turned his back to the bar, and looked out on the floor. Sargon stayed just like he was. "I meant what I said, though. Dad gets particular about his females. I mean, he hasn't had many since mom died a while back, but still. He doesn't like the idea of somebody encroaching on what he's chasing after."

"Nobody is *encroaching* on anything."

"He only needs the idea you are. Get what I'm saying?"

"She's hard not to admire. And he is showing her off."

"Fair enough." Dash turned and snatched one of Sargon's three new shots before quickly slamming it back. Letting out a hard breath, he set the shot glass back to the table. "It's fucked up to think the next woman my dad might marry—technically it would make her my step-mother—is the same age as me."

Yep.

That did it.

Sargon waved a hand at the bartender to get the guy's attention. "Just get me the whole bottle."

"Sir—"

"I want the bottle."

"Sir, I can't give you the bottle. I can give you a couple more shots instead."

Fuck it all to hell.

Whiskey was going to make *something* better. Sargon would call one of Jett's other men to drive him to the mansion.

Sargon was not drunk.

No.

He was … buzzed.

Yes, that worked.

Slightly buzzed, but definitely not drunk. Buzzed enough that he had not been able to drive the car home, but that was fixed easily enough when another man stepped in to help. Frankly, Sargon was a lucky fuck.

Jett had been far too caught up in Cozen to even realize Sargon was not on his game. So much so, that he hadn't even looked for Sargon when he left the restaurant. He just assumed the man would follow right behind.

Which he did.

Sort of.

"You owe me," the man told him as he parked the car in the estate's driveway.

Sargon was only half listening. "Mmm."

He was too busy watching the driver of the limo get out, and move around the back to open the passenger door. Jett exited first, and then Cozen soon followed. Helped by the hand Jett held out to her.

"Did you fucking hear me?"

What was the man's name again?

Brad.

Ben.

Barker.

Something that started with a B, anyway.

"Yeah, yeah," Sargon said, waving a hand at the guy. "Owe you, and all that good shit."

A couple of hours, and Sargon would be fine. He would sober up, and get back to his usual self. Not any worse for wear, either.

The whiskey hadn't helped, though.

Not like he hoped it would.

Sargon exited the car just as Cozen and Jett stood to chat beside the limo. He leaned against the car, and pulled out a pack of smokes to light one up. This job was bad for his health—he was smoking far more than he ever had before.

The voices of the two across the way carried to him with the light May breeze. He could have done without hearing more of their conversation. He didn't like the way Jett spoke to Cozen in a familiar way, and he couldn't possibly like how she fed into it, either.

"You couldn't find something to replace this with?" Jett asked. "The jeweler didn't have anything that caught your eye?"

As he asked, he fingered the golden band tight around Cozen's thumb. She quickly pulled her hand back, but offered a brilliant smile that would distract any man.

As long as it wasn't Sargon …

He was catching on to this woman's tricks.

"I don't like to take it off," she said. "I've worn it for so long now."

"I see." Jett gestured at the house, saying, "Guests are waiting. Care to join me?"

Like she could say no?

Cozen didn't refuse.

Sargon wished he had more whiskey.

"You moved from California to New York?" the blonde asked.

Cozen had not listened well enough to remember the woman's name when she was introduced to her an hour ago. She was regretting that now, considering she had been left alone with the chick to chat. "I did, yes."

"God, *why?*"

"To do something different," Cozen replied.

Yes, that worked.

It wasn't entirely the truth, but it wasn't entirely a lie, either.

"But ... good weather, the beach, and all the beautiful people!"

Cozen tipped her wine up for a sip, and hid her smile in the glass. Swallowing down the sweet liquor, she finally replied, "Sometimes you just need a change. That's what this was for me. A change."

"I see."

The blonde wasn't too bad to talk to, really. Unlike some of the other guests who had been invited to the mansion for the evening, this woman didn't make comments about Cozen's job, or her status, and she had yet to give her a backhanded compliment. Something all women liked to do far too often to their counterparts.

Of course, out of the six guests there, Cozen found none interesting. They were all the same faceless, nameless rich people. Dripping in wealth, and arrogance. A touch too ignorant, too. Their snobbery couldn't be matched when they thought Jett's back was turned.

Cozen wasn't going to tattle on Jett's friends—she wasn't a wilting flower, and they couldn't exactly wound her pride with a couple of low-grade insults. They were not anything she couldn't handle on her own.

And she had been doing that just fine.

Besides, Cozen was all too aware that they didn't know her at all. They only knew the person Jett and she presented to them. The waitress he met—living in a small Manhattan apartment, and prettied up because Jett arranged for it to be so tonight.

To them, that probably screamed low class, and gold digger. She certainly wasn't up to their kind of snuff, anyway.

It was amusing.

Cozen bet she had more zeroes in a Swiss bank account than they did. And even if they met her under different circumstances—in her real life, not playing this character for a job—she doubted they would know the truth.

Unlike them, she didn't need her wealth or to show it off in order to feel validated or successful in her life. The money was nice, sure. Stability and reassurance money provided couldn't be matched except for the feeling of having someone love you, but it was good, too. Good to have, and good to keep.

Just in case.

"Do you think we should get back to the rest of them?" the woman asked.

Cozen's gaze slid in the direction of the entryway to the large library. "Why don't we walk around some more? My legs are restless. I feel like I've been sitting down too much."

That was her being nice.

And *sly*.

Cozen had zero interest in returning to the other guests where they were probably still drinking too much wine in the entertainment room at the Griffin estate. Jett had gotten a phone call for something, and excused himself to take it. That was a good hour ago, now. Maybe a little more.

None of his guests had seemed very surprised. One of the men even happened to mention that it was all too common for Jett to just up and go during social things because he never stopped working. Someone was always calling him back to the job. They didn't seem very offended about him leaving them high and dry, either.

This was also a good chance for her to look around, and so, she had done that a little bit. She slipped out of the entertainment room while the others' backs were turned. It wasn't like they would miss her presence—maybe they would miss insulting her, though.

Who knew?

Cozen managed to look around several rooms on the bottom floor of the one wing. Two kitchens, staff quarters, and a living room with a television the size of one wall. Attached to both kitchens were two separate dining rooms. One very large, and another smaller one—more intimate in size and decoration.

She had also checked four bathrooms, what appeared to be a small office, though mostly unused and with nothing valuable inside, and a goddamn coat closet. It seemed—at least on the bottom floor—the entertainment room, the living space, the main kitchen, and the big dining room were the largest spaces and took up most of the square footage in the wing.

That, and the massive library she stumbled into. Out of all of the rooms on the bottom floor, she found this one *most* interesting. Cozen figured if a man was going to hide something valuable, or hide a safe *keeping* something valuable, this would be a great room to do it in. It was large, excessive, and distracting in far too many ways.

From the floor-to-ceiling shelving stained a cherry oak, to the silk draperies hanging from the tall windows. It all screamed riches and wealth. Not to mention, the gold and crystal chandelier hanging from a vaulted ceiling.

She would be remiss if she didn't mention the constant displays of Jett's wealth all though the bottom floor of the mansion estate, too. It was everywhere. From the gold plated crown molding, to the trim around the doorways. He liked gold—he also seemed to like anything that was crystal. Leather was another common theme in different rooms.

She wondered what was upstairs.

Or what was over in the second, smaller wing.

The blonde answered one question when one of Jett's sons—the youngest—passed by the library entryway. "I wonder if Dash is ever going to move out of the second wing. Silas moved out long before he ever got married."

"He lives there—just him?" Cozen asked.

She didn't like to prod Jett with too many questions. She could not afford to raise his suspicions with her for any reason. But she *was* getting work done—she was learning about Jett, parts of his home, and he was letting her into his life.

Just like she needed.

One step closer.

"Yep," the blonde said. "Just him. It's closed off from this wing with a hallway and a locked door. Sometimes it's left open, but you know, Jett doesn't like for people to wander around beyond the bottom floor very much, or out on the back of the property. Dash, on the other hand, *loves* to show off the place."

Cozen heard the woman, but she wasn't really listening. She had heard a couple of important things, and tucked the information away to keep.

One—the second wing was a useless zone to her. She doubted anything over there was going to help her find the Astor ring if Dash had practically taken over the wing, and lived there full-time.

Two—Jett kept his people, including close friends—downstairs. Or outside. He didn't want them going upstairs to the second floor of the wing. She suspected that was because they were his private quarters. His real *home*, essentially. Bedrooms, and offices. Spaces he used to work, or do business in a private manner. And since she knew his work as a black market broker could be sensitive, he probably didn't want people stumbling on anything.

Upstairs.

That's where it'll be.

That's where she would find the ring.

But *where* upstairs?

That was the better question.

"I think we better get back to the party," the blonde repeated. Her gaze traveled upward as she added, "I heard Jett doesn't invite people back when he finds out they were snooping through his home."

Cozen found what the woman was looking at. A camera tucked into one of the corners in the ceiling. It's positioning made it hard to notice at first, but Cozen had been aware of it since damn near the moment she came into the room.

She was in tune to things like security cameras. She had been taught to look for them first, recognize possible angles it was capturing, and then work accordingly in a space. That was why she had been careful not to make it seem like she was doing anything more than just looking around at the books when she came into the library.

It was not the first camera she noticed, and it wasn't even the fifth. There wasn't a camera in every room or hallway, but in the main rooms, and the large dining room. A hallway or two, as well. Places where people would be, she noticed.

Jett didn't trust anyone.

Rightfully so—look at her.

She was more curious, though, if someone was watching the cameras all the time, or if they simply just went back and checked the footage *after* events or gatherings. That was an important detail to know, should she need to use it.

"There you are, darling."

Cozen plastered on one of her brightest smiles at Jett's voice coming from the entryway of the library. She found him standing there in his three-piece suit with his own smile. Although it looked like he had loosened his tie a bit.

"Sorry if I worried you," Cozen said, and then waved at the library. "I couldn't help but explore."

"And let me guess, you got lost in the library?"

"What woman doesn't love books, Jett?"

"Ah, I see."

The woman beside her shot Cozen a smile. "I will go find my husband."

"Thanks for walking around with me."

"It was very nice to meet you, Cozen."

"And you."

She still couldn't remember the woman's name, and now, she felt kind of bad about it. Out of all the guests, she had been the nicest, and didn't make Cozen feel out of place.

It was a shame, really.

Had it been any other time and Cozen met the woman, maybe they could have been friends. Who knew?

Once the woman was gone, Jett joined Cozen in the library. He snagged her hand in his, and then tugged her to follow him to the brown leather loveseat sitting in front of the large windows. His gaze never left her as she thumbed through a paperback that had been sitting on the side table.

"You can take that home with you, if you like," Jett said. "I finished reading it yesterday."

"I would like that, thank you."

She actually wasn't all that interested in the thriller. She was more of a romance kind of girl, but whatever made the man feel like he was doing something to make her happy. She only needed him to let her into the most private areas of his life.

And *fast*.

Her time to get this done was running out.

"Did you enjoy tonight?" Jett asked. "Your gifts, and meeting new people?"

Cozen gave him a simpering smile. "Of course, I did. And you have a spectacular home, really. I almost got lost, actually. The house is big."

"I would have found where you went," Jett replied, pointing to the camera up above. "At least, in most cases. I keep cameras out of the upstairs, and downstairs they're placed where I entertain, mostly."

Good to know.

Cozen filed that information away for later.

"I imagine this is … foreign to you, isn't it?" Jett asked.

"What is?"

"My wealth."

Cozen's smile dropped a bit, but she didn't take too long to respond. "I don't have a lot of money, if that's what you're asking."

Lies.

"And I didn't grow up with a lot of things—stability, love, or otherwise," she added.

Not a lie.

Jett nodded. "I'm aware."

Cozen lifted a single brow. "Are you?"

She knew about Jett looking into her past—obviously—the one that was on record, anyway. She had wondered if he would bring it up to her that he had done so, though.

"I don't want you to be angry with me," he murmured, "but you have to understand that I can't allow people into my life without knowing them. I may seem like only a businessman on the outside, but it is behind closed doors where I am something else entirely. I have to know everything about the people I allow inside so that they're safe, and so am I."

Cozen wet her lips, and set the book aside. "And what does that mean, exactly?"

"I had someone do a bit of a background search on you, that's all."

"Oh."

"Oh?" Jett smiled a bit, though she could see his worry. "Is that all you have to say?"

Cozen shrugged. "Did you find anything interesting? My life has been pretty boring."

"Hard and difficult, I thought."

"Pardon?"

"Your life," he clarified, reaching out to cup her cheek with his warm palm. "It has been hard and difficult."

Cozen swallowed hard at the feeling of his thumb stroking her skin. She had no real attraction to this man—no desire to want him, or love him. And yet, he seemed to genuinely care about her in some ways.

She had long since learned to play her part in a job, and shut off the tap of emotions that might trickle down with something useless like guilt, or otherwise. Sure, Jett seemed like a decent man from the outside. An older man, but still good-looking, and holding onto his prime. He had lost his wife, and was left with two adult sons. He was like any man, but he was not like every other man, too.

He was also a criminal.

He lived in shades of gray.

Like her.

He just didn't know about her.

She *knew* about him.

"But did you enjoy yourself tonight, and your gifts?" he asked again.

"I said yes."

His gaze looked her over. "I think blue is definitely your color."

Cozen smiled, finding her chance to drop a hint. "I think you should see me in red, then."

His laughter colored up the library.

Jett came closer, and Cozen reached up to pat his hand still resting on her cheek. He pressed a quick kiss to her cheek, and then backed off just as fast.

"Something came up in my call," he explained, "and I have to get back to it. I asked the guests to leave, and it's well after one in the morning, so I know you must be tired. Someone is waiting outside to drive you home."

Cozen frowned. "Oh, okay."

His thumb stroked her cheek again. "Don't be sad. We'll have another day."

"Soon, right?"

Because *time was running out*.

And she was so close to the prize, now.

Jett grinned. "Very soon, Cozen."

"Maybe next time *you* could be the one to show me around the mansion, then."

"Would you like that?"

Yes.

Far more than he knew.

She only needed a little bit of time to work.

"I would," Cozen settled on saying.

"Then, we will definitely have to do that," Jett replied.

Cozen was entirely unsurprised to find it was Sargon waiting outside by a black town car. Smoke puffed from the tailpipe. It told her that the car had been running for some time.

"Sorry," she said as he eyed her, "I didn't mean to make you wait."

"I have been waiting all night."

"Excuse me?"

The edge of his mouth lifted into a half-sneer, but he simply shook his head before nodding toward the car. "Come on, and I will take you home."

She wasted no time climbing into the front seat—though she probably should have taken the back—when Sargon opened the door for her. He gave her a lingering look, and his gaze traveled over her body before he closed the door.

She had felt it, though.

The way his gaze sunk into her.

Searched her.

Jesus.

It was only once they were on the road with the mansion far behind them before he spoke again. He never took his eyes away from the road as he talked.

"You're lucky it is me to drive you home tonight," he said.

"Why is that?"

"A few hours ago, I would have been over the limit to drive."

Cozen frowned. "You were drinking?"

"Whiskey. It makes everything better."

"Does it?"

"Not tonight," he muttered heavily. "I wasn't drunk—a little buzzed. I took a nap in the backseat of the car, and woke up fine. Shouldn't be drinking on the job, anyway."

She eyed him from the side. "Was it because of me?"

Somehow, she just *knew* ...

Sargon cleared his throat. "I don't like watching you with him, Cozen. I don't like the way you smile for him—I know it's fake, but I don't know why. I don't like it when he touches you, or how he shows you off. I hate that you let him do those things, and you keep the act up all the while. I hate all of it."

"I have let you do far more to me," she murmured.

Finally, he looked over at her. Those dark eyes of his bore into hers, and pinned her in place. Just like that, her heart picked up, and her breaths came faster. She felt a shiver race over her skin, and it left her feeling warm and beautiful.

All it took was a look.

From him.

"Have I?" he asked, going back to the road.

"What?"

"Done more to you than he has?"

Cozen bit the inside of her cheek. "What are you asking?"

"Did he fuck you?"

The heat in his voice couldn't be missed. A warning lingered there— unmistakable and dark. A promise of violence in a whisper.

"No," Cozen said, "but certainly not because he isn't interested."

Sargon's jaw tightened, and so did his fingers around the steering wheel. "That's a good, and bad, answer."

"I only lie to work, or save my life."

His gaze darted to hers again before he asked, "And what is it that you do, Cozen—for *work*?"

"I play a part to get what I need."

Not a lie.

Sargon smirked. "I'm not sure if that falls into the good or bad category for an answer this time."

"It's all you're getting." She twisted the gold band on her thumb. "And what do you do, Sargon?"

"You already know—I am a bodyguard, or an errand runner, depending on his need."

"For *Jett*, sure. But what else?"

"I'm usually the one making sure shit doesn't go bad, Cozen. I blend in well, and I like to be on the move. So, what I do this month may be vastly different from what I am doing next month." Sargon chuckled dryly. "Did he try at all?"

Cozen gave him another look. "Try what?"

"Jett—did he try to fuck you?"

"No, he sent me home, although it's clear he's invested."

"Invested ... that's an interesting way to describe what he was trying to do tonight."

Cozen's brow furrowed. "Excuse me?"

"He was showing you what you could have, Cozen. His people, and his beautiful things. You could be one of those beautiful things if you wanted to be. All the wealth, and the lifestyle he leads. It could all be yours, if you asked for it. If you *wanted* it bad enough."

And yet, she didn't.

"I know what I want," she murmured, staring straight at Sargon.

He looked back, unashamed. "Do you?"

"I will always know, Sargon."

Sargon pulled the black town car into the parking lot of Cozen's apartment building, and cut the engine. "I will walk you up."

Cozen passed him a look. "Will you stay, too?"

He lifted a single brow, but didn't reply. He hadn't expected her to be so bold or brazen in asking him to stay the night, but he really couldn't find himself to be surprised, either. This woman was constantly doing things that stunned him silent.

Instead of answering her, Sargon stepped out of the car. He quickly moved to her side, and opened the passenger door before offering his hand to Cozen. She took it, and he helped her out of the car with a smile.

"Lead the way," he murmured.

Cozen gave him another one of those half-amused, half-annoyed looks, but she did what he said. Sargon stayed a couple of steps behind her as she headed for her apartment building. He considered it a win-win, anyway.

He got to watch her ass move beneath that dress.

The way her hips swayed …

It was memorizing, really.

Like this, when it was just the two of them, Sargon didn't have to pretend that he wasn't interested in Cozen. Like everything about her—all the things he knew, and even the stuff he didn't know—called out to him like nothing else ever had before.

She was a siren.

Her song sung just for him.

Fuck him for wanting her.

At the back door, Cozen fiddled with keys until she found the right one to unlock the building. Sargon held the door open as she slipped inside, and then he quickly followed. When she looked back at him and caught him staring at her backside again, her gaze narrowed a bit before her laughter lit up the hall.

"See something you like?" she asked.

"What's not to fucking like, Zen?"

She shot him a simpering smile that promised all sorts of naughty things, and made his cock semi-hard at the thought alone. The smoky eye makeup gave her a demure look, and he bet it would look even better when she was staring up at him.

Like maybe those painted-red lips of hers wrapped around his cock while she was on her knees. He liked the thought of smearing her lipstick a bit while he fucked her mouth, and watching that makeup smudge under his handling.

It was a pretty image.

His mind was creative.

And entirely *punishing.*

"What's on your mind?" Cozen asked him as they took the stairs to her floor. He still opted to stay a couple of paces behind her. "You look like you're thinking awfully hard about something back there, Sargon."

"You on your knees with your mouth on my dick, water in your eyes, and your makeup a mess. I was trying to decide whether I would leave your hair up, or take it all down. I like it down, you know. Makes it easier to wrap my hands in."

She had not been expecting that response. Sargon saw it in the way her shoulders tensed, and she almost missed a step. Then, she shot him a look over her shoulder—those russet eyes of hers darkened with lust instantly.

Sargon winked. "You did ask."

"Is that all you think about when you're around me?"

No.

Not even close.

"I also wonder why you prefer to sleep in a pile of blankets rather than on a proper bed. I'm curious if you're a morning person, and if so, do you take coffee, or tea. You wear red a lot when you're not working—is it a favorite color, or is there another reason you like the color? Have you ever been in love; what are your motives here; can I trust you?"

Cozen turned to face him just as they came to a stop in front of her apartment door. She glanced between the door, and him before whispering, "Come in and stay the evening. Maybe you'll get all the answers you're looking for, Sargon."

"That sounds like more games, Cozen."

She peered up at him through thick lashes. "I thought you liked my games?"

Sargon moved close enough to Cozen that he could smell the lingering perfume she had worn that day. A perfume he had smelled on her more than once. He figured it must have been a favorite of hers.

A sugary scent mixed with cinnamon, or something in that area. It soaked into his lungs with every breath, and he swore he would never be able to forget that smell. He associated sugar and spice with her, now.

Sweet.

Hot.

The memory was strange.

The brain was stranger.

A single scent—one tied to good or bad events in one's life—could bring back a swell of memories. And all someone need to do was smell it in passing.

Sargon knew this scent was going to be that for him.

A trigger.

A trigger of her.

"Come in," she whispered. "Stay with me tonight."

Sargon slipped his hands under her jaw, and tipped her head back a bit so he could stare right into her eyes. Quickly, he dropped one kiss, and then a faster second one, on the seam of her softly smiling lips.

Then, he stepped back.

Cozen frowned.

"Get comfortable," he told her as he turned around to head back down the hall.

"Seriously, you're leaving?"

Sargon chuckled.

Didn't she like her games?

"Sargon!"

"I told you, get comfortable for me."

He didn't bother to turn around. No, he just waved his hand high over his shoulder before he disappeared out the hallway door. He took the stairs two at a time, and then exited the apartment building just as fast as he had come in.

The cool May breeze from earlier in the evening had died down a bit. It was slightly warmer—comfortable, even. Summer would soon be there.

Sargon scanned the parking lot, and the streets as he slipped into the Mercedes. The engine purred to life under his handling, and he spun the tires a bit leaving the lot. He wasn't sure how long he drove around the city.

Enough to lose anyone following him, anyway.

That was his plan.

Sargon didn't know who to trust—he didn't have the first clue if he was being followed, or watched. After all, Jett had *him* following Cozen on a regular basis. Who was to say the man wasn't having someone else keep an eye on Sargon, too?

He parked the car in a hotel's parking lot, and then used back alleys to get himself lost.

Well, not really.

He just needed to disappear for a bit.

A cab took him back to Cozen's place, and then he hit all the buzzers at once to trick someone into letting him inside the building. He'd pick up the car again tomorrow sometime in the morning. Just in case … GPS, and all.

Sargon trusted no one.

Except …

He had a feeling he could trust her because they were kind of in this mess together now. The brown-haired, russet-eyed beauty that opened the apartment door to greet him.

Cozen had changed out of her dress, and slipped on something silky, and pretty.

It even had lace trim.

Black lace.

"Black lace is my favorite," he told her.

Cozen grinned. "Good to know."

"I wasn't really going to refuse your offer."

"I figured that out when you told me to get comfortable *for you*."

Good.

Sargon kicked the door closed behind him.

The phone was ringing—Sargon's cell—but he wasn't paying attention. He didn't care to roll over and find the goddamn thing when he had far better things to be doing at the moment. He was far too busy imprinting the scent and taste of Cozen to be worrying about who was calling him at …

Sargon glanced up from the spot where he was kissing on Cozen's spine to peek at the clock on the wall. *Six in the morning.*

Fuck that.

He was not picking up the phone.

"That's the second call this—"

"Hush," Sargon demanded before going back to kissing a path down Cozen's spine. Naked in her nest of blankets and pillows, one probably wouldn't even know it was just the floor beneath them. It was quite soft, and comfortable, all things considered. "Hush, and let me enjoy you for five more minutes."

Cozen laughed breathlessly. "Only *five?*"

"Don't test me, woman."

To make his point, one of his palms smacked down on her ass. He felt the heat rise to the surface of her skin damn near instantly. He grabbed her backside firmly in the same spot, rolled to his side, and dragged her with him. Tucking her against his naked chest, he buried his face in her neck, and sucked on her pulse point.

Her heart raced as his hand skimmed her curves, and then dropped down between her thighs. She spread her legs open even more for him.

"You're terribly fucking needy this morning," he said, letting his fingers stroke her pussy. "And wet. Shit, feel how wet you are, Cozen."

Her hand slipped down to meet his between her legs. He nipped at the spot where her throat met her shoulder as her fingers sunk into her pussy alongside his two. He pulled out just to stroke her clit while she fucked herself.

Cozen's sweet cries turned into soft mewls. Her leg hooked around his, and tangled tight to lock her into place. He kept those circling strokes at a firm pressure against her clit as a tremor began to work its way through her body.

Jesus.

He could smell her all around him.

Feel her all over his skin.

Her taste was in his mouth—the best thing he'd ever tasted first thing in the morning was her pussy on his tongue.

Nothing was ever going to compare to that.

Cozen tipped her head back on the pillow to look up at him. All mused hair, swollen lips from waking him up by sucking him off, and eyes darkened with lust. All her makeup from the night before was gone, and he'd ruined that pretty, silk nightie of hers when he all but ripped it off.

Not that she minded.

Now, it was just them, and skin.

And sex.

"An amber brown," Cozen whispered.

She was so close to coming—he knew it. He could feel it in the way her heart raced under his kiss, and the shake in her thighs. Her voice had turned breathless and high. The sounds of her fingers thrusting in time with his circles filled the space.

"Amber?" he asked. "For what?"

"It's the color of your eyes."

Sargon smiled. "It is."

"And it's my favorite color."

He couldn't hold himself back from kissing her sweet mouth any longer. His lips came down on hers, and he felt all her soft sounds muffle against his kiss. His tongue flicked against the seam of her lips, demanding entrance. She came around her own fingers and his teasing touch as their tongues danced a now-familiar rhythm.

Sargon couldn't control his needs long enough to let Cozen relax again. He rolled them back over, and put Cozen on her back. She was already widening her legs for him, and pulling him in close.

She pulled him in for another searing kiss as he found heaven in that first thrust. She surrounded him in peace. The rest of the world ceased to exist while he was fucking her.

What more could he want?

"Oh, my God," Cozen breathed in his ear.

Her fingers tangled in his hair while his teeth left imprints on her throat. He had the most indescribable urge to leave his marks behind.

So even after he was done fucking her—even when he was gone—she would still feel him. She could still see him, and that he had been there.

Sargon's phone started ringing.

"Fuck," he muttered against her throat.

Cozen answered him back with a laugh.

He just fucked her harder—a brutal pace that left him with lines down his back from her fingernails, and her bite mark on his shoulder. All that sweet, soft love was gone, then. There was no sweetness or softness left between them.

Just her begging.

And him taking.

"I want to come," he heard her say. "*Please.*"

Oh, he would give her that, too.

Sargon pulled out of the heaven between her thighs, and quickly flipped Cozen over to her knees. He yanked her back to him, likely dragging her knees a little too roughly against the blankets. Once her ass was perched high, he dove right back in.

One of his hands wrapped around her middle to pull her harder into his thrusts.

More, more, more …

That's all he heard her ask for.

"You want more—you need *more*, Cozen?"

"God, yes."

Her words were a hiss beneath her whisper. It was still a balm to his soul. All of her words were like that for him.

He pulled his cock from her pussy, and slid the head through her folds again. Cozen stilled, but then one of her sweet little sighs echoed when he used his fingers to smear her wetness from her pussy up to her ass. He fucked her ass with his fingers, stretching her full and wide, while his cock slid back into the wet, tight heaven of her cunt. It didn't take long at all for the neighbors to start hearing his name being shouted after that when Cozen came again.

"Jesus Christ," she breathed.

Cozen's voice was a hum in the back of his mind. Her words urging him to a finish he knew was coming on quick. He could feel it in the tightness of his spine, the heat in his gut, and the ache in his fucking balls.

Sargon used Cozen's slick, trembling back to catch his come when he pulled out. He painted her overheated skin with streams of white.

Her breathless laughter teased him again. He flipped her over to see her eyes.

Cozen wet her lips, and smiled sinfully. "You made a mess."

Sargon reached for his phone he'd discarded earlier into the blankets. "You don't care."

"As long as you wash me off before you go."

"Deal, sweetheart."

He checked his phone—it hadn't stopped ringing.

Two voicemails.

Five missed calls.

All from Jett.

Fuck.

Sargon gave Cozen a look as he dialed the messaging inbox, and put the phone to his ear. Soon, Jett's messages were playing back to him. The first was just demanding to know where he was since he wasn't picking up the calls.

The second was worse.

"I want you to pick up Cozen and deliver her to my favorite breakfast spot," Jett said. "And give me a call when you're going to do it since you can't seem to pick up the fucking phone this morning. She'll say she has work today, but I already called her in. I promised her I would see her soon, after all."

Sargon tossed the phone away when the message was done—his high from fucking Cozen almost entirely gone.

It was only eased slightly by Cozen reaching for him. Her small arms locked around him like bars holding him tight, and then she pulled him to her. He didn't even mind falling down on the blankets, and burying his face into her sweet-smelling, warm skin again.

"Good morning," she said into his hair.

Sargon chuckled. "For now, sure."

"Who was calling?"

"Who do you think?"

She stiffened. "Jett?"

"You've been summoned. For breakfast, apparently."

Her russet eyes searched his before she said, "Okay."

And just like that, his high was gone again.

"And of course, you saw the library the last time you were here," Jett said.

"Show me again," Cozen replied, smiling widely. "I'm sure you'll have something new and interesting to show me. I didn't get to see very much the last time I was in here."

Jett Griffin was the kind of man who loved to be praised. And adored. He enjoyed attention being on him, and his home. Cozen had come to learn these things easily, and she didn't mind feeding in to the man's whims to get what she wanted and needed.

"The library, then," he said.

At the same time, he dragged her close to his side, and planted a quick kiss to her temple. His affections were becoming more physical with each meeting they had, and he was no longer attempting to hold them back. Cozen was still doing her best to deflect them when she could, but this time, she didn't.

Instead of distracting Jett, she pushed closer to him, and slid an arm around his side. She needed to get him out of her hair for a while—long enough to be without him and look around alone.

Her hand slipped into his pocket as he grinned at her, clearly enjoying the fact she had brought him closer, and she made quick work of sliding his phone from his pocket. A phone he rarely let out of his sights, as far as she had noticed. It was always ringing, too. He would likely be in a terrible fit should he ... lose it for a while.

Jett turned them quickly to face one another as they strolled into the library, and Cozen hid his phone at her back when he grabbed her face in his hands. "Have I told you how beautiful you look today?"

Please don't ring yet, she silently begged the phone.

"I think you did," she replied sweetly.

"Shame. You should be told more often." Jett reached over her shoulder, and pressed his palm against one of the bookshelves. "Now, here's an interesting secret for you about this library."

Cozen deftly slipped his phone into the pocket of her dress when she turned at his urging to find the large bookshelf had opened up to reveal a staircase behind it. "And where does that lead to?"

"My private quarters ups—"

"Mr. Griffin," came the nasally voice of one of the maids, "Jones wanted me to let you know that a call came into the landline."

Jett barely even looked over his shoulder at the woman when he replied, "Have him put it through to my cell."

Cozen stiffened.

Shit.

Then, Jett patted at his pocket when the maid left, but his gaze narrowed. Cozen kept her expression neutral, but inside, she was screaming.

"Where in the hell ..." Jett flashed Cozen a smile before he said, "I think I left my phone in the dining room. Are you okay to look around a bit? I'll find you, darling."

"More than fine," she assured.

Seems her little trick did work.

The second Jett was gone from the library, Cozen considered herself free to do as she pleased. At least until Jett got tired of looking for his missing phone, and came to search for her instead.

Whatever.

Anything helped.

Cozen slipped into the hidden stairwell just as the phone in her pocket started to softly ring with the call that had been put through to Jett's cell. She slipped her hand in her pocket, and hit the button to mute the ring, and took the stairs a little bit quicker.

She didn't think Jett meant for her to go upstairs into his private quarters alone, but she had the chance, so ...

Taking it.

Cozen came to the top of the stairs only to find a wall she had to push open to get to the other side. Like the bookshelves, it swung outward but this time revealed a long hallway with opened doors. Directly across from her looked like ... a spare bedroom.

"Shit," Cozen muttered.

A spare bedroom was useless.

Still, she stepped into the hallway and went further down. Again, Jett's phone rang in her pocket, but once more, she silenced it.

She passed several rooms—none that interested her. Spare bedrooms, living quarters, and even an entertainment room. Similar to the downstairs layout, really, but with more personal touches from Jett himself.

Finally, Cozen found herself in a room that might be of some interest. A bedroom, but not a spare. Definitely the master bedroom by the looks of it. On the nightstand, Cozen found a Rolex watch haphazardly tossed into a glass bowl, along with a couple of rings.

One of the rings being the one she had stolen from him after their first date.

Seemed Sargon had gotten it back to the man.

None the wiser.

Cozen made quick work of opening drawers in the nightstands, and then moving onto Jett's dressers, too. She kept an ear out as she carefully dug through the man's personal items trying to find any sign of the Astor ring, or even something that might point her in the right direction.

Occasionally, Jett's phone would ring, and she would silence it.

She had been trying to keep time in her head of how long she had been gone from Jett—so far, less than ten minutes.

He wouldn't let her go much longer, she figured.

Cozen slipped into the attached walk-in closet, and was surprised to find Jett's *very* expensive jewelry and watch collection on display inside glass cases. The watches rotated on mechanical arms while the jewelry rested on top of black velvet.

No ruby.

No Astor ring.

Cozen's frustration picked up, but she moved to the racks of hanging clothes, and moved things aside. Maybe there was a safe behind them, or something. A man like Jett had to have a safe.

She found fucking *nothing*.

Frustrated, Cozen didn't even bother checking the two bathrooms attached to the master bedroom. She had a good clue that nothing was going to be inside them, anyway, and it would be a waste of her time to check.

She was running out of time.

She had to move on.

One door down, Cozen found an office.

She was half way into the office when she heard Jett calling for her.

"Cozen, darling?"

His voice echoed.

The stairwell, she figured.

Shit.

Cozen's heart raced as she slipped Jett's phone onto the seat of the large leather chair behind the big oak desk. The office was a sprawling room with vaulted ceilings, richly stained wood, and a desk big enough to be a dining table for a dozen people. Jett favored his leather in there, and dark whiskey. Shelves had been lined with old, leather-bound books.

She pulled out a couple of drawers on the desk as Jett called out her name, and then muffled like he had gone inside a room.

Maybe the entertainment room she passed.

Nothing was in the desk.

She turned, and her eye caught something else.

A painting just above the desk that was slightly angled away from the wall on one side. As though it was on hinges, or something.

Cozen reached for it, and pulled it open.

Her heart stopped.

A grin split her face.

An electronic safe rested behind the painting.

Jackpot.

Cozen closed the painting just as Jett's footsteps echoed in the hallway, and then disappeared again. She was quick to step out of the office, and move down the hall. Slipping into a bathroom, and closing the door behind her.

She only came out of the bathroom when she heard Jett calling for her once more.

"There you are," he said, not looking the slightest bit concerned.

Her heart was racing.

A little too close for comfort.

Cozen smiled brightly. "Sorry, I didn't hear you."

Jett reached for her hand, and Cozen let him take it. "Lunch is waiting downstairs. You'll have to wait for the rest of the tour."

She didn't even mind, now.

Cozen looked over the plans she had spread out on the kitchen floor. Using heavy coffee mugs on each corner of the paper, it kept the ends from rolling back up while she worked. The kitchen was the best room in the apartment when it came to light, so she was using that to her advantage at the moment.

She stood above the plans and chewed on the end of a black pen. Letting it hang from her mouth, she put her hands to her hips, and stared at her work.

A whole two weeks of work, actually.

Two weeks …

Of having Jett continue to pursue her. Of accepting invitation after invitation to his home. Of being taken out to place after place—although with a bit of her trickery and suggestions, they almost always ended up back at the mansion.

And despite finding the safe in the office, and also *not* finding the ring, she had not gotten the chance to get back inside the man's office. Not with her tricks, or her distractions. And she was going to need time to be able to crack that safe, too.

She was going to get her chance, though. Eventually, it always happened. And, of course, Jett kept bringing her back time and time again to his home.

Without sex, of course.

Cozen didn't even put the offer—or the idea of it—on the table. She often wondered how long it would take before Jett got tired of her flirtatious nature, and how quick she was to find some excuse to dodge his physical advancements.

He was a man, after all.

He clearly wanted something from her.

It wasn't all innocent.

However, those two weeks gave Cozen *access*. And that was what she needed the very most when it came to Jett Griffin. Accessibility to his home, and private areas. Time to check out the property and the inside of the mansion. The ability to watch for cameras where they might be hidden, and learn the view angles.

The tour Jett had given to Cozen inside the mansion was a godsend, too. She figured he might be so arrogant as to point out something she had missed on her own.

And he did.

The secret staircase hidden by a bookshelf that led up to the wing of his private quarters. Another passageway that led between downstairs rooms.

None of that was important, though. Not like the office with the safe was. Anything that was everything important to him was kept in the office—or that's how he put it when he finally gave her the tour of the upstairs.

Cozen went back to her plans, and marked more down on the blueprints of the mansion's downstairs floors. Every little detail she could remember. How many steps long a hallway was. How many cameras in one area, and where they were located. Although all the cameras were simply downstairs—not one was upstairs.

Anything helped.

All of it.

Writing it down, or sketching out floor plans, helped her more because she could memorize it, and keep it in the back of her mind.

She didn't have any reason to actually believe the ring might be in Jett's office, but she didn't have a reason not to believe it, either. She suspected the piece would be important to him.

Sacred, even.

Especially considering the Astors wanted it back. Not to mention, how Jett had taunted the Astors with the ring by having some floozy chick wear it to an event. No doubt, he was absolutely keeping the ring locked up, and safe.

She didn't like to take risks that might expose her, but she was kind of running out of time here. This job needed to get done already, and she was starting to think she might have to take more risks just to get back in front of that safe again.

Cozen went back to her plans for a moment—her bread and butter of this whole goddamn thing. This heist was made impossibly more difficult by the fact that the thing she needed to steal had not yet been in her sights.

The ring, that was.

She suspected she knew where it was, but that wasn't a certainty. And an almost certainty was not entirely good enough for her, but it was all she had to go on at the moment. Since this was the first time a job left her without every piece of knowledge about the mark in question, she had to do what she had to do. Whatever it took to get this done.

Her hope was that it would all be far easier than any of this—the ring would be in the safe, most likely, and she could open it with the program she developed with a friend.

Shit was never that easy, though.

Still … Cozen hoped.

For now, though, her phone buzzed. A reminder popped up on the screen as she slid it closer to be able to see it. Her mind was so super focused on finishing this job that other things were sometimes falling to the wayside on her.

Hence the need for reminders.

Like this one.

She had to work today.

The act had to be kept up.

Joy.

"Zen, I'm going to need you behind the bar for the rest of the shift," Chase said as he strolled on past Cozen. Like he hadn't just dropped that bomb on her, or something.

"Wait, what?"

"You heard me."

"I can't mix The Kingdom's specialty drinks," she said.

Chase was already gone. He didn't even hear Cozen's refusal.

Fuck.

"Um, do you need a moment, miss?"

"Yeah, we're okay here," the guy's wife said.

The people she was supposed to be serving.

Cozen gave the couple at the table an apologetic look, and waved at another one of the servers to come and help. Once she was free, she darted after Chase to find out what cold hell she had slipped into.

A beer, or a specific wine was one thing. Cozen—and most of the other servers—were fully capable of pouring a drink like that. They usually did just to make things a little easier on Marissa because she was typically busy enough.

But working the whole bar?

Entirely different.

Cozen found Chase in his back office. A place he rarely left unless it was to bark orders in the kitchen, or to meet a particular diner on the floor. He didn't own the restaurant; he simply managed it. He sure liked to pretend differently, though.

"Didn't you hear me?" Cozen asked.

Chase opened his laptop, and passed her a look over the screen. "Hear what? I thought I told you to get behind the bar. Marissa wasn't feeling well, and had to go home. I don't need her puking in someone's glass of wine. The girl who usually takes her place isn't answering her phone, and the dinner rush is coming."

"That's thoughtful, but—"

"Cozen, go do your job."

"I can't mix the specialty drinks for the restaurant. I don't know the mixtures."

Chase shrugged. "If somebody asks for something off the restaurant's menu of exclusive drinks, just say you're filling in. Unless they want something you know how to make, you're not capable."

"You think that'll fly over?"

Because The Kingdom was famous for its special menu of drinks only their bartender could make. A good ten percent of the revenue every day came from only those drinks. People had their favorites, and often stopped in just to get their drink.

"Not particularly, but it will work for tonight."

"Great," Cozen muttered.

Cozen didn't even wait to hear what Chase had to say. She untied the small, black waitress apron around her waist, and hung it on one of the hooks before she exited the kitchen. Making her way behind the bar—one with people already waiting to place drink orders—she prepped herself for another six hours of a whole different kind of hell.

"Who's first?" Cozen asked the waiting people.

A blond, jock-type dressed in a three-piece stepped forward. The equally blonde, plastic-like Barbie on his arm made Cozen want to roll her eyes.

A bartender wasn't like a waitress. She had to be nice and pleasant to the people on the floor, but she didn't have to stay with one table or person for very long before she could move on. She considered that a benefit, despite the eight to ten hours a day in heels that make her feet feel like they were on fire.

A bartender, however, had to be something else entirely. Charming, interested, and willing to engage in conversation. It was kind of hard to talk with food in your mouth, but not as difficult when a person was slightly tipsy, and probably had a reason for drinking alcohol in the first goddamn place.

Cozen was a good two hours in to working behind the bar before the number of patrons started to slow a bit. It was days like today when it became a little bit harder for her to remember why she was here and doing this crap in the first place.

For the job.

It was all for the damn job.

The act she had to keep up.

If anything, it made Cozen all the more determined to finish this job, so she could return back to her quiet, content life where she no longer had to do things like this. She wasn't required to plaster on a fake smile, or spend hours upon hours on her feet in heels. She didn't have to charm a man just to steal from him.

Not to mention … the beach.

God, she missed the beach.

Sargon flashed into her mind, too, in those moments. A brief second of pause where his features graced her memories, and left her feeling spectacularly heavy in her heart for reasons she could not explain.

Like her heart was trying to tie him to something she found comfort and peace in. Like her heart wanted to take him back with her when she went, too.

Cozen wasn't even sure she should entertain those feelings or thoughts. They were dangerous—even more dangerous than the game she had been playing with the darkly handsome, sex God of a man.

So he could play her body like an instrument.

So he could delve into her mind.

So he was beautiful.

So … what?

So you like him, her mind taunted, *a lot*.

Maybe a little more than a lot.

It was difficult and complicated. He had made a hell of a lot of things about a job that should have been somewhat easy and relatively clean very difficult, and particularly dirty for her. He didn't even know it—or did he?

Who knew?

Cozen couldn't really afford the kind of issues Sargon made for her in the grand scheme of the plans. It was one thing for her mind to know that, though. It was an entirely different matter for her heart to get with the plan, too.

She hadn't seen him in weeks.

Two, actually.

Since that morning he delivered her to breakfast with Jett after spending the night with her. She hadn't even gotten a glimpse of him, although she still did occasionally feel like someone was watching her.

Him, specifically.

"Could we order?"

The question drew Cozen out of her thoughts to find a familiar man standing next to the bar with his red-headed wife.

Silas Griffin.

Jett's oldest son.

As for the woman, Marsha was her name. Cozen met her all but once in passing at the mansion, and it was only from afar. They hadn't spoken to each other, and it was Jett who explained that Marsha was his daughter-in-law.

"Silas," Cozen greeted, "and Marsha. Hey, what can I get for you two tonight?"

"Where's Marissa?" Marsha asked.

Oh, Jesus.

The woman sounded like a whistling nasal cavity when she spoke. She was pretty, sure, but the voice was terrible.

"She wasn't feeling well," Cozen explained, "so I am manning—so to speak—the bar tonight. I can make all kinds of drinks, just not The Kingdom's specialty menu. So, what can I get for you two?"

Silas's blue gaze drifted over Cozen in a way that felt cold. As though he were simply about to dismiss her with nothing more than a look. He was a handsome young man—in his late twenties, at least. She could see his father's features reflecting back in a younger version of Jett.

This man, however, did not treat her like his father did.

Silas wasn't fond of Cozen, and hadn't made a secret of his dislike during their brief encounters. Oh, sure, he was respectful, but that was just about all he was willing to offer her. He didn't go out of his way to be nice, or even particularly polite.

He likely thought she was some gold digging woman after his father's money. It had only been less than a year since his mother passed on, too.

Shit, *Cozen* was younger than Silas. He was likely taking that little factor into account when it came to his feelings about her, too.

No doubt, it was awkward for him.

She didn't care.

She was here for a ring.

Not Jett's money.

Not his life.

Not his heart.

"She's certainly pretty enough, isn't she?" Silas asked his wife. "I can see why Dad thinks she'll fit right in with everyone else."

"Well, at least she won't need a dozen surgeries like all the other wives," Marsha muttered.

Cozen straightened on the spot. "*She* is right here."

Silas cocked a brow. "Quite aware, yeah. Shame, too, that he had to pick some woman from a gutter—basically. My father could have his pick of women, and yet he found some strange interest in you. Who are you even, Cozen? Where do you come from that you think you're not reaching way out of your league when it comes to my father?"

Wow.

He wasn't hiding a damn thing. He was so entirely unashamed about his delivery, too.

She respected it.

A little.

It didn't even bother her.

"Maybe you should ask your father that," Cozen returned.

"Oh, I have," Silas grumbled as he fixed the gold cufflink on his shirt sleeve. "And I get told to mind my own business. He forgets that our fortune and family name *is* my business just as much as it is his. What are you going to give him other than a good fuck, and a pretty wife that'll outlive him by a good twenty or thirty years?"

"Not very much," Marsha put in, passing Cozen a stinging look, "other than another name in the Will to take a share."

Silas looked Cozen over again before adding, "Maybe a child or two—boys if you're lucky, or spoiled little girls if the rest of us get to be unlucky."

Okay.

This had gone way too far.

"If there's nothing I can make for you," Cozen said, forcing her tone to remain polite, "then I'm going to have to take my break."

So fuck off.

Silas smiled thinly. "No, you can't make my drink. It's the Griffin, by the way. Named for our family."

Cozen widened her gaze in false amazement. "Fascinating, Silas."

"I do look forward to seeing how you do at the party Dad is having soon. You certainly do okay in a small group of his people—what about a larger group? A whole mass of rich people that will remind you of how far you're actually reaching here?"

A party?

What party?

Silas must have seen the question in Cozen's eyes because he chuckled and asked, "Oh, you didn't know about that? Maybe you're not invited after all."

All right.

Cozen had enough.

She tossed the rag to the bar, and brought up the little sign from underneath that said *We'll be back to serve you soon.*

"We can wait," Silas murmured, looking over the sign.

Cozen smiled. "I'll serve you when hell freezes over, Silas. Have a good night."

Jett was standing in front of Cozen's apartment door when she finally got home. She almost thought about turning around when he hadn't seen her come through the hallway door, but decided against it when the man standing at the other end of the hall caught her eye.

Sargon.

He stood in all black guarding the door. His hands were folded at his front, and his gaze never left hers from the second she stepped into the hallway. It was her first glimpse of him in two weeks, and it left her just as confused as ever.

Before she could think about anything else, Jett finally saw her standing there, and offered Cozen one of his wide, charming smiles.

"Cozen, sweetheart," he said with arms already opening. "I thought you were never getting home."

Fuck.

This was not good for many reasons. She listed those reasons off in her head as she headed down the hall, and took Jett's embrace. His arms did nothing for her, a lot like the kiss he tried to place to her lips, but she diverted to the corner of her mouth at the last second.

The flash in Jett's eyes told her the truth—she was right; he was getting tired of this cat and mouse between them. He might have liked it before when she distracted his physical affections toward something else, but not anymore.

He was looking for something.

He wanted it from her.

Soon.

"Are we going out?" Cozen asked.

"I wanted to drop by, actually," Jett said. He gestured at her door, saying, "Can we go in?"

Not particularly.

He had never been inside her place, and it wasn't exactly up to spec when it came to visitors. It still had very little furniture, the walls were bare, and Cozen rarely used anything beyond the living room, kitchen, and bathroom.

She had packed her plans away of Jett's place before going to work that day. She considered that one win to her benefit.

Jett did not look like he was letting this go. "Inside?"

"Yeah, sure," Cozen murmured.

She glanced down the hall, and her gaze locked with Sargon's for a brief second as she opened her apartment. Their staring contest— thankfully unnoticed by Jett as he was too busy murmuring something in Cozen's ear that she wasn't listening too—was only broken when they slipped into the apartment together.

The second the apartment door closed, Cozen tried to put a bit of distance between herself and Jett. There had never been a time when she was in such tight, closed quarters with him, and at the same time, locked in as to not be able to have a means of escape. He had never done anything to make her feel unsafe, but that didn't mean anything.

Cozen trusted no one.

She quickly moved further into the apartment, and toward the kitchen. Jett followed close behind which she considered a good thing. Maybe if she kept his attention on where she wanted it to go, he would overlook the emptiness of her place.

"How long have you lived here?" he asked.

Shit.

Nope.

No luck at all.

"A few months," Cozen said. "Shortly before I started working at the restaurant."

"It's very ..."

His gaze drifted around.

"Empty, I know."

"A little, darling, yeah."

Cozen shrugged. "Work keeps me busy, and by the time I get home, I am way too tired to be worrying about filling this place up with stuff. I'm a bit of a minimalist, anyway."

All lies.

Jett ate them up, though. "I see. I didn't mean to just show up. That's not usually my style."

Again, he came closer. Again, she was aware of being alone, and unable to get out.

Cozen had sort of backed herself into a proverbial corner because she couldn't move without making it obvious to Jett that she was attempting to get away from him. The goddamn kitchen island was right behind her. She didn't want to offend the man by making him think that she didn't want his attention, or that his physical affection wasn't invited.

That would be a quick way to remove her from his life. No man wanted to feel rejected and disabused by a woman, after all.

Cozen needed to stay *in*.

So, she forced herself not to turn into a statue as Jett came closer. His hands skimmed her trim waist before he rested his palms down on the counter behind her. It effectively locked her into place so that she couldn't go anywhere at all.

Jett came closer still—he really was a handsome man for his age with only that slight bit of salt coloring up his dark hair and a few laugh lines around his eyes. Men were lucky that way. They only became better looking with time. Like a fine wine.

None of that helped Cozen, though.

She did not use sex to get what she wanted. She had never needed to fuck anyone to get a job done, and she wasn't about to start now.

Jett reached up, and his thumb stroked across her lips. "My son mentioned running into you today."

Cozen swallowed hard. "Did he?"

Her words whispered along the pad of his thumb.

"He did. I apologize for the way he might have acted."

Cozen lifted a single brow high. "He didn't tell you how he acted?"

"I got a good enough impression. He won't do it again."

"Okay."

What else could she say?

Jett stroked her lips again, and then said, "He's entirely wrong about you, Cozen. There is far more about you that I am interested in other than how beautiful you are. Mind you, that is also a very important part."

"He mentioned a party," Cozen said.

If she kept him talking, she might be able to keep their distance at a respectable space. Not that he wasn't already beyond that line—and getting closer to her with every breath.

"Yes, I wanted to ask you about that. A new dress, pretty shoes, and you can have your pampering day again," Jett said, smiling softly. "What do you think?"

"I would love that."

"Good."

With that, Jett finally closed the distance between them. Cozen had not been expecting the kiss, as it came without warning, and she had all she could do not to turn into a cold, unmovable statue.

Somehow.

Jett's hands left the counter, and grabbed tight to her waist before he dragged her impossibly closer. Panic welled inside her because this was an even more delicate dance, now. She couldn't stiffen for fear he would feel it and know she was a liar. She couldn't respond more than a closed mouth kiss because she would not be able to hide her disinterest or disgust.

She was a good actress.

A damn good liar.

Not that good, though.

It was only when his tongue struck out against the seam of her lips that Cozen decided enough was enough. A ringing phone saved her from making it an issue. Her phone.

Thank God.

Cozen pulled away from Jett with a small smile. "Sorry, let me grab that. I've been waiting for a call about—"

Jett's gaze had darkened with desire, and he didn't try to hide it as he looked her over. "No worries, darling."

He wanted more.

Far more.

Cozen could see it, and she had to figure out a way to get him out of her apartment before she was stuck doing something she would very much regret. For now, she focused on the ringing phone. She found it in her purse by the front door, and didn't bother to check the caller ID before she answered the call.

"Hello?"

"Cozen, it's Fourth."

Jett rounded the corner in the hallway at the same time.

"F—"

"Astor," the man murmured on the phone.

Oh, shit.

"Now is not a good time," Cozen said.

Putting it lightly.

"Any time an Astor calls is *always* the right time. Good is a matter of semantics, and you answered the phone."

Fuck.

"Cozen, is everything all right?" Jett asked at the end of the hall.

"Oh, you have guests?" Fourth asked. "I hope you're not lounging around when you're supposed to be getting my grandmother's fucking ring. Speaking of which—why do you keep ignoring our phone calls?"

"Cozen?"

Jett again.

"Well?"

And then Fourth.

What had she gotten herself in to this time?

Sargon itched to do anything but what he was doing in those moments. His gaze hadn't left Cozen's apartment door from the second Jett had disappeared inside, and he heard the click of it shutting completely. He was frozen in place, and counting down the minutes of how long the man had been in there.

Alone.

With her.

Seven, now.

Seven minutes, but almost eight.

Closer to eight than seven.

Jesus.

Too damn long.

Long enough for him to have touched her. For him to have kissed her. For him to have had her, too, if he was the type to finish quite sadly and quickly.

The jealousy burned bright and hot in Sargon's gut. The rage was far worse—an uncontrollable inferno threatening to swallow him entirely whole. Every short, painful breath he took only made it that much worse, too. Like wind fanning the flames. And yet, if he didn't take those short, painful breaths, he couldn't remain calm and steady.

It was a double-edged sword.

Every part of him screamed to go—to *move*—and do something.

Interrupt whatever was happening in some way. Maybe a simple knock on the door would do it.

But then what?

What would he say to justify his sudden appearance? The excuse of a fake emergency might work, but only until Jett figured out there was no emergency to leave for. Sargon would then have to explain all of that nonsense.

It was a lose-lose situation.

He stayed put even though it almost killed him to do so. Even though the rage and jealousy continued to wreak havoc on his thoughts and heart, he didn't move a muscle.

She can handle herself.

She knows what she's doing.

It was the jiggle of a doorknob, and the creak of an opening door that brought Sargon from his thoughts—for the briefest second, his mask had almost slipped off. Even in his thoughts, he kept that mask on.

He had to.

It was how this always worked.

"Come," he heard ordered.

Down the hall, a very frustrated Jett stood waiting for him. Maybe Sargon really was losing his goddam mind. The man waved a hand at him impatiently, and then shot a look over his shoulder when the apartment door was closed again. A deep scowl etched its way onto the man's face.

"Well, what are you doing still standing there, Sargon?" Jett demanded.

Well …

Sargon raised a brow. "The car is out this way, Jett."

"Oh … yes, that's right. Let's go then."

Jett stormed down the hallway looking no different than he had before he went into Cozen's apartment. It was the second thing Sargon noticed about his boss after the frustration he showcased. His suit wasn't crumpled, and his salt and pepper hair was still perfectly slicked back.

The deepening scowl the man continued to wear only confirmed it further—he had gotten nowhere with Cozen. Nowhere physically, anyway. Nothing that would be worth doing if he was still perfectly coifed in every way. Certainly not enough to satisfy whatever Jett was looking for, or whatever he went into that apartment wanting to do.

The frustration made sense. That woman could frustrate anyone with the way she teased and went on. Sargon knew that firsthand.

Sargon followed behind Jett as the two navigated the stairs leading to the back door of the apartment building. Jett, who was usually quite animated and liked to talk, now seemed to have nothing to say at all.

"Where to now?" Sargon asked as they headed out of the apartment building. "We have other things to do today, don't we?"

He was fine, now.

The further away Jett was from Cozen, the better Sargon felt.

"Home," Jett said in a grunt.

"I thought you mentioned a meet—"

Jett waved a hand high. "I want to go home, so take me there."

"Whatever you want, boss."

Sargon sped up his strides to move ahead of Jett, and open the back passenger door of the black Mercedes. Jett slipped in without as much as a thank you, and Sargon closed the door after him. The whole time, Jett kept his eyes averted to anywhere but on Sargon.

Shame, he thought.

Or it could have been embarrassment.

For men, those two things were one in the same. At least, it certainly felt that way when it came to women. Men did not like the way rejection from a woman felt when they thought they were God's gift to womankind.

It would all be amusing.

If it wasn't so fucking disgusting.

Sargon quickly slipped into the driver's seat, and before long had the car on the road. They were driving for a good thirty minutes or more before Jett finally spoke from the backseat. Sargon almost wished the man had just stayed quiet.

"She plays games," Jett muttered.

"Who?"

He knew who.

Sargon didn't want Jett to know that he knew who, though.

"Cozen," Jett said flatly.

In the rearview mirror, Sargon could see Jett staring out the window. The scowl the man had been sporting was now replaced with something of a pensive stare. Hard, cold eyes that showcased no emotions when they drifted in Sargon's direction like Jett knew the man was watching him or something.

It was with that look Jett wore that Sargon knew—Cozen was about to find herself in a whole lot of trouble.

Her tricks were no longer working for Jett. The things that might have been drawing the man back to her time and time again before were no longer interesting to him.

"Maybe she enjoys that sort of thing—the cat and mouse, if you get what I mean. There are some woman who think that's foreplay. They like to push you away for as long as they can before you finally *catch* them."

The words made Sargon even more pissed off, but he managed to say them without the bite to his tone. Somehow.

It was a fucking miracle, really.

Jett made a noise under his breath, and went back to staring out the window. "No, I don't think that's the case here. And if it is, I am not interested in the cat and mouse any longer. I think I have chased her more than long enough, don't you?"

Sargon chose not to answer.

Jett apparently didn't need him to when he added, "I will get what I want from that woman one way or the other, and soon. I think I have made my intentions with her more than clear. I always get what I want in the end."

Well, what was it that Jett wanted?

Sargon knew better than to ask. He didn't think he would like the answer if he did.

So he didn't ask.

He didn't say anything at all.

"You busy?"

Cozen's head snapped to the side when Sargon asked his question. "What are you doing here?"

"I'm here more often than you realize, Zen."

"I realize," she returned just as fast. "I just don't usually *see* you."

Sargon shrugged. "Again, are you busy?"

"Kind of working."

"Take your break."

"I can't—"

"Yes, you can."

He snagged her arm in his grasp, and pulled her off the restaurant floor. The patrons whose orders she had been taking before he stepped in didn't look very pleased to have their server removed.

Oh, well.

Sargon wouldn't be long with Cozen. He only showed himself to give her a warning, and let her do with it what she wanted. Then, she could go back to work like nothing had even happened.

"What are you doing?" Cozen hissed.

He didn't let her go until they were at the very end of a back hallway in the restaurant. The offices were further up, but all the doors were closed. For a moment, they had a few seconds of privacy. That's all Sargon needed.

Once he stopped, Cozen jerked her arm out of his hold. "What in the hell are you trying to pull with manhandling me like that?"

"You weren't going to come with me."

Her russet gaze narrowed. "I am working!"

"This is important, Cozen."

"What is?"

"Jett—that's what."

Cozen stilled on the spot. "What about Jett?"

"Whatever little stunt you pulled on him yesterday in your apartment … he's not pleased about it. The little cat and mouse game you've got going on with him? He's over it."

"I didn't *pull* anything," she said quietly.

"Nothing?"

"He … kissed me."

Sargon stiffened a bit. "And what?"

"And it got interrupted by a phone call."

"Does that happen a lot?"

"What, the kissing or the phone call?"

"Both, I suppose. Him being physical, and interruptions in general?"

"Lately he's trying to be more physical in his affections," Cozen said. "And yes, I have been trying to distract them elsewhere if I can."

Sargon wet his lips, and stared over Cozen's shoulder at a space down the hall. He didn't stare at anything in particular, but it gave him a moment to think without looking at her. He couldn't think properly when he was staring at her.

"What are you *doing?*" he finally asked.

"I don't—"

"With him, Cozen. Stop playing this fucking shit with me. Jett is not the kind of man you screw around with. He no longer likes your games, and if you continue to play them with him, you're going to find yourself in a world of trouble. So just tell me … what is it you want from him?"

"It's not him," she muttered.

"Then what is it?"

"Something he has."

Sargon didn't entirely know what to make of that statement. She was here to take something from Jett—to *steal?*

"Except you've gotten tangled up with him in a personal way, now," Sargon said. "Was that part of your plan, too?"

"Do you need me to answer that?"

Sargon's jaw hardened. "He's settled himself with the idea that you owe him something, Cozen. And he wants to collect."

She straightened a bit in her heels, and nodded once. "Fine."

"*Fine?*"

"I've almost got what I want. And then it'll be over with."

"Are you—"

"I have to get back to work," she interrupted. "Thanks for letting me know … this, I guess. It helps."

"Helps with what, Zen?"

Cozen didn't answer. Instead, she turned on her heel, and moved to head back down the hallway. Sargon couldn't let that happen. Either she didn't care that her safety was in jeopardy, or she was willing to risk it.

Either way, that didn't sit well with him.

Sargon didn't let her get very far. He grabbed her wrist hard, and pulled her back around. Anger flashed on her face, and he saw her swinging hand coming in just enough time to catch it before she landed the well-aimed slap.

Instead of the slap, he pulled her in close, and pressed a hard kiss to her mouth. Instantly, her body relaxed in his arms, and her lips moved in a familiar rhythm against his. The second her lips parted to allow him entrance, he deepened the kiss to get another taste of her sweet heat.

She still tasted like cherries and vanilla.

Sweetness and sin.

Her hands came up to grab his jaw as their tongues warred against one another. Those fingernails of hers—always manicured to sharp little points—dug into his skin and left one hell of a sting behind.

But he loved it.

Jesus, he loved it.

And her, he thought.

He loved her.

It was a strange feeling, but it was true. A thick rope wrapped around his heart and with every tug from Cozen—her words or her actions—the rope became tighter. Pulling him even closer to her.

Somehow, he did. Somehow, this happened. Somehow, he too had found himself tangled in a mess with this woman.

If only …

Cozen pulled away, and her gaze dropped from his. "Again, I have to get back to work, but thank you for—"

"You're not being safe, Cozen. This is not a game."

"It's always a game when there's a prize to be won."

"Just say it," he murmured. "Say it, and it ends. I will make sure of it."

Cozen patted a hand against his chest. "It never ends until I win. And I always win."

Sargon slammed the door of the Mercedes shut a little harder than was necessary. Anything that got too close to him today was on the receiving end of his anger. Usually, he was a little better about hiding this kind of thing, but not today it seemed.

He blamed Cozen.

She wouldn't *listen*.

"Hey, Sarg!"

Sargon glanced up at the late May sky, and almost wished it would just fucking fall in on him or something. "It's Sargon."

You useless fucking cunt.

Jett's main man—the one who was in charge of guarding the grounds—took the steps of the mansion two at a time. The guy came close to Sargon, but didn't act like he had been corrected on the name thing.

Clearly, Sargon was going to have to crush someone's throat in to get his point across about his name. Fucking idiots.

"The boss wants to see you," the guy said.

Sargon scowled. "I'm here to check in like I always do. What's he in a rush for?"

A shrug answered him back. "Listen, I was just told to tell you to hurry the fuck up, Sarg."

His little control snapped.

Sarg, again.

Sargon let his hand snap out as he walked past the guy. He caught the man's throat in his grip, and tightened his hold enough to take the man's breath away, and hurt him. He did it so fast that the guy didn't even have a chance to react.

By the time he did react—by trying to grab onto Sargon's wrist—he was already seconds away from having his vocal cords crushed.

"If you call me that again," Sargon told him, "I will make sure you are never capable of uttering another word in your lifetime. Test me, and I will make sure you eat from a straw until they put you in a grave. Do you fucking understand me?"

He squeezed a bit harder.

The guy nodded.

Sargon let him go, and didn't even bother to look over his shoulder when the guy dropped to the ground. Useless fools.

All of them.

Sargon took the entrance steps of the mansion quickly. Inside, he found a couple of maids scurrying down the hall as a shout echoed from the living room. A shout belonging to Jett, of course.

The boss was in a bad mood.

Entirely unusual for Jett.

In the entryway of the living room, Sargon leaned against the wood, and waited for a very pissed off Jett to notice him. The man was too busy shouting something mostly unintelligible into his phone.

What happened?

Sargon would soon find out.

Once his boss finally noticed him standing there, Jett slammed the phone down to the receiver, and turned to face Sargon. "*You*."

"What about me?"

"You didn't think to call me today?"

Sargon lifted a brow high. "There was nothing to call about, boss."

"Nothing *at all?*"

For a brief moment, Sargon wondered if he had just walked into the lion's den without even knowing it. Had someone seen his moment with Cozen at the restaurant earlier, and reported back to Jett? Had he been so distracted that he put both of their lives in danger for nothing more than a kiss in the shadows?

"Nothing," Sargon murmured. "I babysat as I always do, and once she was at home, I was off duty. As has been the—"

"She's gone," Jett interjected sharply.

Sargon blinked. "I beg your pardon?"

"Cozen. She's left the city."

No, that wasn't right.

"I followed her home," Sargon said. "She went into her building. I waited a while, and when she didn't come out like usual, I left. She's—"

"She must have taken off after, then."

"How do you know she's gone from the city?"

"Her manager called me. I pay the man to keep me in the loop about her on things that *you* might not know."

Well … fuck.

That was good information to know now.

Sargon tucked it away.

"And what did he have to say?" Sargon asked.

"She called in shortly after leaving work to say an emergency came up out of state, and she had to handle it. She wouldn't be back to work for a while—he gave her the time off."

Sargon nodded. "So, she'll be back."

"Will she?"

A wildness stared back from Jett.

The man was obsessed.

Sargon could see it.

Cozen had no idea what she caused—no clue of how much danger she was likely in all because Jett Griffin suddenly decided that Cozen was his to have.

"I want you to find her," Jett said, "and report back to me on what she is doing. You're the one with the information about her. You got all that, right? So, go and find her now. California, I imagine. That's where she comes from. Do not contact me unless you have something usable."

Sargon cleared his throat. "I—"

"*Go!*"

Spinning on his heel, Sargon got the hell out of Jett's mansion as fast as he fucking could. His first order of business once he got to the hotel room he had been calling home for several months should have been to open up the folder on Cozen, and make a few calls. Maybe even book a plane ticket to follow her.

Instead, Sargon turned off his phone, and went to bed. Jett was clear—he only wanted a call if Sargon had anything to report.

Well, there would be nothing.

He didn't follow her.

He didn't need to.

He didn't want to.

The private terminal at Miami International airport gave Cozen a sense of safety as she stepped off the jet. A jet that had been flown *to her* in New York from the Astors. She had been expected—without argument—to take the plane ride back to Miami within forty-eight hours.

Their demands, not hers.

Cozen knew better than to deny the Astors. As it was, she had already pushed their hospitality a little too far by ignoring their calls, and never responding to their messages. Whose fault was that, though?

Pearl had been the one to tell Cozen not to call back unless she had news worth sharing. Well, she didn't have anything to tell except the fact she was just trying to get this goddamn job finished.

Unsurprisingly, Cozen found a man dressed in a three-piece black suit waiting for Cozen inside the private terminal. His ice-blue gaze looked her over as she shifted the messenger bag around her shoulders.

"Miss Taylor?" the man asked.

"Just Cozen, thanks. And you are …?"

"Not important." Again, his gaze took her in. Not in a sexual way—Cozen gave him credit for that—but it still made her uncomfortable. "You don't look like any thief I have ever met, pardon me for speaking. A little too sweet and innocent, maybe."

Cozen lifted a single brow, replying, "That's kind of the point, Mr. Not Important."

The man laughed, and nodded. Waving a single hand as he turned on his heel, he said, "Come with me, then. I will deliver you to where you need to go."

"I know where I'm going."

"Shame you don't know what will happen once you get there."

Touché.

Soon, the two were in a black Mercedes, and navigating the busy streets of Miami. Cozen kept her gaze on the road, and her mouth firmly shut in the backseat. The man driving said very little after he realized she was not going to engage him in conversation.

She shouldn't even be here.

She had a job to do.

Soon, although the drive was just long enough to let Cozen relax, the Mercedes was granted access to the gated, private community of Coral Cables. The sprawling estates they drove past to get to the Astor mansion and property were both large, and beautiful. A sure showcase of wealth if there ever was one. Impeccable grounds protecting massive homes.

All with a view or access to the ocean.

Cozen liked Miami, but her fondness for the beach and the ocean hadn't come from here. It started in California, and it was going to stay there, too. She didn't think there was enough room in Miami for the Astors, and another criminal.

They didn't like to share.

The black Mercedes pulled in the long, winding driveway leading to the Astor estate. Eventually the driveway merged into a circular piece of asphalt that showcased several parked, luxury cars sitting in front of the mansion.

Aston Martin.

Lamborghini.

A gray Porsche with *pink* interior.

These cars had not been parked in front of the mansion the last time Cozen visited. And if they had been there, she didn't notice them.

To be fair, she had been a little distracted the last time she visited. It was entirely possible that she just missed it.

"Fourth will be waiting for you in the grand entry," the man behind the wheel said.

"Inside?" Cozen asked.

The guy's gaze darted to hers in the rearview. "That's what I said, is it not?"

Apparently, all kinds of new things were going on today. Including allowing Cozen inside the Astor mansion.

Maybe she should have felt unsafe—the Astors were not known for their kindness when it came to people they felt overstepped their boundaries, or otherwise. They were known for their punishments, and violence to make a point.

And yet, she wasn't all that worried.

After all, she was *in*. She was their current hope at getting a piece of Astor history—their treasured property—back without causing an entire uproar in the world of the criminal underground. She was their way of showing their power, status, and ability without going to more violent means first.

Essentially, the Astors hiring Cozen to steal from another powerful crime figure was their family saying, "See what we can take from you, and watch how we can do it."

Should they remove Cozen from the equation, then that meant they would need to start over. Entirely. From ground zero. A new thief—a new plan. More time separated from their precious thing before they would get it back. That was, if they ever did get it returned.

Why would they bother?

She was already in.

The job was almost done.

"You shouldn't sit there for too long," the man in the driver's seat muttered. "Fourth does not like to be left waiting."

"Sure," Cozen replied dryly.

She made a move to grab her messenger bag, but the man said, "Leave it."

Cozen laughed. "Why, for you to dispose of it after?"

She was joking.

Kind of.

The man only smirked before glancing out the driver's window.

Asshole.

She stepped out of the Mercedes, and shrugged off the thin cardigan. Miami was already hot in late May where New York was bearable, and comfortable. For a few seconds, she simply stared at the marble pillars greeting the guests to the entrance of the large Astor mansion.

The place really was amazing.

And a bit scary.

Or maybe intimidating was the word she was looking for.

Cozen's thoughts continued to ramble inside her brain as she headed up the steps of the grand entrance. She didn't even get the chance to reach and knock on the door as someone opened it for her before she could.

A maid, it seemed.

The woman—dressed in gray and white—gave Cozen a polite nod, and tight smile. She took Cozen's cardigan without as much as a single word, and then disappeared into a connecting room.

Turning, Cozen faced the entry.

Grand was an apt description. The space was the size of a normal home. A crystal chandelier hung from a vaulted ceiling and nearly touched the floor between two winding marble staircases on either side of the entry. The floor—buffed and polished enough to gleam and reflect her staring back at it—was also made up of marble tiles.

Money.

The place reeked of money.

In front of the chandelier stood a man Cozen recognized. Fourth Astor.

"I'm happy to see you *can* follow directions," Fourth said quietly.

There was a lilt in his tone that couldn't be missed—a threat, maybe. Just the way his tone stayed level and calm, and yet managed to also be entirely cold told her all she needed to know. This family was not pleased with her at the moment.

No surprise there.

"I came within forty-eight hours," Cozen returned. "As Pearl wanted."

"As *I* wanted," Fourth said. "I am the one who called you back here, not my great-grandmother. Or anyone else, for that matter."

Cozen nodded. "And why is that?"

Fourth checked his watch, and then brushed a piece of invisible lint from his suit jacket. A black Armani number, it looked like. It likely cost more than most people's salaries for a month, if she were being honest.

"Well, I am here," Cozen said. "So, what do you want?"

"Where is the ring?"

Right to the point.

"With the man I still need to steal it from, I assume."

Fourth's gaze darkened. "You *assume?*"

"I haven't taken it yet. I haven't gotten the chance."

"You have been working this job for almost five months, and you *don't have it* yet?"

"First, I haven't been working *Jett* for five months, Fourth. I have only been in his sights for half of that time. The first three were dedicated to getting my shit together for this heist."

"And—"

"Second," she interjected, not giving a shit if it was rude to interrupt him, "if your great-grandmother wanted to make a show of stealing the ring back from Jett Griffin, then she should have hired a team who would do exactly that, Fourth. Instead, she hired *me*."

"Yes, and I am still not sure why she bothered."

Jesus.

This man was something else.

"She hired me because I am a thief who integrates into the lives of their mark, and then leaves as quietly as she came. I try—if at all possible—

not to draw attention to the heist until I am already gone. There was a reason why I was contracted for this job. I assume you will know the details for that reason better than I will, but that's your business."

Fourth stiffened, and Cozen didn't miss how his jaw tightened. "You were given six months, and already, that time is nearly up."

"Except it isn't up yet."

"Your time has gotten shortened," Fourth said coolly. "Two weeks— that's all you have left. Two weeks to return our property, or you can expect to answer for your failure, Cozen."

A cold chill slipped down Cozen's spine, but she refused to acknowledge it.

"Why?" she asked. "Why the change?"

"Your job is to steal a fucking *ring*. Not some big affair that should take this long. It is a ring. Get it done."

Cozen sucked air through her teeth. She tried not to let the irritation overwhelm her, but it was goddamn hard to do. "And yet, you called me away from the job. You took precious, valuable time away from the work I have to do to call me here and threaten me. You're risking my cover, and the job with this bullshit, Fourth."

"Nothing the Astors do is ever bullshit."

"So says you."

"So says anyone who wants to live or be paid," Fourth returned. "Make of that whatever the fuck you want, Cozen."

Point taken.

"Be that as it may," Cozen said, "I was still put in a job that has no visible mark."

"I beg your pardon?"

"The *ring*. The thing you think should be so fucking easy to steal, Fourth. My *mark*, next to Jett. You tell me the ring is with Jett—it has to be with him because of your aunt, or whoever the fuck."

"It *is* with Jett," Fourth replied, cocking a brow. "We've had eyes on the ring before we contacted you—he has it, no question."

"Then *where*?" Cozen shot back. "Because my mark is invisible. I have been through that man's house, in his life for a while now, and not once have I seen it, and he's never brought it up. The Astors put me in an impossible job. You want me to steal something that I can't see, haven't found, and don't even know if it actually *exists*!"

Fourth straightened a bit, and his jaw tightened. She could see in his dark eyes how her words pissed him off, but like all men in his position and of his standing, he was a force to be reckoned with. A pillar of strength, calm, and violence … but only when provoked.

Cozen knew better.

Still, she held her ground.

"You're telling me that you haven't even gotten eyes on the ring yet?" Fourth asked.

"I am *trying*."

"Try harder."

Fuck him.

Cozen knew how people like the Astors could be. Excuses were not wanted, appreciated, or accepted in any form. All they needed was for their jobs to be done, and done well. They wanted what they wanted, and nothing less would do.

It didn't matter how many times Cozen explained that this job was not simple. This heist was not like almost every other job she had taken on as a thief. With an invisible mark, a man far too enamored with her, and no real chance yet to steal something she *couldn't even fucking see* ... this job was entirely abnormal.

Everything that should make her take a wide step back, and say it was impossible. Never going to be done, at least not her way.

She knew just by looking at Fourth Astor that no matter what she said, there was no way in hell the Astors would release her from this job. They wanted their ruby back—they figured she was already in, and now it was just time to ramp up the heat on her a little bit.

More pressure, so to speak.

Pressure worked for everyone.

"Pearl doesn't want to speak with me, I assume?" she asked.

"My great-grandmother is not well lately. Pneumonia, it seems. Usually she bounces right back from illness, but this time, it's hanging on strong. At her age, that can be a very dangerous thing. As you should know."

Finally, Cozen got it.

A light switch went off. All of this made much more sense, now. This whole show could be summed up in Pearl Astor's sickness, and her family's concern about it.

"That's why my time is shortened, isn't it?" Cozen asked quietly. "Not because you are impatient to get the ring back, or you think I am taking too long to get this done, but because *she* might be running out of time."

"I promised her that she would have the ring back." Fourth shrugged, and his smile faded as he added, "And you will make sure she gets that gift. Two weeks—don't make me come find you, Cozen."

Cozen sucked in a sharp breath as the plane touched down to the tarmac. It was always the freakiest part of flying for her—it didn't seem to matter how many times she had flown, either. Her heart would still lurch, and her fingers still grasp tightly to the arm rests on the seat to give her a sense of stability. Not that holding onto the seats would help if the goddamn plane crashed.

It wouldn't.

It was another twenty minutes of taxing into New York's LaGuardia Airport before Cozen was allowed to deplane.

She was hoping that the fact she had left on a Saturday and returned on a Sunday evening meant Jett wouldn't have noticed her missing—or at the very least, he wouldn't have gotten concerned.

Cozen knew that was a false hope. The man was far too enamored with her *not* to notice she had taken off for a couple of days. Jesus, he even had her schedule for the restaurant faxed to him every week, so he knew when her hours were.

It hinted away from him being simply enamored with her, and more towards obsession, really. It was certainly concerning, but Cozen was far too close to finishing this job once and for all to back out now.

She could handle Jett.

Surely …

She worked on what story she would tell Jett as she came down the escalator at the arrivals gate. She was almost entirely lost to her thoughts when a waiting form at the bottom of the escalator caught her eye, and made her freeze like a deer in the headlights.

He smiled.

Cozen relaxed.

Sargon.

As she stepped off the escalator, he reached for her bag. Taking the item from her shoulder, he easily slung it around his own before his arm snaked around her waist and pulled her closer. To anyone one else, it would have looked like a couple greeting each other in a modest way.

It took nothing more than his touch—his hand fitting tightly against her trim waist—to ground her again. Being close to Sargon was dangerous for Cozen's heart, and her mind. He made it hard for her to keep up the mask she had to wear.

He made her pretense fall.

He didn't even care.

Cozen's gaze scanned the crowd. "Did Jett send you?"

Did he know she had come back from Miami?

Did he know why she had gone there?

"He has no idea you're back, actually," Sargon replied.

Cozen glanced up at him. "How do *you* know?"

"You are not that hard to trace, Cozen. All it took was a couple of phone calls to find information on where you went—or the general area. I think you should remember that when you want to take off for the weekend to have meetings with a family that Jett Griffin considers to be his enemy. Just a word of advice—take it or don't."

She swallowed hard.

Sargon kept his arm tight around her waist, and didn't let her move even the slightest inch away from him. "He wanted me to track you while you were gone. In case you're curious, he knew you left the city almost the second you did."

Cozen scowled—just as she suspected. "Chase?"

"Is he the guy who runs the restaurant?"

"Yes."

Sargon nodded. "Yes, that's who called to fill Jett in on the fact you called in for a couple of days due to a family emergency."

"And he wanted you to follow me."

"Getting uncomfortable yet?" Sargon asked.

Cozen let out a slow breath. "Listen—"

Without a word, Sargon's hand grabbed tight to Cozen's wrist, and he pulled her down a long corridor in the airport that was used for old gates that were currently not in use. He ripped down the caution tape keeping people from going too far, and continued dragging her along with him until he felt they had gone far enough.

Swinging her around to face him, Cozen found genuine fear staring back at her. "He wanted me to *follow* you. Don't you get that?"

Sure.

"And clearly you did," she said.

"Not technically. I made some calls," Sargon replied.

His expression remained aloof and calm, but his words were delivered with a sharp coldness that burned on impact. She could hear his worry, but there was nothing she could do for him right now. He didn't need to be focusing on her—he didn't need to be getting too wrapped up in her.

It was dangerous.

She was dangerous.

"And you found out I was visiting with the Astor family," she said. "I hear his dead wife was an Astor before she gave up the family namesake to be with Jett."

Sargon's gaze flashed with a dark warning. "I know better than to deliver that kind of information to Jett, but he will expect *something*. He will want to know where you were, and he will need to believe that I followed you there. That's what he wanted."

As he spoke, his hold on her became tighter and tighter to the point it was almost painful. He moved closer and closer until his nose grazed hers, and all she could see were his dark, russet eyes boring into hers.

His smell soaked into her lungs.

His presence wrapped around her.

His heat warmed her.

"And will you do that for me?" she dared to ask.

The corner edge of Sargon's mouth curled upward. "Why do you even ask? You know I will."

"Because you want to protect me. Because you care."

"Too much," he returned. "Clearly."

"It's never too much. Sometimes it's just enough, Sargon."

"He was *crazy*, Cozen. Out of his mind when he learned you left. Raging mad, and he probably still is. It's gone way beyond a little infatuation with him. He's out for something with you, now. Do you get that?"

"Crazy is good—crazy means he'll do just about whatever I want to get what he wants."

His fingers dug into her arms again.

Cozen stayed still.

Jett was not all that different from Sargon, in some ways. Both men were tangled up with her in dangerous games that might not end well for them. She was all too aware of just how easy it would be to ruin both of these men.

And yet, she didn't want to hurt Sargon. If anything, she might want to keep him forever.

Those feelings fucked with her head. They kept her off her game when she had to be laser focused.

Sargon's lips grazed hers with a whisper of a kiss, but nothing more. She couldn't deny the way her blood sang all the same. She couldn't even try to pretend like she didn't want to immediately bring him closer for a better kiss.

And so she did just that.

Pulled him closer.

Kissed him harder.

Wished for different things.

When she opened her eyes, reality was still there. Sargon was still staring at her, and he was still being a giant fucking complication.

"You make me feel like I can't trust you, Zen."

"You shouldn't, Sargon."

No one should.

Cozen was a thief. Her name was most appropriate. She took; she stole; she kept by means of trickery or deceit. She did not, however, give in return.

She had not been taught to give—only to take.

Sargon sucked in a hard breath before saying, "Enough of this. It's enough."

"I have two weeks," she returned.

Sargon's lips flattened into a grim line. "For what?"

She was grateful he went that route.

Grateful he gave her another chance.

"To finish my business here. You can let me have those two weeks, can't you?"

"I don't think I have a choice. You've backed me into a corner here, too. I wonder, is that purposeful? Do you use me like you use him? A part of your plans—whatever they are. Am I something disposable, and easily replaced, Cozen?"

She didn't even have to lie.

That's probably what scared her the most.

"You are not either of those things," she whispered.

"Are you sure?"

Cozen pushed up on her tiptoes, and kissed him again. A soft, ghost of a kiss that still managed to tilt the world around them. "This is how it has to be. This is how I have to be."

"And what comes after, Zen?"

"I don't know."

Lies.

She knew.

Didn't he?

"I have tonight, then," he told her.

Cozen met his gaze. "Tonight for what?"

"To have you before you'll technically be back in the city—or that's what I told him, anyway. And then you go back to …"

"Him and the job," she finished for him.

Sargon smirked, and shook his head. "You've never been his. You can't be when you're mine."

Cozen drifted around the hotel room with a keen eye. She moved from thing to thing and touched anything she could find. The suit jacket he'd discarded on a chair a couple of days before. A glass half-filled with water. Even the edge of the bedspread that he hadn't made before leaving.

"So this is where you've been staying?" she asked quietly.

"Seems so, Cozen."

She glanced at him over her shoulder, and smiled. Despite the sweetness in the camber of her lips, he could still see a warring heat blazing in her gaze. Every single time he found her looking at him, he saw that same heat.

"You don't want an apartment, or what? Do you just enjoy shelling out large amounts of money every day for a decent hotel room in New York City?"

"There's no point in me getting an apartment."

"Why not?"

"I don't stay long enough in one place to need one," he replied honestly. "I get bored with whatever I'm doing, and move on. Or something comes up, and I have to leave. Like almost everything else in my life, New York isn't permanent. It'll never be. It's pointless to make the effort to settle in to a place where I have no intention of staying."

"Seems like a waste, Sargon."

Her gaze met his again.

He grinned back.

"So be it," he murmured. "I only put roots down where my heart is. Where it goes, I go. The rest is all details."

"Details," she echoed.

It came out like a whisper.

"Yes, *details*."

Sargon passed by Cozen to grab two things—a silk robe hanging off the back of the chair, and the landline connected to the desk downstairs. He offered the robe to her, saying, "Make yourself comfortable. You're all mine tonight."

Cozen's gaze lingered on the robe, but she didn't take it. "If you want to fuck, just say so. You don't have to make some show about it."

"Actually, I want to eat. Then, I want to use the hot tub. Maybe watch a movie. Who fucking knows? Whether or not we fuck depends on your attitude up until then."

Her sharp little gasp made him grin.

"You're such an—"

"Asshole?" Sargon shrugged. "Get a new insult. That one's been used on me too many damn times, sweetheart."

Cozen yanked the robe away from him, and gave one of her glares before she headed for the attached bathroom. "Don't worry. I will figure out a new insult for you. One you won't like, Sargon. Oh, what about *Sarg*?"

Fuck that noise.

"Call me that name in bed, and I'll shove my dick right up your a—"

She slammed the bathroom door, but not before giving him a sexy wink over her shoulder before she did so.

Behind the door, he heard her shout, "Maybe that's what I want!"

Minx.

Cozen had her own kind of foreplay. That's what Sargon had come to learn about the woman. It wasn't just a hard, dirty fuck that she liked. No, she also liked the chase—the *game*. She got off on playing games.

Sargon didn't mind playing along.

Mostly.

"Try this one now," Sargon said.

Offering the forkful of raspberry cheesecake to Cozen, he couldn't control the way his dick perked to life when her lips encased the fork. Her eyes fluttered closed, and she let out the softest moan before releasing the fork.

"Good, hmm?"

"Very good," she replied.

"Another?"

"One more, maybe."

"New favorite?" he asked.

"I'm still pretty partial to the chocolate one," she said.

"Do you want that one, then? There's still some left."

Cozen peered up at him from her spot in the hot tub. Beneath the bubbling, steaming water, she was entirely naked. He could only see the tops of her shoulders and an occasional peek of the swells of her breasts when she moved.

"Are you going to feed it to me, too?" she asked.

"I will if you want me to."

"Why are you spoiling me like this?"

Isn't that what men should do for a woman like this?

For the woman they *loved?*

"Because I want to," he settled on saying.

"Chocolate, then?"

Sargon nodded. "Chocolate, Cozen."

He left Cozen in the hot tub as he went back inside the hotel room through the sliding glass doors. Quickly discarding the small piece of raspberry cheesecake, he picked up the plate with the small bit of chocolate cheesecake left on it. By the time he got back out on the balcony, Cozen was stepping out of the hot tub.

Naked.

Dripping wet.

Fucking *beautiful.*

"Stare much?" she asked.

Sargon leaned against the sliding glass door. "How could I not stare when you look like that?"

For a brief second, her gaze drifted downward before coming back up to meet his. "You have a strange way of doing that to me."

"Doing what?"

"Making me feel like the most beautiful woman in the world."

"You are—the most beautiful in *my* world," he returned easily.

Cozen laughed. "And what's that world like, huh? Your world, I mean."

"Strange and beautiful."

"Huh."

"Not the answer you were expecting?" he asked.

"I never know what to expect with you."

Sargon stepped out onto the balcony fully with the cake in one hand, and the fork in the other. He pulled a small bite from the cheesecake with the fork, and held it out to a still *very* naked Cozen. Without question, she took the bite he offered. His dick only grew more painfully hard at the way her pink lips wrapped around the fork again.

"Before morning, that needs to be my cock your lips are wrapping around like that," he said.

Cozen released the fork with a grin. "Give me a good fuck out here where anybody can see, and you've got yourself a deal."

Goddamn.

"You're a wicked woman," Sargon said, chuckling.

"You assume I got this way by myself."

"I bet you were always like this—maybe you just needed a little bit of help to showcase it better."

"Maybe."

"You want more cake?"

Cozen wet her lips. "No, not particularly."

Instantly, Sargon discarded the plate and fork to the tiny table next to the wicker chairs on the balcony. Cozen was reaching for a towel on one of the chairs, but he didn't let her get that far. She'd asked for something else, after all. He planned to give it to her.

The towel fell from Cozen's hand when Sargon grabbed her around the waist with one arm, and pulled her to his body. Her back fit tight to his chest and he swung them around, and pushed her up against the banister.

Her breathless laughter melted into a surprised gasp when his teeth sunk into her shoulder, and his fingers slipped down over her stomach before finding the heaven lower between her thighs. *Jesus.* She was already wet—so warm, nice and tight, and damn slick on his fingers when he pumped two into her greedy pussy.

She didn't hide her desire, instead opening her legs even wider for him as his kisses rained down on the back of her neck.

"Did you know your pussy tastes like candy to me?" he asked in her ear. "I can't fucking get enough of it—it's addicting, Zen."

"Oh, my *God.*"

He felt her hand slip down beside his, and one of her fingers joined his two before it was gone from between her thighs once more. She offered her finger—wet with her arousal—over her shoulder to him like it was a gift.

It *was.*

He grabbed her ass hard while he fucked her deeper with his fingers, and sucked her offering into his mouth at the same time. Tart and hot, her flavor coated his tongue, and it instantly made him get down on his knees to find more.

"Open up—spread for me," he demanded.

Two quick snaps of his palms slapped against her thighs. She widened her legs, and spread herself for him with another one of those teasing, sexy laughs. He stopped her laugh really fucking fast when he buried his face into her cunt from behind.

His tongue tunneled into her pussy while his fingers worked at her clit. Every little drop of her arousal that he could get into his damn mouth, he lapped it up like liquid gold. It was too precious to waste.

She was too fucking precious.

"Love it when you eat my pussy," she said.

All breathy.

So high.

Christ.

His tongue and fingers worked her faster until he felt the telltale signs of her oncoming orgasm. The shaking in her thighs, and the clenching of her muscles. The way her cries came out louder—loud enough to echo down to the street below them.

When she did come, he kept his fingers rubbing tight, fast circles against her clit as he stood back up quickly. His pants were already unbuttoned; his fly already unzipped from when he had just yanked them on after jumping out of the hot tub earlier when the food came.

He pumped his hard cock with a firm fist a couple of times, but he didn't linger too long there. He wanted to be inside her—was dying to get her pussy wrapping him tight, and sucking him deeper.

It was better than a drink.

Better than a drug.

"Fuck," Cozen breathed when he slid inside her pussy.

The lingering tendrils of her orgasm fluttered around his dick, and took him all the way in. He put a hand to her back, and forced her to lean further over the rail as he leaned back to watch his dick come out when he pulled away.

He came out hard, and soaked in her. He could see his heart beat pulsing in his dick.

Cozen pushed back against him, and took him in again. He smacked her ass for that fucking trick, and held her tighter to the railing to keep her in place.

"Behave," he warned.

"*Fuck me.*"

"Behave, Zen. Or I'll make you wait for the next orgasm. Pleasure is earned, sweetheart. And you should know by now how to earn it properly."

"Pl—"

He slapped her ass again.

Her moan answered him back. He liked the sight of his red handprints coloring up her backside. Rubbing his hand over the spots, he could feel the heat rising to her skin, and the way she shuddered with every stroke.

Slowly, he pulled his cock out of her again.

"I want you to *fuck me,*" she demanded.

"You're going to wait."

"No, I won't."

"Oh, you will, or—"

"You asked for this, *Sarg*."

He grabbed hard to her waist with one hand, and fisted her hair with the other. "Fucking little—"

"Bitch, slut, your *whore*? Pick one and stick to it," she gasped out. "I like them all."

Sargon pumped harder into her. A fast, brutal rhythm that sent Cozen slamming into the railing with every single thrust. He was sure she would have marks left behind from his hands, and from the railing, too.

He was going to paint her back with his come.

Then he would turn her around, and fuck her again.

"Well, which one is it?" Cozen asked, backing into every thrust. "Your bitch, slut, or whore?"

"All three—but only for me," he grunted.

Cozen peered over her shoulder. All darkened eyes, trembling lips, and sex on her tongue. "Only for you."

Sargon knew he was alone before he even opened his eyes. He could tell by the coldness of the sheets against his palms when he reached for the other side of the bed. He knew it when he reached for her, and found nothing but air slipping through his fingertips.

Cozen's scent—a teasing, sultry mix of vanilla, cherries, and sex— wasn't as strong as it had been the night before when she was beside him. Now, it only lingered around him like an afterthought that he couldn't quite get out of his mind.

Peeling his eyes open, Sargon rolled to his back, and stared up at the white ceiling of the hotel room. He tried not to be pissed off about waking up alone, but what was the point, really. Of course, he was going to be pissed.

Scrubbing his hands down his unshaven jaw, Sargon resolved his irritation for the moment by remembering the night before.

Sex on his tongue.

Cozen on her back.

Buried in her pussy.

It was just enough to get him up and out of bed to take care of the erection making itself painfully known under the thin, white sheet. He was just about to step in under a too-hot shower when his phone rang in the other room.

"Fuck," he snarled.

Why could nothing go right?

Sargon didn't even bother to check the caller ID before he picked up the phone, and put it to his ear with a sharp, "What?"

"Is that anyway to greet your boss?"

His spine stiffened like someone had shoved a rod up it at the sound of Jett's voice. He could tell by the barely contained frustration lacing the man's tone that Jett was still in some kind of a fit about Cozen being gone.

Or … Jett thought she was still gone.

"I have news for you," Sargon said.

"Oh, do tell."

"Do you want it over the phone, or face to face?"

"I just *want* it," Jett snapped back. "Considering you only have one job at the moment, any news you relay to me had better be about that. So, what is your fucking news?"

Yeah.

Definitely pissed.

Most certainly obsessed.

Sargon wondered if Cozen understood the fire she was now playing with. He also wondered what was it about her that had gotten Jett so entirely fucked up over her like this.

He knew why *he* was messed up over her.

But Jett?

The man was rich enough that he could have any fucking woman he wanted. Sure, he was in his mid-fifties, but he didn't look a day over forty or so. He still kept up with his appearance, and fitness.

So, why?

"It is about Cozen," Sargon said.

"Good—did you find her?"

"I didn't have to go looking very far. She's back in the city. Got in this morning."

"I beg your goddamn pardon?"

"By the time I had found where she went—Florida, I guess; she has family there—and set up a flight to get in, she was already on her way back. I didn't see the point in leaving the city."

"I told you—"

Sargon interrupted Jett's roar with, "My flight was to leave this afternoon. Soonest one I could get. Hers came in at six. Still want me to fly down there?"

Jett quieted for a long while. A deathly silence, really. Had Sargon been in the man's direct vicinity, he probably would have made himself scarce for safety reasons. No need to push the man's buttons more than he already had.

"Have you laid eyes on *her*, yet?" Jett demanded. "This morning since she flew in?"

"No."

And that wasn't a lie.

"I need you to do that—*now*," Jett said firmly. "Go to her place, and get eyes on her. Make sure she is okay, and … not up to something."

"Jett, I assure you, she is not—"

"Do what I said, and then get to my home to fill me in on everything else. Do not fucking question me this morning, Sargon, I am not in the mood!"

Clearly.

Jett didn't even let Sargon respond before he hung up the phone.

Fucking wonderful.

It looked like his shower would have to wait.

Jett paced with heavy strides behind the large dark oak desk. He barely even passed Sargon a look as the man entered his office. It was the first time Sargon had ever actually been inside the space during the months that he had worked for the man.

He took in the dark tones, leather furniture, and gold accents around the room. Shelves lined with leather-bound books, and portrait paintings on the walls of men that Sargon suspected to be long-deceased Griffin men if the resemblances were to be trusted.

"Finally," Jett said.

"I had to wait to get eyes on her, as you wanted," Sargon said.

Jett waved a hand blindly. "Just … knock on her door!"

"Wouldn't that be a little … obvious?"

The man stopped pacing. "I beg your pardon?"

"Pardon me for saying this—"

"Don't preface whatever you're going to insult me with by trying to excuse it, Sargon. I am not a stupid man."

All right, then.

"If you think that woman will take kindly to the fact you are having her followed more than you already are, then you are mistaken. Do you think she wouldn't freak out just a tiny bit to know that you immediately had someone looking for because she left the city? Not to mention, you knew exactly when she got back in?"

Jett swallowed hard, and sat down in the chair behind his desk. "Well—"

"Your purpose of having me approach her, and keep an eye on her, was because you felt I was not threatening to her. You thought she was not scared of me. Do you want me to frighten her? Because knocking on her door shortly after she arrives home from being out of town will definitely do that."

For the moment, Jett seemed content to agree with Sargon. He considered that as a battle won, of sorts.

At least, for now.

"And you did get eyes on her?" Jett asked.

"Yes, and I even took a picture."

"Where is it?"

Sargon tipped his head to the side. "You're quite ..." *Don't use obsessed, you stupid fuck.* "Well, enamored with her, aren't you?"

Jett raised a single brow. "I enjoy a good chase, we'll say. I enjoy ending the chase much more. It's even better when something as beautiful as her is the prize."

Something invisible tightened around Sargon's throat. He forced himself to speak through it. "The picture is on my phone."

"Send it to me, now."

Sargon knew better—just by the look on Jett's face—whether than to ask if the man was serious or not. He pulled out his phone, and texted the photograph of Cozen drinking tea as she stood in her living room window.

Not two minutes later, the same photograph was printing out of Jett's printer behind his desk. The black printer rested beneath a large painting of Jett and his two sons.

"How does she have *family* in Florida when she has practically been an orphan her entire life?" Jett asked.

Shit.

"It was a couple—young, like her. I don't have all the details on them. I didn't get that far as I was focused on getting to her after that. Do you want me to run some info on them?"

Jett grunted under his breath. "Maybe; I will leave the option open. You didn't even lay eyes on them, then?"

"No—I told you, I didn't get the chance to get there before she was already coming back. It's possible they're simply people she met on her travels, or maybe they were kids in foster homes she also lived in, and they remained friends. Whatever the emergency was, it was quickly cleared up."

"How did you find out she went to Florida, and not California, anyway?"

Fuck.

"Made some calls—flight itineraries were sent over. You're not the only man in this city who knows people that can get shit done for them on a fast schedule. I just don't call in my favors very often. That's how I got the info she was back in the city, too."

Might as well add that info in before the bastard asked it.

"Ah."

It was all doable. As long as someone had the right contacts. Jett had no reason to question Sargon, or distrust him.

Besides, the man was more distracted by looking over the photograph in his hands of Cozen drinking her tea.

"I like this," Jett said, "I think I will keep it."

Sargon blinked, and replied, "Okay."

What else could he say?

Without another word, Jett turned his office chair around, and stood. He grabbed the edge of the painting of him and his sons, and pulled it away from the wall like it was a door.

Sargon supposed it *was* a door, of sorts.

It hid a safe.

Jett didn't even attempt to hide the six numbers he keyed in to open the safe. *Seven, five, nine, nine, five, seven.* Each beep that accompanied the numbers rang heavily in the back of Sargon's mind.

He memorized the numbers.

He eyed the items inside the safe once the door was open, too. Particularly, the cash stacked high on the top shelf. So much cash, that it filled the shelf entirely.

Jett shoved the picture into the middle shelf with what looked to be other paperwork, although Sargon wasn't close enough to tell.

Then, the man pulled out a black box from the bottom shelf. He popped it open, and surveyed the ruby ring inside. A large, square-cut ruby—likely worth the cost of a large home, or a luxury vehicle.

"I thought I might need to have this cleaned," Jett murmured, "but it's still quite beautiful."

Sargon eyed the jewelry. "I could have it cleaned for you."

Jett passed him a look, and shook his head. "No, I take good care of this. My first wife barely wore it for fear someone might take it from her— it has an interesting history, you could say. I think someone else would appreciate it far more than she did, and they won't fear wearing it every second they have it on. She did say red was her color."

"And what exactly are you going to use that ring for?"

Jett smiled.

Slyly.

"Propose. I have waited long enough to put another beautiful woman on my arm and in my bed. My wife has been dead for an appropriate amount of time. Cozen will fit my lifestyle and public persona quite well. So yes, I intend to propose to her with it. What else?"

Time was counting down faster than Cozen could work. She had all of one week left before her deadline to return the Astor ring was up.

One week.

The Griffin party, on the other hand, was just five days away. It would be the one—and the last time—Cozen had the chance to get the ring. A ring that she still had not seen since inserting her presence into Jett's life. A ring she was not even one-hundred percent sure the man still had in his possession.

Her instincts told her that Jett did still have the ring. He was not the kind of man to simply give something up just because. Considering he wouldn't return it to the Astors—claiming it belonged to his wife—he was unlikely to give it to anyone.

He *had* to have it.

All of Cozen's planning and careful attention to details about Jett, his life, and his home made her pretty confident that yes, he did have the ring. Likely hidden in the safe in his office.

Cozen didn't like to work on maybes.

It wasn't smart, or safe.

This was the first job she had in a long time where she was going into the home stretch—because of a deadline she had no choice but to follow—with far too little knowledge about the mark, and how she was going to extract what she was there to find. It made her uncomfortable. Like needles swimming in her bloodstream.

Yet, she couldn't back down.

She couldn't *not* try.

Cozen would much rather return to her fate with the Astors and tell them that she had tried and failed, rather than the fact she hadn't tried at all.

It was that simple.

"I am *sure*," Tye said.

"How sure?" Cozen asked.

Her long-time friend, and programmer-slash-hacker-slash-fucker, sighed on the other end of the phone. This was the first time Cozen had called him since she started this job for the Astors. She didn't think she would need his help.

Now, she was just making sure.

"Cozen, I designed the fucking program," Tye said quietly. "You were the one who worked with me on it to make sure it was perfect. I know what it will do."

"*Any* electronic safe?"

"Yeah, girl. Shit, just use the adaptor like I taught you, get the program app on the phone booted up and ready to go, force back the keypad on the safe, and you will find the plug to put the adaptor in. All electronic safes have them—how else can they recalibrate an electronic safe without access to the *brain*?"

"I know they all have them, Tye."

"Exactly."

"And you're sure—"

"Zen, I am fucking sure, okay? As long as the safe works in numbers from zero to nine with no special characters, no letters, and no need for fingerprinting entry, then it will find the code and open it for you. You know I wouldn't fuck with you like that, right?"

"Well ..."

"Okay, so I wouldn't fuck with you when you're on an actual job, then. Outside of work, I would mess with you all the time."

"Yeah, yeah."

Cozen tipped her head back, and stared at the clear sky overhead. Fluffy white clouds danced in the sea of blue. All in all, it was a beautiful day. She wished that helped with the way she felt.

Nothing helped lately.

She was too close.

Almost done.

Then she would be better.

She would be perfect.

"By the way, how's your g—"

"I'll call you when I get back to California to let you know how it went," Cozen interjected. "Thanks for everything, Tye."

She hung up the phone, and shoved it back into her pocket. Silently, she added, *if I even make it back to California alive, that is.*

Cozen figured Tye wouldn't have appreciated that little tidbit. Although, she did feel slightly better to—once again—get confirmation from the man who had built and installed the program for electronic safe cracking into her phone that it *should* work.

As long as the safe was standard—the quick look she had gotten of Jett's said it was—it should get the code, and open it for her. Without alarming any security systems attached to it, and it should do it within three to four minutes.

Cozen just needed to get at the safe in the office, and make sure she had the time to spare to get inside it. Nothing more, and nothing less.

And of course, these were all still *maybes*. Maybes because what if she got that safe open, and the ring wasn't there? Who was to say Jett didn't have the ring stored in a lockbox somewhere across the city?

Christ.

She kept her back against the cool brick—being it was the first of June, it felt like it was the only thing around her that was cool. Even the air was muggy, and hot. The black uniform The Kingdom required her to wear was constantly sticking to her skin.

Seemed like New York was going to have a heat wave this year. She couldn't be more grateful that within a week, she would be gone from the city.

Gone from the smell of pollution, and the over packed streets. Back to her small house on the beach, and sleeping in her bed instead of a nest of pillows and blankets. Soon, she would be home again.

That was, if the Astors didn't kill her first.

Think good thoughts. Think only good thoughts.

Even her mantra felt like it was patronizing her lately. It was times like now when she couldn't help but think that maybe the life of a thief just wasn't meant for her. Maybe she wasn't as good at her chosen trade as she assumed, never mind what others whispered about her.

She knew those thoughts were garbage.

Self-doubt creeping in.

Anxiety working through.

She could do this—she *would* do this.

She didn't give a fuck if she had to blow a wall out of the man's house to get it done—she would do it.

Somehow.

"Zen!"

Cozen blinked out of her daze, and found the manager leaning out the back door. It seemed like her fifteen minute break was up, apparently.

Joy.

"What?" she asked.

"Your favorite patron just walked in. He's asking for you. Get back to work."

Cozen swallowed hard. "Jett, you mean."

It wasn't even a question.

Chase nodded. "Yeah, Jett. He's—"

"In the private room, I know."

For a moment, Cozen considered lying about having a migraine just so she could go home. Over the last week, she hadn't needed to deal with Jett all that much as he seemed to be in the middle of a lot of business and his upcoming party. His dinners at the restaurant were shorter, and he had not taken Cozen out to dinner, a show, or anything else for that matter.

He did still have someone—probably Sargon—watching her every move. She only suspected it was Sargon because she could feel that man's eyes on her when he was looking at her. No one else made her feel that way.

"Well, hurry it up," Chase barked.

The exit door swung closed.

Cozen sighed, and pushed off the wall. She fixed her hair by running her fingers through the strands a bit, and put her game face on.

Sure enough, Jett was already looking in the direction of the private dining room's entrance when Cozen walked in. His gaze scanned her over, and he didn't even try to hide the way he lingered on her breasts under the tight, black bodycon dress, or the shape of her hips. Inside, she felt disgust. Outside, she kept her smile firmly in place.

"Hey, you," she said.

Across from Jett at the table, Sargon kept his gaze trained firmly on the phone in his hands. Cozen was grateful.

"Good afternoon to you, darling," Jett replied.

Cozen came to stand beside Jett, and moved to pull out her pad and pen to scratch down his order. She didn't get the chance.

Jett pulled her in his lap.

In his lap.

She stiffened at the sudden change, but thankfully, Jett didn't seem to notice as his hands skimmed her thighs. He pressed a quick kiss to her cheek, and then used two gentle fingers to move the few strands of hair that had fallen over her eyes out of her face.

Across the table, Sargon finally looked up.

Heat blazed in his gaze.

Hatred swam heavily.

Not for *her.*

She thought, *never for her.*

"My apologies," Jett murmured in her ear, "but I missed you. I've been way too busy lately, haven't I?"

Cozen let out a little laugh, and tried to relax a little more. It was hard to do when the man was touching her, his lips were close enough to kiss her, and another man who tempted her at every step was only a couple of feet away.

"I have to *work*," Cozen teased.

"Ah."

Jett gave a little grunt, and pushed her up from his lap with a slight pat to her backside. Cozen didn't miss how Sargon's gaze narrowed at that sight, either. But when Jett looked in the direction of his bodyguard—wasn't that Sargon's job for Jett?—the man was looking back down at the phone in his hands again.

"We'll have lots of time to catch up soon," Jett told her, smiling cunningly. "The party is coming up—I intend to spend a good portion of my night catching up with you, Cozen."

She didn't think he meant that literally. More like he planned on doing something else with her entirely.

Great.

Cozen had never needed to give up her body before for the sake of a heist. Somehow, she always found a way around it. Trickery, or whatever the case may be.

She wasn't *that* thief.

She stayed true.

Jett didn't look like he planned on giving her much of a choice.

And time was still running out.

The knock on Cozen's apartment door sent her out of the meditational heaven she had finally just achieved. All it took was a knock to pull her out of it almost violently, really.

Shame.

Cozen knew what was going to be waiting on the other side of the door before she even opened it. The week had flown by fast—Friday settled closer and closer with every beat of her heart.

Tonight was the night.

Showtime.

Cozen pulled open the door, and was immediately bombarded with *people*. One carried a garment bag slung over their arm. Another carried two large silver cases—makeup, likely. Right behind the girl with the makeup came another woman wielding clear cases full of different hair products and tools. A man dressed in a sharp black suit came in second to last with velvet boxes piled in his arms. Jewelry, probably.

Jett's people.

Here to spoil her.

Cozen put on a smile.

A mask, now.

She was anything but happy.

"I think you're going to like this dress, Miss Taylor," the girl holding the garment bag said.

The others started setting up on the small table and two chairs that Cozen had finally broken down and bought for the kitchen. She didn't pay them any attention because for one, they weren't speaking to her, either. And for two because they wouldn't care to hear what she wanted for her hair and makeup. They were going to do whatever Jett had told them to do in order to get her ready for the party.

Cozen didn't need to be told.

She knew.

"Will I like it?" Cozen asked. "I didn't pick it."

"Mr. Griffin assured me it is very much *your* style," the woman said.

"You'll like the dress," a voice murmured behind her. "But that's about all you will like, sweetheart."

Cozen stiffened at his voice.

Heat flooded her veins.

Turning slightly, she found Sargon leaning in her doorway with his signature grin. Despite the playful note in his tone, and his sexy smile, she found discomfort and unhappiness staring back in his eyes.

She hated that was because of her.

Because of *this*.

Cozen glanced back at the woman. "Let me see it, then. The dress, I mean."

The woman smiled brilliantly. "Of course."

Soon, the garment bag was unzipped, and torn away from the dress it was keeping hidden. The woman—and Sargon—had not been lying. She did love the beautiful piece of art that was this dress.

A dark wine-colored evening gown with long sleeves, a deep V-neck plunge in the front *and* back, with enough length to sweep the floor, and a slit that went all the way up the entire skirt. A wrong step, a move too fast in one direction, and a woman would probably flash more of her private bits than she intended to.

Five white pearl buttons closed the back of the dress at the mid-spine, but was still a deep enough plunge in the back to show off all kinds of skin. The deep red color of the fabric was rich, and vibrant.

"Red is my color," Cozen murmured. "It's beautiful."

"Wonderful," the woman said. "And you have the proper shoes to match. I have all your sizes, so I have no doubt everything will be a perfect fit."

Of course, she did.

Jett would have made sure of it.

The woman turned around to handle the other people, and it gave Cozen a second to let her mask slip. Not to mention, *breathe*. She spun on her heel to face Sargon who had also let his grin flatten into a grim line.

His sharp jaw was so tight, she could practically feel his irritation and stress wafting from him. She had to be careful with what she said to him with these people around—she didn't know how close any of them were to Jett except for the fact that he kept sending *them* anytime Cozen needed to be dressed properly for something.

"The red is beautiful," Sargon said quietly.

"I wonder what made him pick it."

Sargon tipped his head to the side. "Could be that it matches the ring he intends to propose to you with. A beautiful ruby—keeps it hidden away in his office safe. Maybe he's trying to find out if red really is your color, Cozen. Wasn't that what you told him?"

She didn't miss the heat in his worlds.

The fire in his eyes.

Cozen heard other things, though.

Important things.

A ring; a ruby; an office safe.

The rest was not important. The rest, she didn't give a shit about because it would never come to fruition.

Did he even realize the kind of information he just gave her, and how fucking valuable it was? A life saver, really. A confirmation she had been waiting for.

"Did he make sure to put the ring back to keep it safe when he was done?" Cozen asked.

Sargon's gaze darkened as he stared hard at her. "*That's* what you care to ask me right now?"

"Yes."

The man nodded, and sneered. "Yeah, Zen, he put it back."

Perfect.

Cozen was acutely aware of the eyes watching her as she moved through the Griffin mansion. Each step she took was careful and slow lest that slit in her red dress open a little too much and flash parts of her that were not meant for public consumption.

She had lost sight of Sargon the moment he helped her out of the car, and Dash—Jett's youngest son—was there to greet her, and take her inside to find his father.

Guests turned to watch her walk by on the arm of a Griffin son, but she simply kept her head turned forward, and on her next task at hand. Dressed to the nines, everyone looked a hell of a lot like she did in that moment.

Perfectly coifed.

Beautifully dressed.

Impeccable.

Flawless.

Fake.

Dash patted Cozen's hand tucked into his elbow. "I see why my father likes you so much, Cozen."

She gave him a smile. He was not like his older brother. Still just as arrogant and spoiled, sure, but he was not quick to insult her like Silas did every time she was in the man's presence. It was a nice change.

It wouldn't last.

"Thank you," Cozen said.

"Smile," Dash murmured.

"I am."

"Not nearly wide enough, Cozen. My father likes it when beautiful women smile like they mean it."

She didn't have the chance to reply to his statement. He turned sharply at the large dining room where Jett was holding court like a king. Cozen had come to learn the man only really preferred a few rooms in the downstairs portion of his wing when he had to entertain people.

His dining room with a too-large chandelier and all its gold accents was definitely a favorite spot for Jett.

Cozen stood on display in the entryway to the dining room with Dash, but quite quickly, the young man—although frankly, he was the same age as her—stepped off to the side when his father came forward. Jett set his glass of what looked to be whiskey aside as he came closer with his arms already outstretched and opened to take Cozen into his embrace.

She heard the whispers murmuring amongst the guests. She certainly wasn't blind, either. She could see how they watched her, and the half-sneers they made as Jett finally came close enough to pull her into his arms.

One of Jett's arms wrapped tightly around Cozen's waist as he pulled her into his side, and turned them to face the room.

"Now we can party—my beautiful Cozen has arrived."

Cozen gave Jett a look, and asked quietly, "Did you purposely make me late tonight?"

Jett winked. "I might have. A woman who looks like you do should always be appreciated by anyone who can see you, Cozen. And I wanted everyone to see just how beautiful you are."

His hand came up fast, and before she knew what was happening, his thumb stroked across her lax lips. A gentle touch, sure, but absolutely indicative of his wants when it came to her. His gaze darkened as he looked her over, and stroked her mouth once more.

Without warning, Jett kissed Cozen. A hard kiss that forced her to gasp a bit—the opening of her parting lips giving him the idea, and the chance, to deepen the kiss.

Every part of her wanted to revolt.

Fight or flight kicked in.

And yet, Cozen forced herself to relax. To take the kiss, though it made her skin crawl, and her blood run cold. Thankfully, it didn't last long as someone hollered something disgusting from the other side of the room, and Jett pulled away.

His grin was still firmly in place.

So pleased with himself.

Soon, Cozen would be the one pleased. She made sure to keep a tight hold on her clutch as she moved across the room at the urging of Jett's hand at her lower back.

"Don't go too far from my side," he murmured in her ear. "I intend to show as much of you off as I can tonight."

Cozen flashed him a brilliant smile. "I won't leave your side."

For now.

Jett raised a single brow high, and his smile turned suggestive in a blink. A lot like his tone when he said, "And then later, I intend for you to show me everything about you that I haven't already seen, Cozen."

Well, then …

Cozen simpered him with another smile. "I look forward to it."

Jett was on his third drink, and his fourth trip around the mansion to do the rounds again with Cozen. The man couldn't help himself, it seemed. He had to show his beautiful thing off to the rest of the worthy people.

To her credit, Cozen was doing well ... if keeping a fake smile plastered on for every rich fuck to either gawk at her, whisper about her, and for some, to actually *touch* her. Her mask never faltered. It never failed.

Sargon might almost be proud of that achievement of hers, if he wasn't so goddamn irritated about it. This whole night was irritating for him—all because it was *the* night. The end of line for Cozen when it came to Jett.

Tonight was the night Jett expected her to pay up, so to speak. The man wanted what he wanted from her. He wanted *her*—all of her that she had to give. And he was not going to accept any kind of excuse if she wasn't willing and ready to hand it over to him.

Jett was tired of the chase. That much was clear. Cozen would be expected to be the mouse too tired to run, now.

Just the thought ... *Jesus.*

Just the thought of someone touching Cozen, of them seeing her body, or having her like he did was a little too fucking much for him. It was enough to make Sargon want to burn the entire city of New York down just so that another man couldn't ever look at Cozen the way he did, or enjoy her the way he had been allowed to.

The *idea* of her being with Jett beyond what Sargon had already witnessed was enough to make his fucking blood boil. He could barely think the word *sex* without his rage spiraling into a dark place.

Was this what she wanted? Was whatever she was after worth the price of her body?

Sargon didn't know anything.

Not anymore.

"Wait a second," Sargon told the server as he passed.

The guy turned with the silver tray in his hand, and Sargon grabbed a flute of champagne. Quickly tossing the alcohol back with one swallow, and ignoring the bubbles that made him *hate* champagne, he set the flute back on the tray.

"Is that all, sir?" the server asked.

Sargon weighed his options, and then shrugged before grabbing one more flute of alcohol. He could have just went to the wet bar, and had the man working there make him a far stronger drink. He really didn't need Jett noticing him doing anything but what he was there to do, though.

He settled on shitty champagne.

Tossing the drink back, he swallowed it down, and set the empty flute to the tray once more. The server's brow lifted as he gave Sargon a look.

"Now, I'm done," Sargon grumbled.

"All right," the server replied, never batting a lash, "thank you, sir."

Quickly, the server turned on his heel, and headed out of the nearest doorway. Likely to go back toward the kitchen for a refill. Sargon emptied the man's last two drinks on his tray, after all.

It was almost comical, really.

Sargon wondered how much these servers seen or heard in their jobs when it came to the rich fucks they catered to. How much nonsense and private scandals were they afforded a glimpse of during their short stays at parties, or otherwise?

Like flies on the wall.

Amusing.

Sargon should have been working, in a way. His job tonight was solely to keep an eye on the guests, and make sure they didn't wander beyond the bottom floor of the first wing. Jett didn't like people hanging around upstairs, or drifting into places they had no business being. The man's personal and public lives were kept entirely separated by nothing more than a staircase, and a ceiling.

Jett's business dealings, both legal and illegal, happened in the privacy of his sanctuaries. His office, private library, and bedroom. *His* space, not anyone else's. He liked to keep the rest of the world out of that space.

For obvious reasons, Sargon supposed.

Sargon *was* working, to an extent. He followed Jett around as the man made his rounds over and over with Cozen. He kept an eye on the guests all the while, and it seemed like all of the people knew not to wander off too far from the party.

None of them even tried.

Sargon suspected the cameras up above helped. A reminder to all the guests that they were being watched, and should behave as such. While Jett kept working security cameras in the downstairs, there was nothing upstairs to capture *anything*.

Another wise move.

Who would want to hand over video proof of their illegal business dealings to officials should someone come looking?

Jett was not a stupid man.

Maybe that was one of the reasons why Sargon grew increasingly concerned over how attached—obsessed, really—Jett had become with Cozen. To play a game with a dangerous man was to make moves you hoped would not kill you.

Was she making the right moves?

Sargon didn't know.

"Everything has been fine on my end," Sargon assured Kirk.

The guy was considered to be Jett's head of security, but frankly, Sargon answered to no one but Jett when it came to his job. Lately, he wasn't even answering to Jett all that well, either. But that was another matter for a different day.

"Good, good," Kirk said.

The guy's gaze never left the many flat-screen monitors in front of his face. He was the only man on the grounds—besides Jett—to be allowed in this room to run the security cameras, and keep an eye on the footage. He was afforded an eagle eye view of everything happening at the party without actually being there.

"Thanks for checking in," Kirk said.

Sargon nodded. "No problem. Anything else before I get back out there?"

"Nope."

"Perfect."

Sargon waved a hand over his shoulder as he left the security room, and figured he wouldn't need to check in with Kirk again unless something particular came up. It was the only thing he agreed to for the night was to check in with Kirk periodically to let the man know if everything was fine on the main floor, or if he should be watching someone in particular.

He had not realized how painfully paranoid Jett could be at times. He didn't understand why the man threw parties like this if it was such a taxing event when it came to stress. Why not just have the goddamn parties where your personal life and business did not intermingle with the guests you invited?

Because that would be too easy.

Clearly.

Jett—like most everyone else in attendance at the party—had too deep of pockets to shy away. Showing off the expensive things he had amassed over the years came with the territory of being as wealthy as he was. Keeping a good public persona, and seemingly inviting people into his life allowed for a little more trust when it was needed.

It was all a well-crafted lie.

A spectacular charade.

Sargon doubted that most—maybe only a handful—of the guests knew what Jett really did behind the scenes. They likely had no idea that they were shaking the hand and breaking bread with a man who had brokered deals with some of the biggest, and most feared, names in organized crime all over North America.

Or … shit.

Maybe they did know.

Who was he to say?

Sargon found Jett had finally separated from Cozen's side for the first time all night when he made it back to the main rooms hosting the party. The man of the hour was having another two fingers of whiskey poured for him at the bar.

Quickly scanning the room and the people, Sargon couldn't find Cozen. Instantly, his heart rate picked up a little bit.

Where had she gone?

He didn't get the chance to even move into the connecting room to check if she was there, or somewhere else. Jett caught sight of Sargon standing just beyond the entryway of the dining room, and waved a hand as if to silently call him over.

What the king wants …

Sargon scoffed internally at that thought. Jett was no king. At least, not to him, anyway.

"How are things looking around here?" Jett asked once Sargon joined him.

"Quiet," Sargon replied, "and Kirk says the same. I just came back from checking in with him."

Jett nodded, and smiled. "Good, good. I assume my guests have spent enough time in my home to know what the rules are. I hate having to repeat them time and time again."

"Yes, well, if there's nothing else, I'm going to get back to my—"

"There is something else, actually."

Jett tipped up his glass for a long swig of the whiskey, and didn't bat a lash at the likely harsh sting it left behind when he set the glass down to the wet bar.

"What is that?" Sargon asked.

"I need you to do me a favor," Jett murmured. "I would have had one of the other guys do it, but I don't even like them being upstairs in my private spaces unless they need to be. I assume you won't be missed out here on the floor. You haven't been mingling."

Sargon lifted a brow. "My job is not to mingle."

"Exactly, and you don't *linger*, either."

Not with these people.

"I won't linger in your private rooms, if that's what you're saying," Sargon replied.

Jett nodded once. "Yes, that's what I am saying."

"What do you need?"

"There's a bag I set on the foot of my bed—a black duffle. I didn't have time to set my things out for the evening before the party got underway. I would appreciate it if you would set my room up for me."

Sargon cleared his throat. "And by set your things up, you mean …?"

"Some of the things are meant to make Cozen comfortable for the evening. You can place those items in the attached bathroom that doesn't have my personal belongings inside. Other things will clearly be *mine*. Put them in my bathroom. Nothing more, nothing less."

That sounded simple enough.

Except it made Sargon want to *rage*.

Jesus.

He needed to get a handle on this shit.

"Well, go," Jett said to him sharply with a wave of his hand. "I would like to end my evening sooner rather than later."

"What about the party?" Sargon forced himself to ask.

Jett laughed. "The party will continue on with or without me. There's nothing rich people like more than drinking and mingling with other rich people. Now go."

That was that.

Sargon figured—at least—he would be able to leave a gift behind for Cozen.

A *just in case*.

Jett was not the only man in the mansion who came prepared to make Cozen far more comfortable with her night. Sargon had been counting down to this evening, after all. It had only been a matter of time before it happened.

He'd prepared for it, too.

207

Prepared to help her, anyway.

She just had to *use* it.

Jett was wrong when he assumed Sargon wouldn't linger in his private rooms. Lingering, and quietly searching through Jett's belongings—not that he found anything interesting, or something that might hurt Cozen—was the only thing that kept him from going downstairs, and ruining Jett's night entirely.

By taking Cozen away.

If she didn't want this—didn't want to do this—the woman wouldn't do it. It was as simple as that. Sargon forced himself to repeat those words even as he set out the things he had found in the black duffle bag at the foot of Jett's bed.

Sargon had even rifled through those things a bit.

Some items were obvious—safety measures, like condoms. Sargon wondered how long it had been that Jett didn't keep a pack of those on him. Or maybe it had been just long enough that he recently ran out. Who was to say?

Other things were not as obvious. The pretty white box wrapped with a red ribbon, for example. Sargon carefully unwrapped that present to find a black lace lingerie set that would make the devil's cock hard, frankly.

It left nothing to the imagination. Scraps of thin, pretty fabric that would be easy to rip off, and would look damn good for the short time a woman wore it.

Jett had good—and expensive—taste.

Sargon hated that, too.

Once he had put everything where it needed to go between the respective bathrooms, he took the chance to look around Jett's master bedroom. It had the same look, feel, and style of the man's office.

A large, four-poster bed that dominated the space in a dark wood stain. Deep, rich colored rugs, bedding, and tapestries decorated the space. More bookshelves lined with old, leather-wrapped books. A small bar meant for one or two people, but with only the very best top-shelf liquor setting next to the crystal glasses. A walk-in closet showcased Jett's love for tailored, name-brand suits, Italian leather shoes, and Rolex watches.

A person could take a handful of the man's jewelry he left sitting out in the open inside his walk-in closet, and make a killing selling the items at pawn shops.

The two bathrooms were polar opposites. One strictly meant for a man, and his business. The towels being a dark, rich brown like the tilework in the shower, and the shiny marble on the countertops. While the other bathroom was more feminized even in its soft colors, and pale beige towels.

Before Sargon thought to change his mind, he moved back into the bathroom, and left his little gift for Cozen sitting under the white box with the red bow. He had used the notepad and pen he found in Jett's nightstand to scribble a quick note that he folded up around the small bag.

Just in case.

It was only when Sargon heard the laughter rumbling from down the hall that he finally decided it was time to stop lingering. Male laughter, and female. Both he recognized. Only one, he loved.

Sargon slipped into the only opened door just down the hall from the master bedroom at the same time Cozen and Jett rounded the corner near the large stairwell.

Jett's office.

Their forms passed by the door, and their laughter continued. Although, he was pretty sure he could hear a soft note of stress in Cozen's sweet laugh. It just wasn't as musical—not as high and free as it usually would be.

Neither of the two noticed him standing just a few feet in the office hidden by the shadows. He always did blend in quite well with the darkness.

Sargon didn't leave the office. Not even when he heard the bedroom door close down the hall. He had other things to do, now.

Cozen's laughter died the very second Jett closed the bedroom door behind them. His subtle touches and whispered words suddenly became far more forward, and clear. She barely had time to turn around to face him, and he was in front of her.

On her.

A hand grabbed her clutch, and tossed it aside before coming around her waist pulling her closer. His other hand snaked into the free waves of her hair to tangle into the strands, and tug firm enough to keep her in place. His body beneath his fitted suit pressing tightly against hers—so tightly she could feel his growing erection pressing into her clenching stomach.

Fight or flight wanted to kick in.

Cozen forced herself to relax; she calmed to give her brain a chance to take in her surroundings, and figure out a way out. Or … something.

Jett's kiss coming down hard on her lips all but silenced her plans. She couldn't afford to make this man think she was plotting against him in any kind of way, so despite the revulsion in her body, she responded back.

Fisted his suit jacket to bring him closer. Answered his kiss with her own. Laughed breathlessly when he murmured something unintelligible in her ear.

"Let me help you out of this dress," he demanded.

Cozen swallowed hard when his mouth traveled down over the column of her neck. "Impatience looks good on no man."

At least, not on *this* man.

Jett's hands tightened on her body and in her hair. To an almost painful point as his gaze found hers again. The hand at her waist slipped lower, and snaked beneath the slit in her dress. All too soon, she felt his hand edging its way closer to the spot between her thighs.

All the while, Cozen grinned.

She didn't show anything else.

Not her panic.

Not her disgust.

She kept that mask on—kept it firmly in place. She only needed to get Jett in a space where he was distracted, and then she was free to finish the rest of her business here. She would never need to deal with him again after tonight.

"Do you know how long I have waited to get a taste of you?" he asked.

Cozen cocked a brow.

She did know.

About as long as she had been waiting for her chance to extract a ruby ring from him. His fascination with her was only caused by her presence in his life, and little else. He never would have known she even existed in any other case.

"Do you know how long?" he asked again.

"Long enough, I imagine," Cozen replied quietly.

Jett flashed a grin. "Then you will forgive me for my impatience. And for my forwardness, too, I hope."

Cozen reached up to grab Jett's jaw, and brought him in for a quick kiss. "You're forgiven."

As fast as she was on her feet, Cozen found herself turned around, and on her back on the bed. She stared up at the vaulted ceiling as Jett climbed over top on her. The slit in her dress had opened up entirely to expose her bare legs and thighs.

Not to mention, the red lace underneath.

Jett's hands skimmed from her ankles to her knees, and then the insides of her thighs, too. He pushed her legs open a little more to fit in between, and his fingers dug firmly into her thighs. Hard enough to leave marks behind, likely.

She didn't want *his* marks. His marks owned no place on her body. She was not his—not his to have, or to claim, or to leave a piece of him behind when he was done. She would never be his despite his foolish notions, and this diversion she was playing on him.

It's a game. It's a job.

Do what you have to do.

Cozen's internal mantra helped to keep her steady. It helped to keep her legs open when all she wanted to do was close them, and put her fist through this man's throat. She didn't think that would work out very well for her in the end.

So instead, she played her part.

She did what was needed.

Widening her thighs, and letting his hands travel. Letting his mouth explore her inner thighs, and then higher on the swells of her breasts, and her throat. She pulled him closer when what she really wanted to do was shove him away, and she let him believe ...

For a moment, he only had to believe this was real. Soon, reality was going to come down hard on Jett Griffin, and it would not be a nice place for him to be sitting. To realize that a woman he had become so attached to had only come into his life to use him, and hurt him in the end.

She didn't feel badly.

This was who she was.

This was what Cozen *did*.

Without warning, Jett was pushing away from her. He straightened to his full height at the foot of the bed while she propped herself up on her elbows. His change in pace gave her a chance to look around, and think.

Knocking him out with something would do the trick. She only needed him down for just long enough to do her business, and get the hell out of there.

Her gaze scanned the room for something to—

Jett pointed at the bathroom nearest to them with the door wide open, the light turned on. "You have some things waiting for you in there—a gift, or two. I wanted you to be comfortable tonight. And every night with me, Cozen. Always."

She smiled.

"I'm comfortable with you."

But five minutes away from him would give her more of a time to plan, so she took that offer faster than he could remove it from her.

"But I would love to see what you got me," she said.

Jett flashed her a grin. "I'll give you a few minutes, then."

She disappeared into her bathroom just as he moved into his across the room. She was quick to close the door behind her, and lock it, too.

Just in case.

Cozen overlooked the items clearly set out for her. A white gift box with a red ribbon. New toiletries to say he absolutely intended for her to stay the entire night, and have things to freshen up with in the morning.

No, instead she looked for something to *use*. Something to make sure Jett would be down for the count while she finished this goddamn job. She didn't want to actually kill Jett—her job wasn't to end his life, and she rarely took on that responsibility during a heist, anyway.

Quickly, Cozen realized there was nothing for her to use in the bathroom. She cussed a blue streak under her breath, and sat her ass down on the edge of the marble bathtub. The gift box on the counter taunted her.

What was inside?

Likely nothing she wanted.

Still, she reached for it. Pulling it from the counter, something else underneath the box fell with it. She opened the top of the gift at the same time she reached for the folded up piece of paper on the floor.

Black lace—racy and sexy—rested inside the box. A note, and a baggie of powder, rested inside the paper.

Cozen dropped the box to the floor, uncaring about the lingerie Jett clearly wanted her to wear. She was much more interested in the note and drug she was holding.

Crushed Quaaludes. In case you need an out. – Sargon

Cozen held tight to that bagged, and crumped the note in her other fist. He was her saving grace, and Sargon couldn't even possibly know it.

Or maybe he did.

She didn't have time to think about it.

Cozen just needed to *act*. Quickly, she stripped down out of the wine-red dress, and let it fall to a forgotten heap on the floor. She removed the red lace bra and panty set to replace it with the black set inside the box on the floor.

The lace hid *nothing*. It barely covered her breasts, and her ass was fully on display in the thong.

It didn't matter.

Not now.

Opening the bathroom door just enough to peer out, she found Jett was still hidden behind the door of his own private space. Cozen came out quickly, and moved across the room to the small wet bar. She grabbed one of the crystal glasses, and used the spirit Jett had been drinking for most of the night to fill it almost to the rim.

Far too much alcohol for just him.

That was okay, too.

Cozen opened the baggie, and dropped the powder into the whiskey. A couple of swirls of the glass, and the powder was gone entirely. Like it hadn't even been there to begin with. She hid the baggie in her palm as a knob jiggled.

She just turned around as Jett's bathroom door opened, and he came out. He'd left his jacket, and shirt behind. His pants were undone, and his shoes were gone. He was not a bad looking man—fit for his age, and aging *well*, too.

Like a fine wine.

Another woman would suit him well, and be what he needed. Cozen was never going to be that woman, though.

"Good God, woman," he murmured.

Cozen smiled, and tipped her head to the side. "Do you like it?"

Jett came closer. "I knew I would. You may like red, but I like black."

"Drink?"

He was right in front of her now—distracted with eyes glazed, and lust on his mind. She could see his erection straining against his pants as his hand came up to stroke down her naked side.

"You poured it for me?" he asked.

Cozen nodded. "You like whiskey, don't you?"

"My preference to water," Jett said, smirking.

"Drink, then."

He took the glass.

Cozen held her breath.

Jett's hand continued to stroke her naked skin as he tipped the glass back, and downed a good half of the whiskey in one go.

Half should do it.

Overdo it, even.

She moved a little closer to Jett. She needed his attention to be focused on her while the powder did its magic, and started to really kick in hard. That was the thing about Quaaludes—though they were illegal in the states, you could get them elsewhere—it didn't take them very long to kick in, and a person could tell once they did.

"Come here," Cozen whispered.

She cupped Jett's jaw, and stroked his five o-clock shadow with her thumb. Pulling him in even closer, she kissed him until he was responding back fully. His arm wrapped around her waist to hold her tight, and his hand slid down to palm her ass.

Cozen moved them—making Jett walk backward toward the bed. A slow walk. Careful and measured with each step. Her gaze never left his, and she kept those sweet whispers going to keep his attention fully on her.

She felt his first step miss—a stumble just before the bed.

He landed where he needed to go. She moved over him. She straddled his waist, and put her hands against his bare chest. Beneath her fingertips, she could feel his heart racing.

Maybe a half of a glass with a half of a baggie of crushed pills was just a little bit too much for Jett. He had been drinking all night.

Cozen put the thoughts aside.

His gaze was hazy, now. His mouth was a little slack. His hold on her ass wasn't as firm as it had been.

"Jett?" Cozen asked.

He was watching her, but not *there*. Seeing her, but not really. Hearing her, but only barely.

Quaaludes were bad that way.

"Jett," Cozen whispered, "the Astors wanted to say hi, and I'm the one they sent to deliver their message."

He closed his eyes, then.

Time to get to work.

Cozen roamed through the top floor of the wing entirely unconcerned that she was being watched, or that she might unintentionally run into someone. Jett had made it quite clear to his men before they went upstairs that he was not to be interrupted, and the guests were not to leave the downstairs wing.

She was in the homestretch.

Almost scot-free.

Cozen went about halfway down the staircase—never going far enough to be seen—and listened. She could plainly hear the party was still in full swing. She doubted the guests would start to disperse until well into the early morning hours.

Their noise relaxed her further.

Spinning on her heel, Cozen headed back up the stairs. She kept a tight hold on the glass of whiskey that she had taken from Jett's room. She couldn't afford for her little trick to be found out in the morning, so she opted to take what was left with her and discard it later.

She flipped open her clutch as she came closer to the room she knew was Jett's office. Just one door down from his bedroom. She had left him right where he fell on the bed—his eyes closed, and breathing steady.

Sleep would keep him warm.

At least until the morning.

Cozen slammed the door to the office as she pulled out her phone from the clutch. She didn't even bother to turn on the light as a dimly lit lamp on the large desk gave her enough to work with. Her gaze was glued on the screen of the phone as she started it up, and moved around the desk.

Sargon's words rang heavily in her mind. She hadn't forgotten what he told her—a safe behind the desk, and a ruby ring inside meant for her.

Of course, Jett might have meant the ring to be hers. It wouldn't be hers at all. It would never belong to her.

Cozen reached for the painting, and pulled it outward only to find … the safe behind it was open. Panic swelled in her heart as she shined the phone inside to look around, and found nothing of any importance.

Sure, there was money.

Jewelry.

Papers.

But not the ring she needed!

Had he taken—

"Looking for this, Zen?"

Cozen's heart leaped into her throat as she spun on her heel. She'd completely overlooked him sitting there on the leather couch next to the far wall. Sargon peered up at her from his spot, and a deep, sexy grin overtook his features. His roughened expression softened a bit at his smile, and yet her thighs still clenched just like her pussy at the sight.

This man was dangerous for her.

Addictive.

Problematic all the way.

In his hand, he held out a ruby ring. It glinted under the dim lamp, and he spun it a bit to show off all the angles.

"Pretty, isn't it?" Sargon asked.

"You couldn't make some damn noise?" she demanded.

He chuckled—all dark and husky.

Like a promise of sex.

The need of sin.

Christ.

"I blend in well with the shadows," he returned.

"Does it have a cursive *A* engraved into the bottom of the ruby?" Cozen asked.

Sargon lifted a single brow before he flipped the ring over, and peered at it. "There is. I'm going to assume it stands for *Astor*."

Cozen swallowed hard. "Like you didn't already know, Sargon."

"You look untouched."

She straightened a bit.

She had put the dress back on before she left Jett's room, but little else. Her hair and makeup was still intact, and nothing looked amiss on her body.

"Did he touch you?" Sargon asked.

Before she could answer, he pushed up from the couch, and crossed the space between them. He left the ring sitting on the side table. She set her clutch and the glass half full with whiskey on the desk just before he crashed into her senses entirely.

His body crowded her space, and took away her ability to think or breathe for the moment. Those dark eyes of his looked her over like he was searching for something unseen, and drank her in silently. His fingers drifted over her face—soft and reckless; damning and sweet.

"You messed me up so much," she told him.

Sargon came closer still.

His lips grazed hers.

She kept talking.

"You got in my way—you fucked with my head," she said.

Sargon grinned. "Oh?"

"You're not supposed to *get in my way*. No one is supposed to get in my way. I don't let that happen. I have a job to do, and I do it well."

His hands cupped her jaw, and she stumbled when he drew her forward. Not that she really noticed her feet tripping over themselves. She was too caught up in the darkly gorgeous man who had damn near fucked up her entire heist, and at the same time, managed to be her saving grace at the end.

"Did he *touch* you?" he asked again.

Cozen peered up, and Sargon kissed her softly. Not dominating and overwhelming like he usually did. No, sweet and precious. Like she was made of priceless diamonds, and the wrong touch would leave her with irreparable scratches.

"Did he?"

"No," she whispered when he pulled away. "Not enough to make it worth it, anyway."

"But enough for you to *know*."

The rumble that accompanied his words only made her more confused. Hotter in her body, and weaker in her knees. Wet between her thighs, and breathless in her lungs.

"Your little gift was more than enough to keep him in line."

Sargon sneered. "I hoped you would use it."

"How could I not?"

"I wasn't sure, Zen."

She had never been surer.

Cozen pulled him in for another kiss, but it was not soft or sweet like the first one. No, it was hard and harsh and oh, so hot. A searing seal of his unspoken promises, and all the things she hadn't said or told him yet.

Things she may never say.

Things she couldn't say yet.

Cozen blinked, and she was lifted from the floor before her backside was set down roughly on the desk. Sargon's hands—warm with calloused fingertips—skipped under the slit of her dress, and grabbed tight to her thighs.

He didn't even have to ask.

He didn't have to make her.

She opened up *for him*.

She wanted him.

Those teasing, skilled fingers of his slipped beneath the thin scrap of lace covering her sex, and stroked her pussy. He knew her body too well—played it like an instrument that belonged to only him.

In no time at all, with only his fingertips toying with her clit, and teasing the slit of her pussy, she was wet, hot, and begging for him.

God, she *needed* him.

Never once had their kiss broken until that moment. And he only pulled away just long enough to kiss her jaw, and then where her pulse raced at her throat. He shoved his pants down, and she was the one who grabbed his already rock-hard length out of his slacks.

One stroke.

Two.

On the third, he grunted into her kiss, and his hips came forward. Those fingertips of his dug tighter into her thighs.

Replacing someone else's touch.

Remarking her.

Making it better again.

Cozen didn't even bother to slip her panties off. She just hiked up the skirt of her evening gown, shoved the gusset of her thong aside, and finally got Sargon where she wanted him. Where he always needed to be.

Fucking her.

Deep in her.

Always with *her.*

That first thrust sent her to heaven. The second sent her sprawling back on the desk as she tried to catch her breath. He didn't give her time to react properly before he was pounding into her relentlessly. The smell of sex was already clinging heavily to the air, and the slap of skin against skin mingled in with their harsh breaths, and quiet murmurs.

A fast, ruthless rhythm that had her cries of his name coming out broken and breathless within seconds. The man could fuck.

Jesus, could he fuck.

Sargon's hand pushed firmly into her stomach, keeping her down on the desk while his other grabbed firmly to her outer thigh so he could yank her into every thrust. Her legs hooked around his hips, and she met him for every brutal flex of his hips. She needed him to be rough with her—needed him to control, and pin her down.

She liked that the very best.

So hard.

So deep.

He stretched her damn good, and filled her like no one else ever could. She hadn't looked fucked before, but she certainly would now.

"Christ, you look so good taking my cock," she heard him say. "You take me so fucking well, Zen."

"Only you."

Her hand dipped between her thighs to feel him filling her. Every beat of his heart pulsed in the veins of his dick, and against her fingertips. He was slicked up with her wetness, and thick between her fingers. He'd pull out all the way to the tip, and then fill her up just as fast all over again. Feeling him fucking her was the next best thing to *watching* him fuck her.

She was convinced of it.

"Play—I want to see you play, sweetheart."

Cozen did with fast, tight circles over her clit aided in his thrusts. Seeing the way he watched her play with her pussy while he fucked her was an intoxicating sight. His muscles tightened and flexed beneath the silk shirt he wore, and his teeth bared when she started to shudder.

"Right there," she breathed.

Fuck yeah.

Her orgasm came on quick—like ice water pooling down her spine and freezing her in place while heat shot through every other one of her nerve endings. A strange, yet beautiful, burst of colors behind her clenched eyelids.

"Oh, my God," Cozen mumbled.

"Fuck," she heard him snarl.

She opened her eyes back up at his harsh grunt. He brought her in hard against his dick—all the way to the hilt—as the last of her orgasm slipped through her veins, and emptied himself as deep into her pussy as he could get. She reached for him then as he pulled from her body—his loss was palpable. Pulling him in close, she found his lips with her own.

Another searing kiss.

A goodbye of sorts, this time.

For now.

"You messed me up so bad this time," she said, repeating her earlier sentiment.

She needed him to know.

To *understand.*

Sargon nodded. "And I would do it again if it meant finding you, and having you, Zen. Do I, though?"

"Hmm?"

"Have you?"

She reached for the glass of whiskey on the desk instead of answering him. She shouldn't need to answer.

He should know.

"Drink," she told him.

Sargon eyed the glass. "Zen—"

"You won't have a drink with me? This is almost over."

He blinked.

Still hard against her thighs, and his come leaking out of her.

He only *blinked.*

"Drink," she whispered. "Toast something for me, Sargon. Celebrate with me."

"Since when do you drink whiskey?"

His question accompanied him taking the glass from her before he lifted it to his lips to down the alcohol mixed with a drug to knock him out. It was a good way to get rid of the rest of the mixture, anyway.

Sargon was far too trusting—despite knowing she was here to steal from the man he was supposed to protect, he still *trusted* her. She thought he even loved her.

"I don't drink whiskey," she said.

"I know," he replied.

It was too late.

He'd already finished the glass. And her time here was nearly over. She only had a few things left to do—the clean-up, so to speak.

Every good thief needed to make it out clean.

Sargon's eyelids felt glued together. No matter how hard he tried to open his eyes, his body just wouldn't cooperate, it seemed. His body ached—limbs heavy and sore, and his mind sluggish and cloudy. His mouth felt like cotton when he smacked his lips, and the taste that accompanied it was disgusting.

He struggled to remember … well, anything. He didn't know where he was, or why the softness under his back was not the firm mattress he preferred. He tried to pull anything from his memories to tell him how he ended up like this, and yet a giant black hole was the only thing he found in his mind.

This was bad.

Bad, bad, bad.

Come on, he urged his body and mind. *Wake up; get the fuck up.*

Still, he got nothing.

Sargon rolled over to his side, and managed to crack his eyes open just enough to see the faintest flicker of morning sunlight filtering into an unfamiliar bedroom. It was no more than a small ray about an inch wide—full of dancing dust, and bright colors.

Yellows.

Whites.

Purples.

Reds.

Red like that dress—the slit up the thigh. Every single time she walked, he felt like ripping someone's throat out for trying to get a peek at what that goddamn slit was showing off. Red was her color, though. She looked like every inch a fucking queen.

Red.

Red like the ruby ring spinning between his fingertips as he pulled the item out of its black velvet box, and removed it from the safe. It sparkled because of the way its angles had been cut. It caught light, and reflected back. A beautiful ring—shame about the cursive A carved into the bottom on the gem, though.

That really removed its value.

Red.

Red like Cozen's lipstick print on his throat. He'd caught sight of it in a hallway mirror as she led him from the office, all confused and dazed.

"It's okay," she kept telling him, "it'll be okay."

"Why?"

"You got too close. You know you got too close."

Sargon's eyes finally peeled all the way open, and he stared at that stream of light filtering into the unfamiliar bedroom as those memories came in hard again. They were fragmented—only bits and pieces; shards of memories for him to put together what had happened, and why he couldn't remember all of it.

Sitting up in the unfamiliar bed only made his head begin to pound. A deep, throbbing bass in his temples and at the very base of his skull. If he didn't know any better, he might think his brain was bleeding—no hangover he knew felt like this.

Being straight up also didn't help with the sudden swell of vertigo he experienced. Like the fucking bed was tilting sideways, and the floor was swimming underneath him. He tried to squeeze his eyes shut just to make it stop, but it really didn't help.

What was happening?

"Jesus Christ," Sargon muttered.

He put his hands against his temples, and pressed hard. The pressure did little to relieve the headache, but it allowed him to at least open his eyes and stare at a fairly normal room. Not one that was swimming and moving in front of his gaze.

Deep breaths.

Take deep breaths.

He glanced down to find his silk shirt was wrinkled like he had been sleeping in it—clearly he had—and his slacks were undone. The button left open, and the fly down. He reached down to fix his pants, but a memory swelled in his mind instead.

He blinked.

He'd fucked her on that desk.

In that office.

Tasted her mouth, and her throat.

He got all of her sounds, and heard her whispers in his ear. She was hot satin—tight and silky smooth. Wet as a fucking lake, and never looking better than she did spread out on her back while he pounded into her pretty pussy.

Sargon blinked again.

Another fragment.

Another answer.

More questions.

"Why—where?"

"Shhh," Cozen told him, looking back over her shoulder.

His hand was firmly in hers. She wouldn't let him go as she navigated the upstairs hallways of the Griffin mansion. Her hold on him was the only thing propelling him to keep moving on unsteady feet, and follow her. He didn't know where she was taking him, or why his head felt like he was living in the fucking clouds.

"You have to be quiet, Sargon. Soon, you'll be able to sleep. Okay? They can't find you in Jett's office tomorrow morning."

Sargon came out of that memory with a wheeze leaving his chest. He moved forward just a little too much on the bed, and toppled right fucking off it. His entire head was spinning, now. His balance was all but gone.

He wasn't quite sure how long he stayed on the floor like that—trying to make sense of the fragments of memories, and the shitty way he felt, but nothing really came.

Eventually, he forced himself up from the floor and onto unsteady feet. He still wasn't quite sure where exactly he was as he stared at a thick oak door leading out of the bedroom, but he assumed somewhere in the Griffin mansion.

Sargon stayed like that for a long while, too. Unsteady, and half leaning on the bed with two hands to keep him from toppling over again.

A few more deep breaths.

A long few minutes.

He finally felt like maybe he could walk without feeling like a baby deer on new legs. He headed for the door, and was surprised to find that his usual strength was all but gone as he tried to pull the heavy oak open.

Or maybe that was just him.

Eventually, he got out.

Sargon peered down the quiet hall—he recognized the things and space staring back at him. He was downstairs in the guest rooms. She had taken him downstairs.

He blinked again.

Memories filtered in again.

"You have to go down there by yourself," Cozen whispered.

Sargon's mouth felt dry—words wouldn't form when he tried to speak. Why wouldn't she come with him?

He wanted her with him.

"There's cameras in this hall," she told him. "If I go further, they'll catch me on them with you. You have to go by yourself."

Sargon nodded.

He went.

By the time he came out of that memory, Sargon was down the hall, and coming into the grand entrance. He felt slightly better. It seemed like the longer he was awake, the more steady on his feet that he became.

Everything started to clear.

His mind.

His heart.

His voice.

"Sarg, where's Jett?"

He glanced to the side, and found a handful of Jett's men waiting there. They all stood around in a semi-circle like a bunch of limp pricks that couldn't do fuck all without their boss's say so.

Which wasn't all that far from the truth.

"What?" Sargon asked.

"Jett—the *boss*. He's not down this morning. It's Saturday."

"And almost noon," another one added. "He should have been at his breakfast meeting hours ago."

Nobody thought to go check on Jett?

Sargon didn't even bother to ask the useless fuckers that question. Instead, he headed for the staircase that would lead into Jett's private wings. Soon, although it felt like it took hours to climb those stairs, Sargon was just outside of Jett's office.

The door was open.

He peered in.

Nothing looked amiss.

The desk was clean—buffed to shine. The painting behind the desk, and the safe it kept hidden, were both shut like no one had ever touched them. The wood around the painting looked like it had been buffed, too.

No fingerprints left behind.

A good thief gets out clean.

Sargon's feet moved him forward down the hall, and further away from the scene of the crime. Only down to the next room, though.

Jett's bedroom.

He knocked once.

Then, twice.

Silence answered back.

"Jett?" Sargon called.

Silence.

"Jett."

Louder the second time.

Nothing.

Sargon pushed open the bedroom door, and stuck his head into the darkness of the space just enough to listen for his boss. Through the silence, he heard almost nothing.

And then there it was.

Shallow breathing.

Too many seconds between breaths.

Struggling for air.

Sargon shoved the door open, and struggled to find a light switch. Once he did, the panic he felt was quickly replaced by a need to act.

The man was blue.

Or … quickly getting there.

"Call for an ambulance!"

Sargon's shout echoed into the hall. He didn't even know if any of them downstairs heard him, or not. It didn't even matter.

He was already on the bed, and straddling over Jett as he forced the man's head back, and tried to give the man more room in his airways to breathe. Jett was cold—not deathly so, but cold enough—and clammy.

Around his slack lips, a blue tint was starting to form. A telltale sign that the man was going without any decent amount of oxygen. The rest of his skin had taken on a rather gray pallor. Every breath Jett did take was not nearly enough, he struggled for it, and his chest rattled.

"Call for a fucking ambulance!"

Sargon stayed back in the hallway as the doctor entered Jett Griffin's hospital room. Both of Jett's sons were waiting inside—one on each side of their father's bed. The tube down Jett's throat was keeping him breathing because his lungs could no longer do the job.

None of the men in the room thought to close the door, and Sargon couldn't make himself move to give them privacy.

He needed to know.

He needed to hear it.

"The blood tests came back in, and it confirmed my suspicions," the doctor explained.

Silas let out a hard breath. "He was drugged, then?"

"Quaaludes by the looks of it—genuine Quaaludes, too, not the fake kind they sell on the streets."

Dash's hands tightened around the rails on the side of his father's bed. "So, people take drugs all the fucking time. Why—"

"Your father has a weak heart," the doctor murmured. "It couldn't handle the stress this caused on his system, and thus, the heart attack he was suffering from this morning."

"So ... I don't understand," Dash mumbled.

"He's *dying*, you stupid fuck," Silas snarled.

"I know that!"

"Then quit—"

A sudden explosion of beeps and flashing monitors interrupted the Griffin brother's argument. The doctor didn't wait around before he moved into action by running to the door, and shouting for the nurses.

"Code Blue! Code Blue!"

Sargon stayed where he was—pressed against the wall, and entirely out of the way. He didn't need to be getting into this mess, and his time here was nearly over.

Nurses rushed past him.

One had a crash cart.

They filed orderly—yet still quite quickly—without panic into the hospital room, and shoved the Griffin brothers aside. By this point, the doctor had already climbed on top of Jett to begin chest compressions.

Apparently, the man's heart was giving out.

Even if he did live through this—the flat line on the screen said he wouldn't—the Do Not Resuscitate form Silas wanted to sign earlier promised the man would be dead before the evening.

Sargon knew it.

The doctor already said Jett's heart was too weak. Without intervention, it was going to keep failing.

Sargon stayed.

He watched.

He waited.

It took thirty minutes before the doctor called it.

Time of death: *June 8th, 2013 at 6:32 PM.*

Sargon left the hospital without a look back. He no longer had a boss to answer to, and he was ready to go home.

"We are now boarding first class passengers of flight ... "

Sargon glanced up from the ring he was spinning around on the leather cord hanging from his neck. Standing from the seat, he grabbed his jacket off the back and headed for the gate's check-in desk.

He stood behind a line of another ten or so first class passengers. The attendant chatted with each one as she scanned their tickets, and smiled all the while.

One step closer ...

Sargon was up next, and already pulling the ticket from his pocket before handing it over to the woman with her hair in a bun. Blue eyes, blonde hair, and peach and cream skin. She was pretty, but she was not Cozen.

No one could ever be Cozen to Sargon.

The attendant glanced down at his ticket as she said, "I think that's the first time I have ever seen this name."

Sargon was used to that. "Oh?"

"Owen Sargon Jones."

"Owen was a family friend, according to my father," Sargon said.

And Jones was the name his mother and father adopted after they faked their death. Despite the fact their accents and features made it clear they were not born and raised Americans, they adopted common American names to blend in better.

At least on paper.

They even gave Sargon the given name Owen under his forged documents—it helped at times like these to use a different name when he didn't want to leave a trail behind for Sargon Makri.

"Oh, not the given name—the Sargon, I mean. Is that a family name?"

"Something like that."

More like … his parents way of holding onto the past they had given up because they had to run from it, and stay hidden.

"Ah. Have you been to California before, sir?"

"Born and raised," Sargon replied.

Not a lie.

"Returning home, then?"

He nodded. "Yeah, finally."

She raised a brow at the lack of carry-on in his hands. "It's a long flight, sir. You didn't bring anything to keep you entertained?"

Chuckling, Sargon tapped his temple and replied, "It's all up here."

He took very little with him when he went.

He left it all at home.

Home was with his heart, after all.

The attendant smiled again, and handed his freshly-stamped ticked back over. "I see. Well, enjoy your flight, Mr. Jones."

"I certainly will."

Pearl Astor was sitting when Cozen entered the grand dining room of the Astor mansion. The old woman barely looked away from the tea she was sipping as Fourth continued to read to his great-grandmother from a newspaper.

"You're looking well," Cozen said.

Pearl smiled, and her aging face cracked with deep lines around her mouth and eyes. "Oh, it takes more than a little sickness to keep me down, darling. Sit."

Cozen eyed the angry Persian cat sitting in the chair closest to Pearl. She didn't think moving the cat would be in her best interests considering it looked ready to fucking kill the first person who touched it.

"Do you want me to read you the review of the opera, or not?" Fourth asked. "It's got some ... well, prose you don't have patience for, Great-Grandmamma."

Cozen took a seat *next* to the cat.

Pearl peered over top the rim of her cup at Fourth. "Oh, is he all flowery with his descriptions?"

"A bit."

"Fuck him," Pearl muttered. "I will go watch it without the review, then. I am getting damn tired of that man—what do I pay him for if he can't write reviews without all that embellished nonsense? Complete garbage. I am going to fire him, and then sell the newspaper. Watch me."

Cozen burst out with a laugh, but quickly clapped her hand over her mouth to stop more from bubbling out. Across the table, Fourth cocked an eyebrow at her.

Pearl only smiled.

"Sorry," Cozen said. "It's been a long day."

"I bet," Pearl replied.

And a long night.

She didn't bother to explain that bit, though.

"I have something for you," Cozen said.

Instantly, Pearl's gaze lit up. Her dark brown eyes were warm with excitement and anticipation as her smile grew impossibly wider. It was as though fifty years dropped from the woman's age just like that.

Amazing, really.

Cozen smiled, too.

It was hard not to.

"Do you have something for me?" Pearl asked. "Really?"

Nodding, Cozen put her clutch to the table, and opened it up. She pulled out the tissue she had grabbed to wrap the Astor Queen's ruby ring in to keep it safe, and hidden during her travel to their home.

Silently, Cozen passed the tissue over.

For a long while, Pearl simply held the tissue in her hands, and stared down at it. Fourth set the newspaper aside, and leaned back in the dining chair as his gaze drifted between his great-grandmother, and Cozen.

"Down to the wire, weren't you?" he asked.

Cozen shrugged. "I got the job done."

"Barely."

"Never barely, Fourth. I never even need to use a backup plan … but this time, the backup was there whether I needed it or not. It never usually works out that way, but life has a way of surprising me."

"Hmm."

"Or maybe it's just luck," Cozen added, shooting Fourth a look. "Someone once told me I was the luckiest woman they had ever met. So lucky, that he never wanted to let me get very far out of his sight for fear the luck he got from being near me would wear off."

"And who is this *someone?*"

Cozen didn't answer.

Her attention was on Pearl.

"Leave her be, Fourth," Pearl murmured softly.

The old woman carefully unwrapped the ruby from the tissue, and lifted it high in the air as she peered at it. She turned it over, and inspected the cursive *A* on the underside of the gem, and then twisted it around and around in her fingers.

For a brief second, she even slipped the ring down her forefinger before she quickly took it off, and set it on top of the tissue paper on the table.

Pearl looked at Cozen, and nodded. "Thank you."

"Never mention it," Cozen replied in kind.

"I take it this wasn't an easy job for you, all things considered."

"One of the most unusual jobs of my life."

"Really—the *most* unusual?"

Cozen laughed. "A mark I hadn't seen, and wasn't easily found. A man in my way who knew better. Another man obsessed with me to a dangerous point. A contractor threatening my life, and shortening my deadline ... yes, most unusual."

Pearl gave Fourth a pointed stare as she said, "Did you do that?"

"Well—"

"Fourth," Pearl admonished.

"I got your ring back, didn't I?" Fourth leaned over, and grabbed his great-grandmother's hand before pressing a kiss to her weathered knuckles. "Just like I promised I would, Great-Grandmamma."

Pearl's severe expression melted into one of happiness. "You did. Astor men always keep their word, don't they?"

"We do," Fourth said.

Pearl's attention came back to Cozen for a quick second. "You'll have to forgive him. He's terribly impatient. I blame it on his father—his raising."

"*You* helped raise me," Fourth muttered. "You forget that."

His great-grandmother paid him no mind.

Cozen shrugged, and waved the whole thing off. "I think this heist was a good end for me. Or rather, a good way to leave this ... world of ours. The job I should have refused because of circumstance, and the job that finally gave me enough of a thrill that I don't have to keep chasing after the next one."

"This one was enough, hmm?" Pearl asked.

"Eventually, all thieves find the job where they know it's the last one. It's a part of the business. We all get out eventually."

Pearl lifted a single white eyebrow high. "And was it satisfactory, Cozen?"

"Pardon?"

"Ending it here. Is it a satisfactory end for you?"

"Almost. I have to tell someone else, too."

Pearl gave a nod like she understood, and then gestured at Fourth. The man was quick to stand from the table, and leave the room. A minute or so later, he was back with a file in his hands that he handed over to Cozen.

"All the details of the transfer are in there," Fourth said, taking his seat again. "The rest of your money will be in the Swiss bank account of Grace

Cozen Jones by this evening. I just approved them."

"Where does the *Jones* come from, anyway?" Pearl asked. "I thought you were a Taylor."

"A Taylor when I need to be—a Jones because I want to be."

"A revolving door of identities, I know. I am sure it does you well when you need documents to back up a story. I asked where the Jones came from, child."

Cozen stood from the table, and twisted the gold band on her thumb. "My husband. It comes from my husband."

"You're married?"

"Five beautiful years," Cozen whispered. "And he never lets me down."

Cozen let her bare feet drag through the warm sand as she strolled down the beach. The sandals dangled from her fingertips—she liked to walk with nothing on when she was here. Her flimsy summer dress blew wildly with the breeze, and cold water came up to wash over her feet with the tide.

The sky was a pretty color.

Reds and purples.

Yellows and oranges.

It reminded her of that day ... that evening ... all those years ago.

Cozen tucked her legs up to her chest on the wicker chair, and stared out at the ocean. As long as the shopkeeper didn't notice her before he closed up for the evening, she had probably found a place to sleep for the night.

Her last boss fired her when he realized she was sixteen. Apparently, it would have been okay for her to strip on a pole, but not be serving liquor.

Something like that ...

Losing her job meant she couldn't use the backroom in the bar to sleep, either. There went her damn bed.

And the roof over her head.

She'd figure it out.

She always figured shit out.

"Hey, you okay?"

Cozen glanced up—worry saturated her insides as she thought the shopkeeper had noticed her, and was about to send her on her way. It was supposed to rain tonight, or so she overheard someone saying. She really just needed a bit of shelter to keep her out of the wetness, and the overhanging roof with the wicker furniture behind the café on the beach would provide that.

She wasn't going to do anything.

Not steal, or whatever.

She only stole when things were really bad.

Instead of the shopkeeper, Cozen found someone else entirely.

A beautiful man.

Brown skin with a golden glow. Dark eyes, and a charming smile. He was a couple of years older than her, at least. Tall, with wide shoulders and a body that looked like he might be a boxer. Something radiated from him that almost made Cozen feel safe.

She didn't know what it was.

No one ever made her feel safe.

Against the backdrop of the colorful sky and the rushing tide on the beach, the guy almost looked God-like.

A saving grace for her, maybe.

She didn't even know if she believed in that kind of thing.

"You okay?" he asked again.

Cozen swallowed hard, and stood up from the chair. "Yeah, I'm just … waiting for a friend."

"A friend?"

She nodded. "Yep."

"So, you won't mind if I sit here and wait with you, then?"

"Uh …"

"Just to make sure nobody bothers you while you wait," he added quickly.

Shit.

Cozen struggled to refuse.

The guy just sat his ass down.

She sat back down, too.

Then, he held out a hand to her, and smiled widely. He showed off straight, white teeth that only added to his gorgeous appeal.

"Hi," he said.

Cozen took his hand, and he squeezed her fingers softly. "Hi."

"Sargon Makri."

"Cozen Taylor."

"You don't have a friend coming, do you, Cozen?"

Her breaths ached.

Her body was tired.

She was hungry.

Alone.

Scared.

"I haven't had a friend coming for me in a really long time," she admitted.

Sargon's fingers tightened around hers, and he tugged a little to bring her a bit closer to him. "Could I be your friend, then?"

She hadn't told him no.

Actually, she told him yes.

He'd taken her home to meet his mother and father—Mia and William Jones. Strangely common American names for people who spoke with a heavy accent, and did their prayers five times a day on beautifully ornate prayer rugs.

And yet, they were the most amazing people she had ever met in her life. People who took her in without question, and gave her all the things she had been missing. Love, a family, and home. They protected her, adored her, and taught her how to do the same for them.

But they were not ordinary people, either.

A family of thieves.

God knew …

God knew Cozen fit right in.

"My little thief—my beautiful woman. You were named most appropriately, Cozen. You took from me; you stole from me; you kept what you took with you. And you won't ever give it back, now. But that's okay. You can keep my heart."

His vows to her had been unconventional.

At best.

And entirely beautiful.

He promised her forever.

As long as she kept his heart.

So she did.

He was waiting for her on the back porch of their beach bungalow like he always did when he knew she was coming home. Leaning against the railing in his signature silk shirt with the top two buttons undone, and black slacks, he was more relaxed than she had seen him in months.

"About time," he told her.

Cozen grinned. "I had to make a stop along the way."

Sargon cocked a brow. "Where to?"

"Had to drop off a ring, for one."

"For two?"

She nodded down the beach. "Took a walk."

Sargon chuckled, and came down the last two steps. "What, a walk down memory lane?"

"I like memory lane when it's for us. Those are my very best memories."

Her husband's grin softened into a smile, and before she could say another thing, he pulled the leather cord up over his head that he had been wearing for months. A quick tug with his hands, and the leather snapped apart. The golden band dangling from the end dropped into his palm, and he held it out to her.

Cozen took her wedding ring back, and slipped it on. Sargon waited patiently as she removed his ring from her thumb, and handed it over, too.

For a moment, they were quiet.

Peace settled back in to their lives.

They were normal again.

Together again.

Perfect again.

"Come here," he demanded.

Cozen found herself wrapped in his strong embrace before her next blink. Home, and love, and serenity surrounded her. Strength, and comfort, and faith soaked into her bloodstream.

She tipped her head back to find Sargon staring down at her. He dropped a quick kiss to her lips, and then another one just as fast and as sweet as the first.

"You almost lost this job," he told her.

Cozen sighed. "It was never going to get to that point. You were too close for it to fail. *That* was the problem. You got too close this time. You never get this close—always just far enough away to watch me work, but never close enough to step in. What happened?"

Sargon shrugged. "Circumstances, I guess."

"Good thing you were there. It helped in the end."

"You could say that."

"You know what amazed me, though?" she asked.

Sargon grinned to show off that dimple of his. "What?"

"I think you made me fall in love with you all over again."

His laughter was a balm to her soul.

Like his life was the balm to her heart.

The breath to her blood.

The sea to her sky.

The spark to her fire.

This man was her everything.

"Mmm," Sargon hummed, "I have many talents."

"Let's not do this one again, though."

He cocked a brow. "No?"

"Every thief has that last job, right?"

"So my parents like to say."

"So *you* say, too."

Sargon cleared his throat and tugged her in close to his chest again, so she could hide away from the world. "My job ends when your job ends, Zen. You know that."

"I found my job—my *last* job."

"Oh, we're going to be like a normal married couple now, or something?"

She laughed lightly. "We're *normal.*"

"I mean … define normal, sweetheart."

"Our kind of normal."

"Fair," he replied. "Mom and Dad are coming over for supper. They want all the details about the job—you know how they are."

"Living vicariously through us, now."

"You love it, too."

She really did.

"I can't believe you fucking drugged me," Sargon muttered.

She pressed her lips together to keep from laughing. "You know that would have looked bad for you to leave the house with me. What if someone figured out we were working together? Better to have the Griffin family looking for the female thief than both of us."

"I don't think they'll be looking for either one of us at all, actually."

"Mmm, why not?"

He squeezed her tighter. "I just assume the Griffin brothers will be a little too distracted to realize the ring was stolen right away. They'll have far too much to deal with, and maybe by the time they do realize it is gone, you won't be the first person they look to."

"I don't understand."

"They have to handle the death of their father. Lots of arrangements, I assume."

Cozen stiffened. "Jett's dead?"

"Yeah."

"How?"

"A weak heart and drugs do not mix, Zen."

Well …

Shit.

Sargon squeezed her again, and murmured against her hair, "I know it wasn't your intention."

"No."

"But the silver lining is that the Griffin family's attention will be elsewhere for a while, and that is never a bad thing in this business."

True.

Cozen tipped her head back to look up at her husband once more. "I made one more stop, by the way."

"Oh, for what?"

"Had to grab something at the pharmacy."

The edge of Sargon's mouth quirked up in a half-smile. Like he just *knew* what she was going to tell him, and he couldn't wait for it.

He'd been asking for this one thing from her for two years—she kept putting it off because *what if.*

What if that job came up, and she had to refuse?

What if she had a little love at home that she didn't want to leave?

What if it wasn't the right time?

What if …

What if no longer applied.

What if no longer mattered.

Cozen pulled the little plastic pink and white pregnancy test from the deep pocket of her summer dress—she loved dresses with pockets. They hid all kinds of secrets.

This one was a good secret.

Sargon kept one arm tight around her waist as he took the test flashing with the word *pregnant* from her fingers, and looked it over with a growing smile. What were the chances her birth control would fail when it was supposed to be nearly one-hundred percent effective?

It felt like another sign.

Something else to tell her now was the time.

Now was *their* time.

"You could have told me …"

"I wanted to wait."

"Until what?" he asked.

"Until it was just us again. Until we were *us* again."

He kissed her again, then. Harder, deeper, and longer. A lingering kiss that seared her soul, and set fire to her heart.

This was love.

He was *love*.

"We're always us, Cozen."

Well …

They always would be, now.

A Note

First and foremost, thank you so much to my editor, Eli, for all her hard work on this book. And for never figuring the last twist out until the very last second. Your voice messages made my whole day.

To my readers, thank you for always coming along on this trip with me. It's fun, right? It's better when we're doing this together.

To the ladies who proofed this book, all my love. I appreciate your help, and am forever grateful.

For London—who put the bug in my ear to write this book, and who made the beautiful cover for Cozen—well, here we are, hon. It's hard to believe from one chat, it went this far, ha. Then again, with us, it's not hard to believe at all. We cannot be contained. Thank you.

To my hubby and my beautiful boys, keep stealing hearts like thieves. Like you stole mine.

Hugs, loves.

Bethany-Kris

Bio

Bethany-Kris is a Canadian author, lover of much, and mother to four young sons, one cat, and three dogs. A small town in Eastern Canada where she was born and raised is where she has always called home. With her boys under her feet, a snuggling cat, barking dogs, and a spouse calling over his shoulder, she is nearly always writing something ... when she can find the time.

Find Bethany-Kris at her:

WEBSITE: www.bethanykris.com
BLOG: www.bethanykris.blogspot.com
FACEBOOK: www.facebook.com/bethanykriswrites
TWITTER: @bethanykris
INSTAGRAM: www.instagram.com/bethany.kris
PINTEREST: www.pinterest.com/bethanykris

Sign up to Bethany-Kris's New Release Newsletter here:
http://eepurl.com/bf9lzD.

Other Books

John + Siena

Loyalty
Disgrace

Cross + Catherine

Always
Revere
Unruly
The Companion

Guzzi Duet

Unraveled, Book One
Entangled, Book Two

DeLuca Duet

Waste of Worth: Part One
Worth of Waste: Part Two

Standalone Titles

Effortless
Inflict
Cozen

Donati Bloodlines

Thin Lies
Thin Lines
Thin Lives
Behind the Bloodlines
The Complete Trilogy

Filthy Marcellos

Antony
Lucian
Giovanni
Dante
Legacy
A Very Marcello Christmas
The Complete Collection

Seasons of Betrayal

Where the Sun Hides
Where the Snow Falls
Where the Wind Whispers
Seasons: The Complete Seasons of Betrayal Series

Gun Moll Trilogy

Gun Moll
Gangster Moll
Madame Moll

The Chicago War

Deathless & Divided
Reckless & Ruined
Scarless & Sacred
Breathless & Bloodstained
The Complete Series

The Russian Guns

The Arrangement
The Life
The Score
Demyan & Ana
Shattered
The Jersey Vignettes

Find more on Bethany-Kris's website at www.bethanykris.com.

www.ingramcontent.com/pod-product-compliance
Lightning Source LLC
Chambersburg PA
CBHW072350020726
47506CB00004B/1093